"I told you, Jennie, I want you. And you want me too, don't you?" Ancel asked.

Jennifer barely stirred. Her eyes opened briefly, then one arm went around his neck, and she buried her head in his shoulder. A soft sigh escaped her lips. She was dimly aware of their faces only inches apart, then touching. Slowly, Ancel brought his mouth down on hers.

It was the tenderest kind of kiss, with just the right amount of pressure. Their mouths fused perfectly. She melted possessively in his arms, feeling his firm mouth on her cheeks, in her hair.

"Ah, Jennie, Jennie," he growled. "What a lovely temptation you are. . . ."

D0645932

Dear Reader,

It is our pleasure to bring you a new experience in reading that goes beyond category writing. The settings of **Harlequin American Romance** give a sense of place and culture that is uniquely American, and the characters are warm and believable. The stories are of "today" and have been chosen to give variety within the vast scope of romance fiction.

Of the few things that can stand the test of time, the land is the most noble. Barbara Kaye has created a heroine who feels strong ties to her homestead. Drawn to the Texas soil from the city, she is reacquainted with the force of nature and realizes that true love can be found close to home.

From the early days of Harlequin, our primary concern has been to bring you novels of the highest quality. **Harlequin American Romance** is no exception. Enjoy!

Vivian Stephens

Vivian Stephens
Editorial Director
Harlequin American Romance
919 Third Avenue,
New York, N.Y. 10022

Call
of Eden

BARBARA KAYE

Harlequin Books

TORONTO • NEW YORK • LONDON
AMSTERDAM • PARIS • SYDNEY • HAMBURG
STOCKHOLM • ATHENS • TOKYO • MILAN

Published August 1983

First printing June 1983

ISBN 0-373-16019-4

Printed in Canada

Chapter One

The light on the interoffice phone winked at her. Jennifer Cameron raised the receiver to her ear and heard the receptionist's voice. "Take one-nine, Jennie. It's your sister."

Jennie sighed in resigned exasperation. Meg was impossible. Jennie could not count the times she tactfully had tried to make her sister understand that receiving personal calls at the office simply was not businesslike. "Please don't call me," she had pleaded, "unless it's really urgent." However, when Margaret Cameron Curtis had something to say, that was urgency personified in Meg's estimation, and so the daytime intrastate calls to the office persisted. Frankly, Jennie couldn't recall a single instance when the call couldn't have waited until evening...or not have been made at all, for that matter.

"Hello, Meg," Jennie said into the receiver. "What's up?"

"Oh, Jen, the most *marvelous* thing!" Meg enthused. "I'm sure you've heard of Gregory Peterson, the oilman...."

"Of course." You couldn't grow up in Texas *without* hearing about the Petersons.

"Well, Steve and I met him and his *adorable* wife Susie at a party in Houston last weekend. Oh, such a party it was, Jen! I wish I had time to tell you about it. Anyway they've invited us to spend a week on their yacht in Galveston Bay. Isn't that wonderful?"

"Yes, Meg, it's wonderful," Jennie said, forcing a modicum of enthusiasm into her voice. "I'm sure you'll have a grand time."

"I'm so excited, but I've been in such a dither—all that shopping! I mean, I was just fresh out of yachting clothes," and Meg's irritating giggle came across the wire.

"Aren't we all," said Jennie, this time not even attempting to disguise the sarcasm. *There has to be more to this,* she thought, Meg's calls might never be important, but they usually had more substance than the mere recitation of social invitations.

Meg's voice gushed on. "Well, there's no sense in beating around the bush. This once-in-a-lifetime chance, which Steve and I just *can't* pass up because Gregory Peterson is such an important and influential man in the state, and if Steve ever decides to go into politics...well, I'm sure you understand. Anyway, this trip has presented me with a problem, and I thought my very efficient sister might be able to help me with it."

"Cut the flattery, Meg," Jennie said dryly. "Get to the point."

"Oh, Jen, worst luck. You remember Jeremy Walde, the realtor in White Rock who's been trying to sell the old homestead for us?"

"Of course I remember him, Meg. Why?"

"He called last night and says he's had an offer on the place."

Jennie straightened in her seat, suddenly interested. She and Meg had been trying to sell the family home for five years, since the death of their father, but to date they had received no serious offers. This *was* news.

"Hallelujah!" she exclaimed. "I don't see the problem. Tell him to sell."

Meg affected the pitiful tone so well known to Jennie. "Unfortunately it doesn't seem to be that simple, Jen. Mr. Walde says he wants one of us there, preferably Monday, for negotiations with the buyer—whatever that means. Actually, he said he wanted both of us there, but I explained that you have my power-of-attorney as far as the house is concerned. Obviously, Jen, it's impossible for me to go to White Rock. Steve and I are leaving for Galveston in the morning, and you wouldn't *believe* all I have to do...invitations have to be refused and there are instructions to the servants—"

"Yes, yes, Meg. I'm sure it's exhausting. But tell me, what do you want me to do?"

"Well, like I said, I've been in such a tizzy over this that Steve threatened to call off the trip, but...then I remembered your vacation." There was a brief pause before Meg's supplicant voice went on, "It *is* coming up, isn't it?"

Jennie clenched her teeth together so hard her jaws hurt. When Meg affected that syrupy tone it was a sure sign she was on the verge of imposing on Jennie, and the worst part of it was that Jennie rarely refused her anything. It was almost as though Jennie was three years Meg's senior, instead of the other way around. The pattern had begun in childhood. Meg always had possessed the uncanny knack for getting her little sister to do all her unpleasant chores, then sitting back and blithely accepting credit for the accomplishments.

"Yes, my vacation starts Monday," Jennie told her sister. "But I have plans, Meg, and I don't want to change them. I'm going to visit Aunt Mary in Tucson."

"Oh, how deadly dull!" Meg cried. "What a dreadful way to spend a vacation!"

"It's at least as exciting as going to White Rock... which is what you're getting ready to ask me to do, right?"

"Jen, surely you could take a couple of days to just run by White Rock and see to this. I'll just *die* if I have to miss this wonderful trip—more for Steve's sake than my own, of course. But I do so hate to let a sale get away. We haven't exactly been besieged with offers for the old place."

Jennie smiled ruefully, as unable as always to understand Meg. Her sister's engrossment with herself was incomprehensible to Jennie, who assiduously avoided inconveniencing others. But nothing was too much trouble for someone else to do, went Meg's theory, and the wonder of it was that she got away with it most of the time.

Jennie sighed. If her sister would only stop to think she might realize how much she was asking. Meg, who lived in utmost luxury in a servant-infested, cedar and brick mansion in San Antonio, was only an hour's drive from White Rock. She could easily meet with the realtor, take care of anything that needed doing, and be home before dinner. Jennie, on the other hand, resided in a small suburban Fort Worth apartment and budgeted nearly every nickel of her salary. She would have to drive for five and a half hours, spend who knew how much for gasoline, meals and lodging, and give up precious days of her vacation in the doing. So much for "running by" White Rock.

But Jennie knew none of this would ever occur to Meg, for the plain truth was that Meg had no conception of the kind of life Jennie led. She was certain her sister didn't realize there was an entire world of people who weren't waited on hand and foot, whose every whim was not indulged, whose every wish was not granted. The biggest decision Meg ever had to make, it seemed, was what to wear to the country club on Saturday night; the most strenuous thing she ever did was to play the piano. There were times when Jennie almost envied her sister; most of the time, however, the thought of Meg's existence merely appalled her.

And of course Meg would have no way of knowing just how much Jennie dreaded returning to the old hometown. She had avoided the place like the plague since Rob Cameron's death. Yet somewhere in the dim recesses of her mind lay the knowledge that she would have to go back sooner or later, if for no other reason than to sign her name on a sales contract; but that was something to be worried about when the time came, not before. White Rock held nothing but a lot of unpleasant memories that were best left buried.

On one point however, she agreed with Meg completely: She didn't want this sale to get away. Meg might only want to be rid of the family home because owning it was a nuisance, but Jennie had a far more compelling reason: money. Save for a small trust fund, the family homestead was her only legacy from Rob Cameron. Her half of the proceeds from its sale would go a long way toward brightening her rather dismal economic circumstances.

"Well...I suppose I could give Mr. Walde a call

when I get home tonight, and if it really seems necessary for me to go to White Rock, I guess I'll go, that's all," Jennie said, swallowing her disappointment.

"Oh, I knew I could count on you! I told Steve, I can always count on Jen. You have everything so all-together, while I just flutter around, accomplishing nothing," Meg gushed. "I told Steve just the other evening—we were having drinks on the patio before going to the club for dinner—and I said, I remember when Jen and I were kids..."

Jennie groaned inwardly. Meg was going into her eastern-finishing-school-cum-southern-belle routine that shouldn't have fooled anyone over the age of twelve, yet time and time again Jennie had seen perfectly intelligent adults fall for it like a ton of bricks. Once, just once, she would have liked to find the nerve to say, "Oh, come off it, Meg! You and I grew up on that old ranch outside White Rock, Texas, and neither of us ever had more than one pair of shoes at a time until we entered high school. You used to like to sop gravy with biscuits and go wading in that old cow pond, so *stow it*!"

But, as usual, all she said was, "I'll see what I can do, Meg, and get back to you. Have a good time on what's-his-name's yacht."

"Oh, I intend to, I intend to! You do whatever you want about the house, Jen—I trust your judgment completely. I'll talk to you in a week or so. And thanks ever so much."

Jennie replaced the receiver in its cradle and stared across the busy office. People were rushing about, typewriters were clacking away, phones were ringing, but she long ago had learned to tune it all out. The normal atmosphere in the editorial offices of *Women Now* magazine was one of organized chaos, and though Jennie found her work exhilarating, she was ready for a vacation. The fledgling periodical's growth during the three years Jennie had been working there had been nothing short of phenomenal, but the work load had grown along with the circulation. The members of the small staff were perpetually behind schedule, and there wasn't one of them who did not occasionally suffer from a good case of taut nerves.

Jennie stuck a pencil into the thick thatch of dark, auburn-laced curls atop her head; her huge dark brown eyes made an all-encompassing sweep of the papers on her desk. Then she stood, picked up a stack of typewritten sheets and carried it with her as she crossed the room, perfect legs making scissoring motions beneath the hem of her simple yellow dress. Coming to a glass-enclosed cubicle, she knocked lightly before opening the door. Gloria Travis, elegant and spectacled, was sitting behind her own cluttered desk, scowling. But, then, the editor of *Women Now* nearly always scowled.

"Got a minute, Gloria?" Jennie asked.

"Barely," the gruff-voiced woman answered.

"I have a manuscript from the slush pile that I'm really excited about. I think it's good, really good, and I wanted to call your attention to it before I leave. We could run it in September."

"Lord! We're getting a slew of unsolicited manuscripts," Gloria muttered.

"That's because *WN* prints so much fiction. There aren't all that many places for an unknown to break into print."

"I had a qualm or two over advertising that we read unsolicited manuscripts, and then when the slush pile started rising like bread dough..." The editor rolled her eyes skyward. "But I have to hand it to you, Jennie—you manage to keep it under control. I don't know how you find the time, though."

Jennie shrugged. "I read a lot of it at home at night. So does Connie. I've trained my new assistant to regard every one of those manila envelopes with hopeful anticipation. I suppose I get a kind of vicarious thrill every time I give a new writer a chance at publication."

Gloria's knowing eyes looked at Jennie, and she shot her a Gloria-version of a smile. "Hoping someone will do the same for you someday?"

"Sure."

Gloria took the manuscript from Jennie, glanced at it briefly, then set it down among the dozens of others awaiting her attention. She personally put her stamp of approval on every word that appeared in the pages of *Women Now,* but everything that passed over her desk with Jennifer Cameron's initials on it automatically was accepted. The editor had long ago learned to trust Jennie's literary sense.

"I don't know how in hell I'm going to manage without you for two weeks," Gloria said.

"Ah, you'll manage. Connie's new, but she's a good, hard worker. However"—Jennie paused, trying to decide the best way to say what she had to say about her assistant—"I wouldn't be too quick to approve Connie's choice of manuscripts. She's still at the stage where she thinks if all the words are spelled right, it's great literature."

"I'll watch her like a hawk. I have to admit, though, I'm not looking forward to wet-nursing a new journalism graduate."

Jennie's dark eyes twinkled merrily. "You wet-nursed *me* when I got out of the University."

"I know, but you were different. You looked like you should have been leading cheers at a football game, but you had a lot of savvy."

Jennie laughed a lilting laugh. She knew she looked younger than her twenty-six years, a fact partly attributable to her petiteness, and she always felt it put her at a disadvantage in the business world. For this reason she considered herself enormously fortunate to have encountered Gloria Travis on her first job interview three years earlier. Somehow Gloria had been able to see beneath Jennie's ingenuous good looks to find the capable, sensible, intelligent young woman there.

"Oh, by the way, Gloria, it doesn't look as though I'll be going to the Tucson address I gave you. I had a call from my sister, and I might have to go back to the old hometown to settle some unfinished family business. But I'll keep you posted, just in case you need to reach me."

"I won't, Jennie. God knows, everyone deserves two quiet weeks away from this madhouse."

Jennie smiled at her editor, for she genuinely liked this gruff woman who had been something of a mentor for three years. The two women often had dinner together, something that neither advertised around the office for fear of charges of favoritism. Jennie knew that most of the women who worked at the journal were terrified of Gloria Travis, but she long ago had ascertained that Gloria was a great deal of bark and very little bite. "Tell me, Gloria—how long has it been since *you* took two weeks off?"

"Now what would I do with two weeks off? I've really no place to go," Gloria said unconcernedly.

Jennie felt a sudden wave of pity for her boss, although Gloria certainly was not the sort who invited pity. Gloria's parents were dead, she had never had any children, and she was long divorced. She resided in a quiet, immaculate beige-and-white apartment; her friends were business associates. The magazine was the beginning and the end, the sum total of Gloria's existence. Sometimes Jennie pictured herself ten or more years down the road—still single, working from sunup until sundown, then going home to an elegant, empty apartment—and she shuddered involuntarily.

"Well, unfortunately it looks as though I *do* have someplace to go. It's not exactly what I had in mind, but..." She left the sentence dangling. "I'll give Connie a last-minute briefing before I leave, just to make sure she knows all the really important things, like where we keep the coffeepot."

"Sure, sure. Have a good time, Jennie. I'll see you in a couple of weeks."

That evening in the serene privacy of her apartment Jennie relaxed, sipping a vodka and tonic while lasagne baked in the oven. Her eyes swept her surroundings, and she approved of what she saw. The small apartment, with its white walls, white kitchen appliances and white bathroom fixtures, had been decorated in the bright yellows, oranges, and greens that she so favored. Every item of the furnishings—from the smallest ashtray to the long print sofa that had been such a bargain because of one tiny flaw on one of the arms—had been purchased by her during the past three years, paid for out of her salary, often on the installment plan. Only her automobile, the beige Toyota that was her pride and joy, had been paid for out of her trust fund. She owned a lot of lovely things, her credit rating was excellent, and she had some money in the bank.

Considering everything, she thought she had done a damned fine job with her life. If she lacked anything, she wasn't aware of it. The thought of what she'd achieved was immensely satisfying to her.

How odd that her inherent Scottish thrift had escaped Meg completely. For the first time, Jennie realized that Meg, while so casually asking her sister to "run by" White Rock, had not mentioned reimbursing her for half of whatever she would be out for this trip on their mutual behalf. Not that that was so surprising to Jennie. Money to Meg was a plastic card with Steve's name on it. Mentally she made a note to keep a record of every cent she spent for this little jaunt and then to present it to her sister. Jennie's magnanimity extended only so far.

She stretched her now stockingless legs in front of her, propped her bare feet on the coffee table, and reached for the telephone on the lamp table. Within moments she had reached Jeremy Walde at his home in White Rock.

The realtor greeted her expansively. Jeremy had been one of Rob Cameron's best friends, and Jennie was confident he had the Camerons' best interests at heart.

"Jennifer! How wonderful to hear from you, my dear! I was speaking to your sister only yesterday. How are you?"

"I'm fine, Mr. Walde. I'm calling because I spoke to Meg this afternoon, and I understand you've had an offer on our place."

"Out of the blue, my dear, out of the blue! Strangest thing...the offer came from one of our prominent local citizens. One would think if he were interested in the place, he would have made an offer long ago."

"Can you tell me something about it, Mr. Walde?

Meg is leaving town and has more or less left this up to me."

"Well, the offer is for substantially less than we're asking, but the prospective buyer says the place is in such run-down condition that he feels his offer is a fair one. We might counter with another figure, and perhaps he'll agree. But either you or your sister will have to be here when I meet with the gentleman Monday."

"I see," Jennie said, regretfully conceding the fact that she was not going to be able to avoid a trip to White Rock.

"I have an appointment with him at eleven o'clock Monday morning. Do you think you could possibly be here then?"

"Well...I suppose I could. By the way, who is our prospective buyer? Is it someone I might know?"

"Probably," Jeremy Walde said. "It's Paul Gunter."

Jennie, who was taking a sip of her drink, almost choked. She bolted upright on the sofa, spilling some of her drink as she did so. "Wh-who?"

"Paul Gunter. Do you remember him? The banking family? Of course, he's quite a bit older than you are...."

Eleven years and two months, exactly, Jennie thought. He was thirty-seven now. Thirty-seven! My God! Her face flushed, and she felt her heart begin to race wildly. "Yes, I know very well who Paul Gunter is," she said finally.

Paul...was a name she had tried conditioning herself never to let enter her conscious thoughts. Paul Gunter was more responsible than anyone or anything for her desire to escape White Rock forever. "What in the world does Paul Gunter want with our old home?"

"I have no idea, my dear, but he's definitely interested, let me assure you."

Jennie's dark brows drew together in acute puzzlement. It made no sense. Paul Gunter was an urbane, sophisticated man who never had evinced any interest in things rustic and bucolic. The bank in White Rock that his grandfather had founded during the grim days of the thirties was only a small portion of the Gunter banking empire. He and his father owned, besides their grand mansion in White Rock, a beach cottage on the Gulf Coast, a "cabin" in the mountains of New Mexico, and condominiums in Houston and Dallas. They certainly did not need a country place fifteen minutes from home.

She was intrigued... but not intrigued enough to want to hazard a confrontation with Paul. Of all her painful memories of White Rock, remembrances of Paul Gunter were the most painful.

Oh, you're being silly! she chided herself. *It's been five years, five long years, and if Paul wants to buy the place, sell it to him. What do you care? You've come a long way from White Rock.... The place means nothing to you, nothing! Make the final break and be done with it.*

The calculator in her brain was activated. A motel room, even for a few nights, would be more expensive an undertaking than she had planned on. But the old house was still there, empty, and as she recalled, most of the furniture was still there.

"All right, Mr. Walde," she said into the receiver. "I'll be there. I don't suppose there's any need for me to arrive before Sunday—that's the day after tomorrow. And I think I'd like to stay at the house. Will you leave a key in the mailbox for me?"

"Oh, Jennifer!" The realtor's voice sounded genuinely alarmed. "Surely you aren't planning to stay out there alone?"

"Why not? Is there electricity, water?"

"Well, yes. I never had them discontinued. With the place unoccupied the utility bills are minimal, and I wanted to keep it ready for showing at all times. But it's so lonely and remote out there, Jennifer. I really don't think—"

"It'll be all right, Mr. Walde, really. I'm not afraid. Just please leave a key in the mailbox, and I'll see you Monday. Where should I meet you?"

"On the second floor of the Gunter State Bank. Do you remember where it is?"

Do I! she thought grimly. "Yes, Mr. Walde, I remember."

When Jennie hung up the phone she was trembling, whether from anger or apprehension or a combination of both she was not prepared to say. She did not want to go to White Rock, she most definitely did not want to see Paul again, and she did not particularly like the idea of Paul's buying the Camerons' house. A faint, faraway warning signal was flashing in her mind, all the more disturbing for its vagueness, and for a brief instant she considered calling San Antonio to tell Meg she could not possibly make the trip to White Rock.

However, the clarion calls of duty, necessity, practicality—all those things that had ordered and measured her life for years—came through loud and clear. Jennie took a deep breath, exhaled slowly, and placed a call to Tucson.

Aunt Mary's disappointment was genuine, as was Jennifer's. Meg might disparage a visit to Tuscon as "deadly dull," but Jennie had always found a two-week stay with Aunt Mary a rejuvenating time. Her aunt, Rob Cameron's only sibling, was the widow of a Navy Officer; she had seen more than a little of the world and had a veritable treasure house of amusing, entertaining anecdotes. Beyond that, the woman was a keen student of human nature, a thoughtful and stimulating companion, and Jennie honestly enjoyed her company.

"A man doesn't have anything to do with this, does he, Jennie?" Aunt Mary asked hopefully when Jennie explained that her visit would have to be canceled.

Jennie laughed. "I'm afraid not, Aunt Mary."

"Oh, that's too bad. You're not getting any younger, dear."

Jennie let that one pass without comment. "This is strictly family business. We've had an offer on the house in White Rock, and I have to go see about it."

"For goodness' sake! Why doesn't Margaret take care of it? She lives minutes away, and it's such a long drive for you."

"Meg and Steve are leaving town, Aunt Mary. They're going yachting for a week."

"Hmm." Jennie could envision her aunt's disapproving expression. Aunt Mary was not particularly fond of Meg, and the feeling was mutual. "That sounds like Margaret. Born to the purple, she was—just a cut or two above us commoners. I don't understand how that darling Steve puts up with her."

Jennie smiled. "Aunt Mary, Steve adores Meg. *I* should be so fortunate."

"Indeed. Jennie dear, do be careful on the highway. One reads such dreadful things in the newspapers these days."

"I'll be careful, Aunt Mary. And I'll come to see you the first chance I get. I love you."

"I love you too, Jennie."

Jennie's next call was to the airline, to cancel her Tucson reservation. Then she replaced the receiver and sighed, realizing she was in the rare position of having a spare day on her hands. She had expected to be winging her way to Tucson in the morning, so everything that needed to be done had been done. She had arranged for the post office to hold her mail until further notice and had stopped newspaper delivery. A neighbor was going to take care of her plants. Her packing had been completed, and her apartment was in spotless condition. Therefore; tomorrow she would have her car serviced, then treat herself to a lazy, lovely Saturday, and she would leave for White Rock sometime Sunday morning.

After adding some linens and kitchen utensils to her list of things to take with her, since the house in White Rock would have neither, she spent the remainder of the quiet Friday evening seeing to herself. She bathed slowly and luxuriously, thinking that time alone was the nicest part of living alone. In her apartment there was no one clamoring for her attention, demanding this and that. The few people whom she called friends invariably were young women like herself, independent and self-reliant with no need to be let in on every facet of each other's lives. Of men friends there were few, not for lack of interested parties, but because Jennifer Cameron's extraordinary self-discipline tended to put off most men. Jennie often thought wryly that even in this age of supposed equality between the sexes men still were looking for a bit of a clinging vine, albeit one who could bring home at least part of the bacon.

It was this apparent lack of interest in the opposite sex that most fascinated her women friends, and even Jennie found it difficult to analyze her ambivalent feelings toward men. They could be quite enthralling at times. She thought there was nothing more pleasant than being held in a pair of strong masculine arms, and she often longed for the day when that certain someone would come along. So in that respect she was not all that different from every other young woman she knew.

What *was* different was her notion of what that certain someone would be like. He would be special, of course—a man who would regard her as a human being capable of intelligence and understanding, a man who would be a companion in every sense of the word, a man who wanted so much more from her than a tumble in bed.

But most of all, he would be strong, someone she could lean on just a little. Throughout her life she had been the one others leaned on. Her father, Meg—both had expected her to be the strong one. She thought it would be the most delightful thing on earth to draw strength from someone else, at least occasionally.

Once she had thought she had found that strength in Paul Gunter. He had seemed so sophisticated, so worldly, so all-knowing. But he had turned out to be the weakest of men, a man who would allow his father to rule his life. Oh, she had always known it was Ernst Gunter, the family patriarch, who had opposed his son's marriage to humble little Jennifer Cameron. Ernst had much better things in mind for his older son, and Paul, Jennie now realized, hadn't put up much of a fight.

As Jennie prepared for bed, the old confusing mixture of hurt and anger churned in her stomach. She considered herself capable of coping with any exigency; she firmly believed a person could do anything that had to be done. But one thing was certain: It was going to take all the strength and determination she could muster to get through a meeting with Paul Gunter with poise and coolness and detached disinterest. But she would do it. By God, she would do it!

Chapter Two

"Ain't you Rob Cameron's kid?" the gnarled, wizened man behind the coffee shop's cash register asked.

"Yes, I'm Jennie," she said, handing the man her lunch check and a five-dollar bill.

"I was watchin' you while you was havin' lunch, and I thought you looked kinda familiar. Don't guess I've seen you since Rob died. That's been...how many years now?"

"Five," Jennie said. "I was still going to the university."

"Five years!" The man shook his head in disbelief. "Time jus' skitters away when you get to be my age. Where you been keepin' yourself, Jennie?"

"I live and work in Fort Worth now."

"You drive down from Fort Worth today?"

"Yes."

"Long old tirin' drive, ain't it?"

"I'll say!" Jennie was desperately trying to remember the man's name—she and Papa had often stopped to have lunch in this coffee shop on their periodic trips to the stockyards in Fort Worth—but nothing came to her. And she was growing a little impatient with the chitchat, wanting to be on her way. The slow part of her journey still stretched ahead of her. But when hill people decided to "visit," it was useless to try to hurry them.

Behind the counter the man dawdled about making her change, while he entertained himself by studying the young woman intently. She was a big-city type now, he decided. Real high-class and just as pretty as could be. Glistening dark curls framing an oval face, enormous dark eyes under thick lashes, a full-lipped mouth. Her simple green dress with its multicolored scarf at the neck looked the sort a career girl would purchase—understated, not faddish, the sort of garment meant to be worn for years. The man rubbed his chin thoughtfully as he recalled the Jennifer Cameron of another time—a pigtailed scamp in jeans and plaid shirt, riding in the pickup with her father and big sister, hauling a fat steer to market in Fort Worth.

"You on your way home now, Jennie?" he asked.

"Yes. There's someone who's interested in buying the old homestead," she explained.

"That's too bad," the man said obscurely. Finally he glanced at the lunch check, slapped the five-dollar bill into the drawer, removed some change and handed it to her. "Now, don't leave these hills for good, Jennie. Hope to see more of you around here."

"Thank you," Jennie said, but she was thinking, *When I leave this time, I'll be gone for good.*

She bade the man good-bye and walked out into the brilliance of the afternoon sun. Of course, she had said that before, right after her father's funeral. Meg had then been the new bride of wealthy Stephen Curtis of San Antonio, and so her sister's future had been secure. Once Jennie had been assured of enough money to see her through college, she more or less had left for good. Now here she was, back again, and all morning long a nagging feeling had persisted, the feeling that she should have left well enough alone. She simply should have given Jeremy Walde instructions to take care of things in whatever way he thought best and gone on to Tucson. She had no business back here in the hill country; she no longer belonged.

Now Jennie was forced to leave the interstate and follow a westwardly course. Suddenly the land seemed to empty of people. Urban sprawl would be a long time reaching these rough cedar hills. How odd that the thought should be so pleasing to her, for she now considered herself a city girl. Fort Worth and Dallas possessed an abundance of urban sprawl, but Jennie was convinced she loved the shine and glitter, the vigor and vitality of the city.

She stifled a yawn and stretched a little. The food had silenced her complaining stomach, but it also had left her drowsy. She glanced at the dashboard clock and determined that she was going to arrive in White Rock later than she had expected. Once off the interstate her pace had of necessity slowed, and she had gotten a later start than she had planned.

Damn Meg and her thoughtlessness! At this moment Jennie could have been landing in Tucson, ready for two weeks of lazing around the pool and gorging on Aunt Mary's butter-rich, cream-laden cuisine. Instead, she was on her way to a place she did not want to be, for a meeting with a man she had hoped never to see again.

As weary as she was, her brain seemed suddenly overactive, and she was becoming aware of a new and disturbing sentiment: the feeling that she was being disloyal to her father. To sell that spot of earth Rob Cameron had loved so much seemed almost heresy. Jennie, unlike Meg, had always understood that Rob's attachment to the land was a somewhat mystical link, something inherited from his Scottish forefathers. She consoled herself, however, with the knowledge that Rob had been a realist above all; he never would have expected his daughters to keep the place, to try to run it and show a profit. His will had stated that she and Meg could dispose of The Croft in any manner they saw fit.

The Croft! Home...or once it had been in earlier, happier times, when the homestead had been the beloved center of her limited universe.

"The Croft?" people invariably would exclaim. "Damned funny name for a ranch. What's wrong with the Double Bar S or Rocking W or something that makes sense?"

"It's a Scottish term," Rob would explain. "It means a small landholding. You really can't call The Croft a 'ranch' without some pretension."

"You run cattle, don't you?"

"Sure, but—"

"Then it's a ranch. And The Croft still is a funny name for it."

Yes, Jennie supposed it was a funny name in these German hills where Shoenkoepper and Stahlberger were as common surnames as Smith and Jones would have been elsewhere. The Scot Camerons were an oddity, but the cedar hills of Texas had reminded Rob of a miniature Scottish Highlands, and it was there he had transferred all of his love and energy and interest to his daughters and to The Croft. They had been his passions.

Jennie pressed the accelerator closer to the floor, and soon she knew she was nearing her destination. The road began winding erratically, and huge granite slabs, some the size of bathtubs, poked out of the earth. Only a true child of these hills would know that pockets of soil nestled between the smooth, pink domes and that wildflowers grew there. In the spring their vibrant color display could take one's breath away. Many Texans had a sentimental attachment to the hill country, whether or not they had ever lived there, and Rob had always referred to it as God's country. Jennie thought perhaps it was because the hills still retained a measure of what the world must have been like before man moved in and started trying to change it.

Jennie's heart palpitated unpleasantly when she sped past the sign proclaiming: WELCOME TO WHITE ROCK, TEXAS—HOME OF TWELVE THOUSAND FRIENDLY PEOPLE, AND A FEW OLD SOREHEADS! The sign, now badly weathered, had been there for as long as she could remember, the whimsical contribution of some long-forgotten city official. And soon she spied another sign, which had also been in the same location for as long as she could remember. The sign on Walter Freidrich's storefront announced: We Buy Pecans, Furs and Deer Hides. She was home!

She noted with pleasure that the river—as everyone called the friendly stream that wound its lazy way through town—was running clear and bright, just as it always had. The river was greatly loved by everyone in White Rock, even though it had the unfortunate habit of flooding every ten or so years. Farther to the south, the river had been dammed to create several larger rivers, all now laden with power boats and water skiers, bringing prosperity and pollution to the river's lower end. Neither prosperity nor pollution had reached White Rock, a fact which half its citizens considered a pity and the other half thought a blessing.

Jennie maneuvered her car along Flach Avenue, the town's main thoroughfare, almost deserted on the bright Sunday afternoon. A few of the stores had undergone facelifts, she noticed, but most had not changed perceptibly since her childhood. Changes came slowly in this part of the world.

Then she spotted the Gunter State Bank, still standing majestically at the corner of Flach and Second streets, its dignified facade seeming to assure one and all that here was a formidable bastion of financial strength and stability. Jennie felt hot tears welling in her eyes as she unsuccessfully tried to stem the flood of memories.

She thought of the impeccable, sophisticated gentleman whose executive offices were on the second floor of that building. Paul Gunter. He of the chiseled face, the thick thatch of dark hair, the gray eyes that could flash like honed steel. The man who had been her introduction to the school of hard knocks. How incredible that merely thinking of him could bring on such a torrent of emotions, none of them particularly pleasant. Tall, handsome Paul. *Damn him!*

The drive from White Rock to The Croft was less than eight miles, but on the winding country road it seemed much farther. Such a queer rush of feelings at seeing home again! The countryside still was very rural and quiet, with many ringtails, skunks, raccoons, squirrels, and deer lurking in those thickly-wooded hills. To Jennie it seemed a century ago that she had roamed the woods, at one with nature, totally unafraid of any living creature, save perhaps for the rattlers and copperheads that any prudent person feared.

A sadness akin to physical pain gripped her when she caught her first glimpse of the homestead. The massive wooden gate marking the ranch's southernmost boundary now was crumbling with decay. Above it, the neatly lettered sign designating this homestead as THE CROFT was so weathered and faded it was nearly illegible. Once it had been so lovingly repainted each spring.

Jennie halted the car at the roadside mailbox and retrieved the key Jeremy Walde had left for her. She was startled to realize she was actually shaking. She returned to the car, drove through the gateway and up the path to the house.

The structure itself was not unlike many others dotting the hills—constructed by hand of native stone and meant to last for generations. The big covered porch, where she and Meg had often slept on merciless summer nights, was badly in need of paint and general repair, but the house, itself, surprisingly, looked in good condition.

Jennie lifted her eyes and surveyed her surroundings. The house and outbuildings stood in a clearing surrounded by a black-green forest of oak and cedar. In the case of The Croft, the clearing had been considerably reduced in size; the tenacious brush was moving in. Jennie heard her father's words from many years ago: "That old brush is just laying out there waiting for us to get lazy, Jennie girl, then it'll be back."

Braking, Jennie switched off the engine, then settled back in the seat for a minute, as though she needed some time to summon the courage to walk into that house. But, deciding she was being ridiculous, she finally got out of the car, walked up the steps, unlocked the front door, and stepped inside.

The interior had a musty, unlived-in smell, but it was cool. It had been designed to be cool, with tall narrow windows to let in plenty of light but keep out the worst of summer's sun. Suddenly Jennie's heart lurched. In front of the limestone fireplace was her father's chair, now covered with a sheet. In all her remembrances of her father, he had been sitting astride a horse, atop his tractor, or in that chair.

Unable to stand the sight of it, Jennie quickly crossed to the stairway and went upstairs. The ranch house was not a large one; the second floor contained only two big bedrooms and a bath, the plumbing circa 1952. The largest of the two bedrooms, Rob's old room, had been stripped of furniture, and Jennie remembered how eagerly Meg had snatched up the antique bedroom suite that had arrived from Scotland with some unknown great-grandparent.

In the other bedroom, the one she had shared with Meg until her sister had gone off to school, there were twin beds and a battered dresser. Jennie felt her spirits sag even more. Everything looked so shabby and worn. Perhaps it had always looked that way. She just hadn't noticed.

Quickly she went back downstairs, crossed through the dining room and went into the kitchen. The big, homey room had been the hub of family life. She ran her hand across the wooden table that had been the site of countless meals, countless schoolwork sessions, countless father-daughter conferences. Rob had been sitting at that table the night Paul Gunter had announced he wanted to marry Rob's younger daughter.

The memories all came together in a rush, and hot tears splashed down Jennie's cheeks. She shouldn't have come; it was just too painful. Slowly she sank onto one of the chairs around the wooden table and allowed herself to lapse into a morass of personal grief and regret.

"Hey! Anybody home?" A booming masculine voice shattered the silence.

Startled out of her reverie, Jennie jumped, wiping at her eyes. She ran into the dining room where she almost collided with a young man dressed in faded jeans and a light cotton shirt, open at the neck with the sleeves rolled to his elbows.

"Whoops!" he said, grabbing for her with strong arms. Jennie looked up into the brightest green eyes, the most dazzling smile she had ever seen. "I saw the car," he said, "so I figured it would be you. How are you, Jennie?"

Jennie's brows knitted together while she studied him. He was tall and slender, very strong and muscular. The hands gripping her shoulders actually hurt. He had thick blond hair and those laughing eyes, but the most singular of his features was his smile. It was like a brilliant burst of sunshine. She was quite certain she had seen him somewhere before...but where? This dynamic brute with his forceful, sunny good looks was not the sort of man who was easily forgotten.

It took a moment, but recognition finally hit her. "Ancel!" she cried happily. "Ancel Gunter! Good heavens, I haven't seen you in years!" She threw herself into his arms out of sheer delight.

He hugged her ferociously, crushing her to his broad chest. "Six years to be exact," he said. "You may not have remembered me, but I never forgot you!"

Now Jennie remembered, very well. Paul's younger brother who had always seemed to be around when Jennie and Paul were dating. Ancel had, as she recalled, gone out of his way to make the shy twenty-year-old girl she'd been feel more comfortable around the Gunters, who were a rather formidable bunch. It had amazed her then, and it still amazed her—the difference in the two brothers. Serious, somber, so-dignified Paul and buoyant, smiling, lighthearted Ancel.

"How did you know I would be here?" she asked.

"I heard that the owner of The Croft would be in town, and that had to be either you or your sister. Then yesterday I saw Jeremy Walde on the street, and he told me it was you who would be coming. So...I've been watching the house. I could hardly wait to see you again, Jennie."

Jennie shook her head in amusement. "Ah, yes, the White Rock grapevine, still operating at peak efficiency. I'd hate to try keeping a secret around this town."

"It's impossible, just like always."

"What are you doing out this way—besides looking for me?"

He seemed surprised. "I'm your next-door neighbor. Don't you remember?"

"Oh, of course!" she cried. "I'd forgotten that the Gunters owned the property adjacent to The Croft. But I don't remember any of you ever living there. You always had tenants taking care of the place."

"Not anymore. I live there now. Built a little cabin until I can get a house put up."

Jennie was genuinely astonished. "You don't work at the bank?"

"Hell, no!" he exploded. "That place gives me the creeps! I've been in funeral parlors that were less depressing." He paused, and his eyes made a blatant sweep of her. "Little Jennie Cameron! You certainly did grow up nice."

"Well...ah...thank you, Ancel," she said with a

nervous little laugh, at a loss for words and a trifle embarrassed by his frank scrutiny. He made absolutely no attempt to conceal his open admiration, and Jennie found that disconcerting, though flattering.

Abruptly his gaze shifted from her curvaceous young body to her face. "Say, Jennie, I brought along a cooler full of beer and sandwiches. It's not all that long until suppertime, and I felt sure you wouldn't have anything here. Care to join me?"

"Why, Ancel, how thoughtful!"

"Not entirely unselfish, though. Sometimes I go for weeks without seeing another human being...and I never see one who looks like *you* do."

Jennie smiled up at him gratefully. She truly was glad Ancel had showed up. He had relaxed her and dispelled the melancholy.

He winked at her. "Be right back."

Jennie watched as his long strides took him to a dilapidated wagon pulled by a sleek chestnut mare that now was tethered to the front porch railing. It seemed only natural that Ancel Gunter should be driving a horse and wagon. He most definitely did not look the part of a banker. When she had been dating Paul she had thought him infinitely more handsome than his younger brother. Now she was having second thoughts. Perhaps Paul's dark, brooding good looks were more arresting than Ancel's sunny blondness, but there was a solid human warmth to Ancel that was completely missing in his older brother.

She recalled Paul's impeccable dress, his smooth manners, his finesse and savoir-faire. By contrast Ancel was every inch the country cowboy—strong shoulders, slender waist and hips, tanned face that was a bit weathered for—what would he be now? About thirty-four Jennie guessed. He was an utterly masculine figure, fairly bursting with vitality. And so open. There was about him the air of a man who had never met a stranger.

Watching Ancel she could not help thinking of Paul, her onetime fiancé who had so casually turned from her to marry the daughter of a man whose fortune matched the Gunter millions. When she had fallen in love with him she had been so young and innocent, so completely besotted with him. His ultimate rejection had hurt deeply, and the scars still were there.

She wondered if Paul was happy in his fortuitous marriage, and she longed to ask Ancel about him. But then she thought better of it. As she recalled, Paul and his younger brother were not close. As a matter of fact, it had often seemed that they plainly could not stand one another. Not too surprising, she supposed, given their disparate natures. So, Jennie decided it was best not to quiz Ancel about his brother.

They sat at the wooden kitchen table, munching sandwiches and drinking beer. Ancel had even thought to bring a cloth for the table. And he was very anxious to know what she had been doing since leaving White Rock.

"Well, let's see..." Jennie said. "I left five years ago, right after Papa's death."

Ancel nodded. "I hated hearing about that. Rob Cameron was one of my favorite people. Damned few like him around these days, I'll tell you. His word was his bond. I'd rather have a handshake from someone like Rob Cameron than an eighty-page contract from someone else."

Jennie smiled sadly. "I know. He used to say he'd rather argue for two years before a deal was made than for two seconds afterwards. Nothing made him more suspicious than lawyers, accountants—and bankers."

Ancel laughed. "So, Jennie, what did you do after your dad passed away?"

"I went back to U.T. Meg had married Steve by then, and I spent most of my holidays with them. But I didn't want to be a complete nuisance, so I went to summer school and got a flunky job on one of the local newspapers. Then, just before graduation, I saw a notice on the journalism department's bulletin board. A job had opened up with a new magazine, a regional publication for women published in Fort Worth called *Women Now*. I applied, and...I've been with them over three years now."

"Like it?"

"Oh, yes!"

Ancel shook his head. "I can't stand a city for more than five minutes...unless it takes me longer than that to pass through." He looked at her levelly. "Ever get married?"

"No. How about you?"

"Nope."

Jennie crossed her arms and rested them on the table. "Now...you tell me what you've been doing."

He pushed his chair away from the table a bit and leaned back. "Lord! That's a tall order. Well, let's see...six years ago Dad was after me strong to go into the family business. He and Paul have interests all over the state, so they sent me to work in their Amarillo bank. I didn't last long there, I'll tell you—I discovered very quickly that I simply wasn't cut out to be a banker. I always figured if you got within a couple of bucks of the transaction, what the hell!"

Jennie giggled. "I can understand how that kind of attitude might upset a banker."

"Poor Dad. I suppose he considers me the one failure in his imminently successful life. Anyway, I just left Amarillo without a word and bummed around the country, working until I had the money to move on. Went to San Francisco, then on up to British Columbia and to Alaska. When I came back I drove a motorcycle from Seattle to Hartford, Connecticut."

Jennie clapped her hands together and laughed merrily. "Good heavens! *Why?*"

Ancel shrugged and flashed the dazzling smile again. "A fellow paid me to deliver his bike safe and sound to his brother's house in Hartford. And I'd never done anything like that before."

"Press on. I'm intrigued. What next?"

"Oh, dozens of things. I worked in a textile mill in South Carolina, hired out on a fishing boat in Florida, picked cotton in Mississippi, hired out on a drilling rig off the Louisiana coast. You name it, and I've probably done it."

Jennie stared at him in disbelief. Here was a man who could have millions, and he had picked cotton in Mississippi! "So what finally brought you back to White Rock?" she asked, burning with curiosity about her companion.

For the first time since their meeting, Ancel grew serious. "I woke up in some strange little town in Alabama one morning, and to be painfully honest with you, Jennie, I had a granddaddy of a hangover. I remember laying there and thinking, 'Ancel, what in the hell are you doing? Are you going to bum around the country until you're too sick or old, or both, to do anything else? What are you looking for?' And do you know what the answer was?"

Jennie shook her head.

"Peace," he said simply. "Peace for my mind, peace for my soul. And I knew I wasn't apt to find it among strangers in strange towns. So I came home. Dad and Paul didn't exactly roll out the red carpet. I mean, there was none of the prodigal son bit, but I'm glad I came home when I did. Mama died not long after that, and I never would have forgiven myself if I hadn't seen her before she passed away. She's the reason I have the property next door. It was hers, and she left it to me. She knew I'd never have a place in the Gunter banking empire, and she wanted me to have something. The property was pretty run-down when I got hold of it, but I've worked my tail off these last two years, and I'm going to have something special one of these days, Jennie."

So Ancel didn't have any of the Gunter millions, just three hundred or so acres of hill-country brush land. Yes, Jennie could imagine his being written out of the Gunter fortune. Remembering Ernst Gunter, the formidable old family patriarch, and knowing Paul, she could well imagine it. A wave of sympathy for Ancel swept through her. She thought she knew how he must feel at times.

"How fortunate you are to have something to work toward," she said seriously.

Ancel looked at her. "And what about you, Jennie? What are you working toward?"

What could she tell him? How could she tell a dynamic man like Ancel Gunter that her thoughts rarely went far beyond tomorrow's workday or the bills that had to be paid on the first of the month or what she would wear on a Saturday-night date? She was sure he would be disappointed in her, and for some reason she hated that. It sounded so...narrow, so limited. Oh, of course she had vague dreams about the future. To do her dead-level best at *WN* and someday possibly receive an offer from a larger, more prestigious publication. But she, unlike some of her co-workers, did not covet Gloria Travis's job. She thought that someday she would write, but that was a nebulous dream, something she would pursue when the right combination of ideas, time, and solitude coincided.

Certainly that time was not just around the corner. So, the truth was, she was working toward just taking things one day at a time and playing it by ear.

"Oh," she said lightly, "I suppose that right now I'm working toward selling this place and getting back to my job in Fort Worth."

As she had feared, he looked disappointed. "How long do you plan to be here?"

"Not one single minute longer than is necessary. This is my vacation, and I hadn't planned to spend it this way."

"You aren't exactly thrilled over paying a visit to the old hometown, I take it." There was no censure in his voice, only a trace of amusement, but Jennie was appalled at her bad manners. White Rock was Ancel's hometown, too, and not many people appreciated having their home disparaged.

"Oh, no! It's not that. Actually, I enjoyed driving into town again, seeing the familiar sights. It's been a long time. I just wish it were more of a pleasure trip, not business."

Now Ancel leaned forward and spoke earnestly. "Word along the White Rock grapevine has it that my brother is the one who wants to buy your place."

Jennie's mouth set in a grim line. "Yes, so Mr. Walde tells me. I was rather surprised."

Ancel rubbed his chin and grew thoughtful. "So am

I . . . so am I. I didn't believe it when I first heard about it. In all the time we've owned the property next to you, neither Paul nor Dad has ever shown any interest in it. I can't figure it out."

"Well," Jennie said sighing, "I'll find out just how serious he is tomorrow morning. I'm to meet Paul and Mr. Walde at the bank at eleven o'clock. The only thing I know for certain is that Paul's offer is considerably less than the asking price because the place is so run-down." She glanced about her with a rueful expression. "I guess he's got a point. I wouldn't have dreamed everything would look so shabby after five years, and I haven't even looked outside."

Ancel got to his feet. "Let me put this stuff away, and we'll have a look around before it gets dark."

Together they cleared away the debris of the meal, and then hurried out the back door. From the porch Jennie could see the sagging clothesline and the decaying chicken coop. Ancel took her by the hand and they crossed the bare dirt semicircle immediately behind the house, past the long wooden bench where beehives once had been kept. Oh, that sweet clover honey! Jennie ran the tip of her tongue over her lips at the remembrance.

They went to stand at the corral fence. Jennie screwed her eyes tightly shut and saw the now vacant corral as it once had been, a ferment of activity, with half a dozen horses milling about, and Rob or one of the hired hands riding among them, whooping and hollering. She had grown up on horseback, and Rob once had told her she rode "just like a man"—the ultimate compliment.

She opened her eyes and was startled to find they had filled with tears. Oh, she had to stop all this mawkishness! Nothing could bring back those days. Nothing!

She swiveled her head in time to see Ancel emerge from the old shed that had housed Rob's tractor. She watched him as he squinted his eyes under the stetson hat that was so flattering to his masculine good looks. He looked so...*unrestricted* she supposed was the word. A man too loose and free ever to be confined within walls.

Finally, his inspection completed, he came over to her. "This is great property, Jennie. Damned shame to sell it." He took her hand and began walking aimlessly, almost pulling her along with him. "You see, your west end joins my place, so I know that's your most fertile pasture, the one for sowing forage crops. A couple dozen head of cattle, a bull, some sheep, and a few goats to get the brush where it's too rocky and hilly to plow, and you'd be in business. Goats are great creatures for hill-country ranchers to have. Of course, there's no way you can get by without some pick and shovel work, but The Croft takes to a plow better than my place does." He then reversed his direction and gave his attention to the house. "The house itself is in good shape. All it needs is some general tidying-up. You could have this place in shipshape condition in no time."

"Wait a minute, Ancel," she laughed. "Slow down. That's for the new owner to worry about. I'm not going to farm the place."

Ancel dropped her hand, shrugged, and thrust his hands into the pockets of his jeans. "Well, sure, Jennie, I forgot. I guess I got a little carried away. You're looking at a man who's spent two years pouring his heart and soul into a place that was in a whole lot worse shape than The Croft is, and, well, I just can't imagine having something like this and wanting to sell it."

"I suppose we look at it in different ways," she said and wondered again why on earth she hated disappointing him. "It's foolish for us to keep the place. I live in Fort Worth, and Meg certainly doesn't care anything about a run-down hill-country ranch. She and Steve are strictly high society."

"I guess I'm just worried," Ancel said, frowning. "Paul, of all people.... It would be such a shame to sell The Croft to the wrong person."

Jennie was puzzled. "Why would it be a shame? Why do you care what the new owner does with it?"

He looked at her for a brief moment, and again she had the strangest feeling she had disappointed him. "You wouldn't understand," he said simply.

Normally nothing irritated her more than to have a man terminate a conversation with "you wouldn't understand," as though she was some sort of simpleminded child. This time, however, she thought Ancel might be right; she couldn't understand why he cared.

They had walked around the side of the house and had come to the front. Ancel sat on one of the porch steps and pulled Jennie down to sit beside him. "Jennie, I'm going to ask a favor of you."

"Of course, Ancel."

"Tomorrow morning when you meet with Paul and Jeremy, I want you to be careful," he said forcefully, his eyes deep and penetrating. A forefinger tapped her gently on her arm, punctuating his remark.

"Careful?"

"*Damned* careful," he emphasized. "Jeremy's in this for the sale. You can't blame him certainly—that's his business. But Paul"—now Ancel's gaze became distant—"Paul I can't figure out. But I know one thing: He thinks he can make some money off The Croft or he wouldn't be interested. And what's a hill-country ranch good for except raising livestock and crops? Somehow I can't see Paul raising chickens and horses and cows and cucumbers. So...just be careful. This place is worth money—I mean real money. I know what hill-country ranches are going for these days and it's plenty! Jeremy knows it too, but he and Paul are old bosom buddies. They might figure a sweet little city girl wouldn't know from straight up what this place is worth."

Jennie smiled ruefully. "I'm afraid they'd be right."

"Let me give you some advice. Don't do anything hasty. Don't let 'em stampede you into anything. I don't care what they offer you, just smile sweetly and tell them you'll think it over. Then bring a copy of the contract to me, and I'll look it over. I'm not too worried about Jeremy. He's an honest businessman, and it's his job to present any serious offer to you. But Paul—I wouldn't trust Paul as far as I can toss him."

Jennie bit her lip nervously. Jeremy Walde had, some years before, given her and Meg a rough appraisal of what The Croft was worth and had told them to count on a ten percent annual appreciation, but Jennie didn't know if those guidelines still held true. And the ranch had been in much better condition in those days. She honestly didn't know what the place was worth, so how could she determine if an offer was a fair one or not? She badly wanted to sell the place, but the thought that she might get taken rankled. However, she was not at all confident of her ability to deal with two prominent businessmen who were experts at this sort of thing, while she honestly knew nothing about it.

She turned to Ancel, who seemed so knowledgeable about these matters. "Ah... Ancel, I know it's probably an imposition, and I'll certainly understand if you don't want to, but... could you possibly see your way clear to..."

He grinned. "To go to the meeting with you in the morning?"

Her eyes lit up. "Well... yes, if it's not too much trouble."

"It's not too much trouble, Jennie, and if you hadn't asked, I probably would have insisted."

"You're really being very, very kind," Jennie said gratefully, suddenly relieved that she would have someone in her corner tomorrow morning.

"Nonsense. What are friends and neighbors for? Besides, I'd give the family jewels to know what Paul's up to." He slapped his knee and stood up. "Well, now that that's settled, I'm going over to my place and get my bedroll and some stuff for breakfast in the morning. I won't be gone long." He paused when he saw the look on Jennie's face. "Oh, well... I guess I should have asked before inviting myself to sleep over, but hell, Jennie, I can't let you stay here alone! I wouldn't feel right about it. You don't even have a telephone."

"I'm not afraid, Ancel," she said weakly, stunned that he would suggest such an arrangement.

"No... no. You've forgotten how dark and deserted the country is at night. I'll sleep on the sofa in the living room where I can keep an eye on things. Or you can come over to my place, but I think you'd be much more comfortable here. There isn't much privacy in my cabin, but whatever you decide, there's no way I'm going to let you stay here alone."

Jennie hesitated. She considered herself a "modern" woman. She didn't bat an eye over some of her friends' live-in arrangements and liberated lifestyles, but that was in Fort Worth. White Rock was a small town with old-fashioned values. And it thrived on gossip. What passed without notice in Fort Worth would be a cause célèbre in White Rock.

Still, she had to admit she would feel better if Ancel were in the house with her. And what did she care what people thought? She was far removed from them now. Even so, she was glad The Croft was so remote that the incident would pass unnoticed, and therefore uncommented upon.

"All right, Ancel," she said finally. "I'll feel much better if you're here. And I honestly don't know how to thank you. You've gone way beyond neighborliness."

"That's because I'm such a prince of a guy," he said, smiling down at her and winking. Casually he slipped an arm around her waist and gave her a little squeeze, causing a warm sensation to spread through her. Then he released her, and he moved toward the wagon in his loose gait, hands in pockets, whistling.

Later, after Ancel had returned and stocked the refrigerator with food for breakfast, he helped her unload her car. Then they passed a pleasant hour or so discussing general matters, and Jennie got caught up on local gossip. It was almost ten o'clock when they said good night and Jennie climbed the stairs to the bedroom.

She unpacked her suitcases, then put sheets on the bed and performed her usual bedtime ritual. Finally she turned off the lights, crawled between the covers, pillowed her head on her arms and stared at the ceiling.

Tonight sleep was elusive, surprisingly so. She had expected to drift off quickly, for she felt numb from exhaustion. However, she half-suspected her exhaustion to stem not so much from physical fatigue as from a nerve-whipped tension. It had not been easy to come home again, and the worst was yet to come.

Jennie tried not to dwell upon how many hundreds of nights she had lain in this very bed, staring at the ceiling, Meg asleep in the bed next to hers. Those had been mostly happy years, those years of her childhood, when her whole world had been these rough cedar hills. It had not occurred to her then that anything exciting or compelling lay beyond this limited universe.

But those years were gone forever, were past tense, just like Paul Gunter was past tense. A beautiful Galveston socialite named Ellen Barton had become Mrs. Paul Gunter, not Jennifer Cameron. That was over and done with, and soon her last tie to these hills would be severed. It was only right that this should be so.

Jennie thought she had done very well under the circumstances. At twenty-six she was a self-sufficient woman with no need for more than she had. Certainly she did not need anyone for wholeness, for completeness. Needing someone had ended with Paul Gunter's marriage to Ellen Barton. The "Dear Jane" letter he had written to her at the university had shattered her small world and plunged her into a despondency that at times had frightened her. When at last she had emerged from her private depths it was with a protective coat of armor around what was left of her heart. She was too suspicious of men's motives, she knew; she also knew that she demanded more than most men were willing to give. At the first hint that a man's love was not unalterable, not unshakable, he was quickly dismissed. She couldn't help it. The damage had been done long ago, and she never, ever, intended being hurt again.

Alone was better, she told herself. She never regretted the past, but she never forgot it either. It had taught her some valuable lessons.

But occasionally, in weak moments when her defenses were down, she could not avoid wondering what course her life would have taken had she fallen in love with someone unlike Paul, someone with more compassion and gentleness, someone less concerned with himself, a man capable of letting a woman into his heart and soul and making her a vital part of his life.

From time to time a nagging inner voice spoke to her, reminding her that being free and independent was fine at twenty-five or thirty. But what about thirty-five or forty? Inevitably she thought of Gloria Travis then, and a large obstruction lodged in her throat and would not go away.

Chapter Three

The sun's first rays were only beginning to rise over the horizon when Jennie awoke to sounds emanating from the kitchen. She considered herself an early riser; in Fort Worth she always allowed an hour for a leisurely breakfast and the morning newspaper before dressing for work. But when she went downstairs that morning it was obvious that Ancel had been up for some time. His bedroll had been neatly rolled and tied and propped in a corner of the living room; coffee was on, and he was standing at the stove, cooking bacon and eggs, dressed and clean-shaven.

"Good heavens, that smells good!" she exclaimed, suddenly ravenously hungry.

"Eat hearty. You'll need your strength," he said over his shoulder. He expertly scooped an egg out of the skillet onto a plate, plopped three slices of bacon and piece of toast beside it, then carried it to the table and set it before her.

"Why did you say that?" she asked, eyeing the tantalizing food. "Do you think the meeting this morning is going to be that difficult?"

"Do you?" he asked, placing his own plate on the

table. He then returned to the stove to fill two cups with coffee and returned to the table.

"Well...I'm not very good when it comes to business negotiations," she admitted.

"That's not what I meant, and you know it," Ancel said, forking in a mouthful of food.

Jennie sighed. There was no use pretending that Ancel didn't know she had once been thoroughly jilted by his brother. "It was over between Paul and me years ago, Ancel. Past history. I haven't thought about it in ages," she lied.

"Good! He never was worth five minutes of your time, Jennie. He's nothing but a conceited opportunist who doesn't give a damn about anything but money. But I might have known a sharp gal like you wouldn't waste your time pining over the likes of Paul. I'll bet there are half a dozen guys in Fort Worth who are just panting to get you to the altar."

Jennie smiled wryly. "I'm afraid there's not even one."

"Has there ever been...I mean since Paul?"

"No."

His eyebrows arched. "Damn! My brother really did a number on you, didn't he?"

His words jolted Jennie; then she couldn't help asking, "What about you, Ancel? Have you ever been in love?"

"Once."

"Only once? What happened, if I'm not being too nosy?"

"Nothing happened. She didn't know I was alive."

Jennie shot him a sympathetic look. So someone had done a number on him, too. They had a lot in common.

After breakfast they washed the dishes and tidied the kitchen, then Ancel left to go to his own place, promising to return before ten thirty. Jennie went upstairs to make her bed and take a bath, then spent a long time deciding what to wear, as though looking her best would somehow shore up her confidence, which she admitted was sagging badly. Many times in the past she had conjured up visions of her next meeting with Paul Gunter, and she had imagined it under every conceivable set of circumstances, but never once had she envisioned selling The Croft to him.

Finally she chose a simple coral-colored dress that had a short jacket. The outfit showed off her slender figure to perfection, and the color was flattering. She screwed gold studs into her earlobes, slipped her feet into beige pumps, and surveyed herself in the mirror. If only she could get the worried look off her face, she thought, she wouldn't look half bad. She wanted to look every inch the successful career girl, as sophisticated as possible, no small task considering the churning in her stomach.

She heard the front door open, then Ancel's voice called up the stairs, "Jennie, I'll wait for you out front. Lock the door behind you. I've got the key."

"Right," she called back. She took one last look in the mirror, grabbed her handbag and went downstairs. Ancel was waiting on the front porch. He had changed into light brown pants and a cream-colored shirt, both western cut, and was wearing the ever present boots and stetson. To Jennie's eyes he seemed as golden as the bright morning. The man's masculinity was overwhelming.

Then her eyes strayed to the vehicle parked behind her car in the driveway. It had to be the most disreputable pickup truck she ever had seen. "Is that...yours?" she asked.

"Yep. Doesn't look like much but it runs like a fine watch."

"Ah, Ancel, why don't we take my car? I need gas."

"Sure, Jennie, whatever. Want me to drive?"

"Yes, please."

Inside the cramped confines of the Toyota, Jennie was amazed to discover she was acutely aware of Ancel, of the sure way he handled the car, of his strong hands at the wheel. She would have loved nothing better than to simply study him, but there was no way she could do so unobtrusively. She had to be content with a few quick glances in his direction, nothing sufficient to satisfy her curiosity.

He had a strong face. In repose it seemed all angles and planes, intensely serious, but when he smiled, which he did often, it changed instantly and became charming, almost boyish.

There was something ineffably kind and gentle about Ancel Gunter, yet powerful too, and Jennie instinctively knew him for a man who could handle himself well in any circumstance. She found that she was warming to him enormously, and that was strange for a woman inclined to hold men at arm's length, to suspect their words and motives.

As though sensing her acceptance of him, Ancel turned and gave her that warm generous smile that was so free of guile. Then he winked at her, and she felt oddly comforted. She had a friend. Her nervousness subsided a bit, and she thought that maybe, just maybe, this morning's meeting would not be as difficult as she had feared.

The lobby of the Gunter State Bank had undergone

extensive redecoration, Jennie noted as she and Ancel pushed through the double entrance doors. It now was a serene world of mirrors and polished wood and thick carpeting and huge chandeliers. Ancel waved to a chorus of "G'morning, Ancel" as they crossed the lobby and made their way to the elevator that carried them to the second floor. Standing in front of a door marked MEETING ROOM was Jeremy Walde. The fat, florid realtor greeted them both warmly, but it was Jennie who received most of his attention.

"Jennifer, my dear! How wonderful to see you! You've grown into such a lovely young woman. Your father would be proud of you."

"Thank you, Mr. Walde," she said, feeling as uncomfortable as always when complimented.

"Paul will be out any moment, and then we can get to the business at hand. I know you're anxious to have this over and done with," Jeremy said. "Unusually mild weather we're having for this time of year, isn't it? How is Margaret, Jennifer? Goodness, I haven't seen you girls in such a long time! Margaret is living in...?"

"San Antonio," Jennie offered.

"And you are still living in...?"

"Fort Worth. Yes, I am."

"Getting to be quite a city, isn't it? Shedding the old cowtown image, I suppose. Why, I remember back in the fifties..."

The realtor's voice droned on, asking questions that required no answers, making pointless observations. Jennie shifted restlessly, and her stomach churned with dread. She hated this feeling of not being in complete control. Twice she caught herself glancing in the mirror behind Jeremy's head and patting her hair nervously.

When a door at the end of the hall opened, she turned frantically to Ancel.

"Don't leave me for a second," she whispered.

"Don't worry, Jennie, I won't," he said in a soothing, comforting tone. He took one of her small hands in his big one and squeezed it sympathetically. Steeling herself for the inevitable, she raised her eyes and watched as Paul Gunter rushed forward to greet her.

He had not changed perceptibly. A few strands of gray now showed in the thick crop of dark hair, but he was every bit as handsome as she had remembered, tall and impeccable in his stylish three-piece gray suit, every inch the sophisticated, urbane gentleman.

And the smooth baritone voice had not changed. "Jennie!" he cried in wonderment. "How marvelous to see you!"

"Hello, Paul. How are you?" she inquired, unsuccessfully striving for a cool, crisp tone. To her own ears her voice sounded weak and unsure.

He had extended his hand, and automatically she took it, which forced her to remove hers from Ancel's comforting grip. That brief contact with his warm flesh sent a rippling shock through her. Quickly she extracted her hand and reached for Ancel's. Her eyes strayed from Paul's penetrating gaze only to run headlong into Ancel's watchful, speculative one.

Only then did Paul appear to notice his brother. The smile that had been trained on Jennie faded, and the smoky-gray eyes showed not the slightest trace of welcoming warmth. "Well, Ancel, what are you doing here?" he asked in a cold and commanding voice.

Jennie frowned, taken aback by the rudeness Paul made no attempt to conceal. Before Ancel could reply, she interjected, "Ancel happened by The Croft yesterday, shortly after I arrived, and he graciously consented to come with me this morning.''

"I see,'' Paul said suspiciously.

Jennie then forced herself to look at Paul fully and honestly, and she was appalled to realize she was experiencing a few unpleasant twists and tugs in the region of the heart. For one awful minute she was back in another time, reliving those days when she had been reeling from the hurt of his rejection. But then she squared her shoulders and pulled herself up. This was absurd! She no longer was a starry-eyed girl poised on the brink of womanhood, and this man no longer was part of her life. Unconsciously, she tightened her grip on Ancel's hand.

Paul was gesturing toward the door. "Shall we go inside?'' he suggested with extreme politeness, while his expression clearly said that Ancel had no business there. Unperturbed, Ancel strolled into the meeting room behind Jennie and held the back of her chair while she sat down.

Once the four of them were seated around the long table, Jeremy Walde withdrew some papers from a briefcase and spread them out. He cleared his throat and began, "Now, Jennifer, I've drawn up a contract that spells out in detail the offer Paul has made on The Croft. I would like you to read it carefully, my dear, and ask any questions you care to.''

Jennie took the long legal form and began reading. She had not gone far, however, before her eyes widened, and she shot Jeremy a quizzical, dismayed look. "But, Mr. Walde, this offer is for considerably less than you said the ranch was worth several years ago!''

At this Ancel leaned over and read the document. Then he groaned disgustedly and sat back in his chair.

Jeremy cleared his throat again. "I know, Jennifer, but—"

Paul interrupted. "But, Jennie, the property is in rather decrepit condition."

"Like hell it is!" Ancel roared, and they all turned to stare at him. Paul's face clouded darkly as his brother went on. "Jennie and I made a thorough inspection of the place yesterday, and it's splendid property. You know it as well as I do," he said to his brother. Then he turned to the realtor and pointed an accusing finger. "So do you, Jeremy. I'm surprised at you."

Jeremy looked pathetically uncomfortable. "Property is worth whatever someone is willing to pay for it, Ancel. This is the first serious reasonable offer that's been made."

"I don't consider that a reasonable offer," Ancel retorted.

Paul spoke up. "Who's selling The Croft anyway, you or Jennie? Jennie, just what does he have to do with this?"

"Ancel is here as my friend and as my legal advisor. It certainly appears that I need one," she said defiantly and heard Paul give a derisive snort.

Ancel leaned forward and placed one hand on her arm. "Jennie," he said earnestly, "selling The Croft for what Paul is offering is tantamount to giving it away. You know Rob wouldn't want that."

"Jennifer, the place has been vacant for five years," Jeremy reminded her. "It must be a bit of a burden on you and your sister what with taxes going up every year, and—"

"The trust pays the taxes, Mr. Walde," Jennie told him. "It's no burden on either Meg or me."

"Jennie," Ancel said, genuine concern showing in

his expression, "the house alone is worth almost as much as Paul is offering—"

"That's preposterous!" Jeremy cut in. "No one would pay that much for that house."

"—and it's sitting in the middle of a couple hundred acres of good ranchland," Ancel continued as though nothing had been said. "It will run several dozen head of prime cattle with ease. A rancher would pay top dollar for it."

"Find me that rancher," Jeremy muttered.

"The house is shabby and neglected, and I intend having it torn down," Paul said darkly, "and I certainly don't intend raising cattle."

Jennie glanced at Ancel with alarm, then at Paul. "I—I don't understand. What do you mean, you're going to tear down the house?"

"Just what I said. I'm going to raze the house and outbuildings and have the land cleared by a bulldozer."

Jennie's heart thudded unpleasantly. She shouldn't care, of course, but she did; she was deeply troubled and saddened by the thought of demolishing the house Rob Cameron had built with his own hands.

Ancel, too, appeared to be acutely interested. His eyes fastened intently on his brother. "May I ask why?"

"No, you may not!" Paul answered viciously.

"Then perhaps *I* may ask," Jennie said.

The rigid set to Paul's face slowly relaxed, and pointedly ignoring Ancel, he gave Jennie what she thought was a rather condescending smile. "Jennie, this part of the world is on the verge of a tourist boom—I'm convinced of it. The developments south of us have been enormously successful, and the people continue to come. They're looking for room to expand, and it's only natural to assume they'll follow the river. It should bring a tremendous influx of newcomers to this area, and with them will come money and new jobs and growth—progress."

"Forgive me, Paul, I still don't understand. What does all that have to do with The Croft?"

"Dad and I have become associated with a development firm in Dallas. We want to take the land The Croft is on and build a beautiful, exclusive resort hotel, something really marvelous that will lure the tourists. It will have a swimming pool, of course, and tennis courts, a sauna and a great restaurant. Even perhaps a small landing strip for private planes." Paul's normally somber eyes were filled with excitement as he spoke of his grandiose plans.

Ancel's reaction to all this was undisguised horror. "Oh, my God!" he groaned. "Do you have any idea what all that will do to ranching country?"

"It's progress!" Paul snapped.

"Funny, the longer I live the more I realize that most of what's termed progress really isn't very progressive," Ancel retorted.

"It's important for White Rock to grow along with the rest of the state!" Paul declared vehemently.

"To whom is it important? To the people who live here or to Gunter State Bank?" Ancel asked bitterly. "You want to ruin this country for the ranchers who have been here for generations. You want to practically steal this girl's land and then turn around and make a tidy fortune for yourself. You picked the right profession, Paul—I'll bet you get a real kick out of foreclosing mortgages."

Instantly Paul was on his feet, his eyes blazing. "Now wait just a damned minute!"

"No, *you* wait just a damned minute!" Ancel cried.

A fierce throbbing had begun at Jennie's temples. She was totally bewildered, appalled. If there was anything she was not in the mood for it was a shouting match between these two antagonistic brothers.

None of this was turning out the way she had hoped. Paul's offer was acutely disappointing, but that did not bother her as much as the planned destruction of her childhood home. It was ridiculous; she didn't live in White Rock any longer, doubtlessly never would be back once she left this time, so it shouldn't matter to her. Still....

Her eyes sought and held Ancel's. He gave her the merest flicker of expression, but curiously she understood him perfectly. *Wait,* he was telling her. *Don't rush into anything.*

Paul was still on his feet. "Jennie, I'm sure we can negotiate this matter and come to a reasonable compromise on price," he said.

A defiant set to her chin, Jennie got to her feet; Ancel and Jeremy did likewise. "I'm not sure money is the most important issue now," she told him. Then, indicating the contract in her hand, she added, "But I'll take this home and study it. I'll let you know what I decide tomorrow."

Paul and Jeremy exchanged glances, but there seemed to be nothing either of them could do or say. "Of course," Jeremy said finally.

"Shall we go, Ancel?" she asked, holding out her hand to him.

"Sure." He opened the door for her, then turned to Paul and the realtor, one corner of his mouth curved upward in a half-smile. "Good-bye, gentlemen. Have a nice day," he said brightly, and then he ushered Jennie across the hall to the waiting elevator.

"So how was it?" Ancel asked, studying her from across the expanse of the small table. They were having lunch at the Kingston Inn, a hill-country landmark. The historic old inn had been constructed in the days before the Civil War, designed to give stagecoach passengers from San Antonio a last taste of civilization before embarking on the perilous westward journey through hostile Indian territory. Its kitchen was justifiably famous, but today Jennie was doing little more than picking at the delicious food on her plate.

"How was what?" she hedged.

"Come on, Jennie," Ancel scoffed. "How was it, seeing Paul again after all this time?"

How had it been? Jennie wasn't sure. Difficult and awkward. Painful, too, as much as she hated admitting it. During the meeting she had found herself staring at him, most of all remembering those long drugging kisses. Well, he had been her first love, the one no woman is supposed to forget. Surely she hadn't expected to dismiss him with a wave of her hand. And surely Ancel understood. After all, he had been through something similar himself.

"Oh"—she shrugged and gave a nervous little laugh—"you know."

"Yeah." He waited a minute, then asked, "So what now?"

Jennie sighed. "Oh, Ancel, I don't know. This hasn't exactly turned out the way I thought it would."

"Don't worry about it, Jennie," Ancel said sensibly. "Relax, enjoy your food, enjoy the day. So you don't sell The Croft. What would be so terrible about that?"

"This whole trip will have been wasted, that's what."

He gave her a brief quizzical look, then his disarming smile was back, more heartwarming than ever. "Not really," he said lightly. "You got to see me again."

That brought a merry, lilting laugh from Jennie. She truly was delighted to be in Ancel's company.

"It's good to hear you laugh like that, Jennie." He reached across the small table and gently touched the space between her eyebrows. "Get that frown off your face and keep it off. You're too pretty to look so worried. Would you like dessert?"

"Oh, heavens no! I couldn't eat another bite."

A uniformed waitress appeared, and Ancel ordered coffee for both. When it arrived he settled back in his chair and looked at Jennie thoughtfully. She returned the look in full measure and felt a warm flush race through her from head to foot. He had the most compelling manner; he was so warm and sunny and open that she couldn't help feeling immeasurably drawn to him.

"You know, Jennie," he said, "I've been thinking. Paul's probably right about some things. White Rock no doubt is going to grow during the next few years. My brother and I might regard that prospect in different lights, but one thing is sure—land values are going to skyrocket. I can't help but think you have three options open to you."

"Which are?"

"One, you can negotiate with Paul, get him to come up on the price. If he wants your property as badly as I think he does, he'll come up. But I have a hunch you aren't any happier than I am over his plans for The Croft. Right?"

"Right," she agreed.

"Good girl! So two, you can leave things as they are, go on back to Fort Worth and tell Jeremy to keep looking for a buyer."

Jennie's expression was crestfallen. "Ancel, I can't drop everything and come running every time Mr. Walde *thinks* he has a buyer. I have a job, responsibilities."

"Exactly. So that leaves one last option."

She raised an eyebrow, intrigued. "And that is?"

"You and I can go out there and get The Croft in tip-top shape. Then we'll tell Jeremy to put it on the market for... well, I'm not sure about the price yet, but I'm thinking well into six figures. I promise I'll watch the place for you, make certain it stays in good condition. You can make me your authorized agent, and I'll screen all would-be buyers. You can be sure I won't bring you back here on a wild-goose chase, and you can be damned sure I won't let anyone have it who doesn't intend to keep it the way it is."

"Oh, Ancel!" she exclaimed, awestruck. "You're talking about an awful lot of money!"

"It would be worth every penny by the time we got through with it, Jennie."

He spoke in such earnestness that Jennie hated to squelch his enthusiasm, though she doubted the feasibility of his suggestion. "Tell me, Ancel...when you say tip-top shape, what are you talking about? What needs to be done?"

"You take the inside, and I'll do the outside. While you're painting the rooms and doing some general cleaning up, I'll repair the barn and mend the fence and get after the brush. If Rob's old tractor still works, I'll use that—if not, I'll bring mine over. Then together we can tackle the yard. You can weed a shrubbery bed, can't you? With everything looking nice and neat and lived-in, the land will sell itself to anyone who knows a thing about hill-country ranching.''

"Ancel—me? Paint? You've forgotten, I'm a city girl now. I've never painted a room in my life!"

"There's nothing to it, Jennie. You'll have it done in no time.''

She was skeptical and told him so, then added, "Maybe we'd be better off hiring the work done."

But Ancel apparently was a man who had no patience with misgivings and hesitancy. "No doubt you haven't hired any work done lately. You wait for days or weeks for the workmen to show up, then pay a small fortune for slipshod work. Take it from one who knows, I wasted an awful lot of money before I decided that if I wanted something done right, I was going to have to do it myself.''

"It just sounds like so much work to me."

"Not so much. Not really. You'll see."

"Time and money too," she persisted.

"What do you have to do for the next two weeks? You've already said your vacation has been thoroughly spoiled. And as for money, I can let you have some if you need it."

"Oh, no, Ancel! I didn't mean that!" He truly was a remarkable man. He would let her have money when he obviously had so little himself, was willing to spend time and effort when there was absolutely nothing in it for him. She shook her head in bewilderment. She simply wasn't accustomed to men like Ancel, men who were naturally generous. Sadly she realized that living in the city had instilled a bit of cynicism in her; she wasn't particularly happy with that realization. Weakly she tried to explain to him. "It's just that, well, I can't let you do all this for me. You have your own work, and—"

"Jennie," he reproached quietly, "I want to do this. I told you—that's what neighbors are for. Besides, I sure would like to see The Croft looking the way it did when Rob was there."

"So would I, Ancel," she said softly.

"And it's for damned certain I don't want swimming pools and tennis courts and *landing strips* over there!"

She smiled. "Neither do I. I don't know why I don't, but I don't. You know, it's been so strange seeing home again. I haven't given The Croft much thought these past few years. Oh, of course I've reminisced with friends about what it was like when I was young, but I can't honestly say I've had any burning longing to see it again. Now, it's the oddest thing—when Paul spoke of razing the homestead, I felt endangered, besieged." She raised her eyes to Ancel and laughed lightly. "Silly, huh?"

He reached across the table and took one of her hands to squeeze it in sympathetic communion. "No, not at all. I know the feeling, Jennie. I've been all over North America, but when it came time to plant roots, I came back here. These old hills are part of you. It's not something you can change just by going away. Wait until you see The Croft looking the way it was meant to look."

She sighed a long sigh. "All right, I'll give it a try. As you say, I don't really have anything to do for the next two weeks. But I'm warning you, I'm the least handy person on earth."

Ancel's warm green eyes crinkled at the corners, and he thumped the table with his fists. "Good! Good!" Immediately he was on his feet and around the table to pull out her chair. "Let's get this show on the road!"

"Goodness, Ancel! Do you mean right now?"

"Well, it's too late to do much today, but we have shopping to do. To the hardware store for paint, then to Walt Friedrich's for groceries. Looks as though you and I are going to be housemates for a while. A nice quiet supper, then off to bed. We want to get an early start in the morning.

Fine way to spend a vacation, she thought sourly. But it no doubt would be better for her than lounging around and gorging on Aunt Mary's fabulous cuisine. She'd sample a bit of the clean life and return to the offices of *WN* looking tanned and fit.

Throughout the afternoon, as they made their rounds of the stores, Jennie found herself studying her companion with growing interest. For one thing, Ancel was an outrageous flirt. He flirted with waitresses, with the cashier at the hardware store, with the elderly woman behind the bakery counter at Friedrich's. He even, she noted with amusement, flirted with her. He fairly oozed charm, and people warmed to him enormously. Jennie herself was beginning to feel like she had known him for years, a feeling Ancel fostered with all his lighthearted bantering.

But she couldn't help wondering if that devil-may-care exterior wasn't a pose, just a barricade he had erected to shield a real and deep wound. She speculated on the woman who "hadn't known he was alive." Did she live in White Rock? Was Ancel forced to see her from time to time? Was it the woman, not his dislike of banking, who was responsible for all those footloose, wandering years?

She sighed. She supposed she never would know.

Chapter Four

When Ancel said an early start he meant it. Once again when Jennie came downstairs his bedroll was propped in the corner, and he was standing at the kitchen stove, preparing breakfast. After they had eaten, she was settling back for a second cup of coffee and wishing she had a newspaper when he brought her sharply to reality.

"Let's get these dishes done and be about our work," he said.

Jennie glanced with horror at the wall clock. "It's seven o'clock!" she exclaimed.

"Yeah, I know. We're running late."

She started to laugh, then saw at once that he couldn't have been more serious, so she stood and carried her plate to the sink.

"First of all," he said, plunging his hands into the sinkful of soapy water, "I'm going over to my place to pick up a load of cedar posts, some leftovers from my own fence-mending a while back. I'll get you set up here before I leave. You'd better change into something old and comfortable, something you won't mind ruining."

She looked down at her rather disreputable jeans and

'sleeveless cotton shirt. "This is it. The oldest things I have."

His eyes roamed over her. "Those look like pretty good clothes to me, Jennie. Don't you have a pair of shorts?"

"Sure."

"Put those on. I'll give you one of my old shirts. It ought to come to about here." He ran a wet forefinger across her leg at mid-thigh level.

A smile tried desperately to escape, but Jennie refused to let it. "You are going to show me what to do, aren't you? I don't know a thing about this."

"Sure. Scoot along and change. I'll get you started."

Jennie hurried upstairs, changed, and glanced ruefully in the mirror. The faded plaid shirt Ancel had given her did indeed come to the point on her thigh that he had indicated. Her bare legs, slender and straight, looked ridiculous beneath the lumpy garment. The big shirt's neckline, though buttoned to the topmost button, revealed an alarming bit of cleavage. She looked, she thought, like a refugee from a storm, but there seemed little she could do about it. Struggling to roll the sleeves so that they would remain rolled, she hurried downstairs.

Back in the kitchen she noticed that Ancel had laid out a dropcloth and was pouring thick paint into a tray. He looked up when she entered, then burst into throaty laughter. "Hello, shirt!" he said. "Where's girl?"

"Very funny."

"It's been my experience," Ancel told her, "that it's best to use the roller first and then go back and do the brush work. This latex paint makes it all a snap. You'll be finished in no time."

Jennie glanced about the room and seriously doubted *that,* considering her lack of expertise, but she said nothing.

"As soon as I get back from my place, I'll be mending fence, so holler if you need me. You won't, though."

He clomped out the back door, the heels of his boots beating out a staccato rhythm as he crossed the porch, and Jennie turned to take stock of the task at hand. It seemed formidable to a novice, but there was nothing to do but wade in. Tentatively she slid the long-handled roller into the paint tray and raised it. To her amazement the thick goo adhered. Even more amazing was the way it looked on the wall. The fresh yellow streak was in marked contrast with the grimy, dull surface next to it. Suddenly she was seized by the desire to see the entire wall covered.

Within an hour Jennie had paint in her hair, on her face, on her eyelashes, all over the big shirt, but she had mastered the art of rolling paint. The brush work was harder—all that climbing and stretching—but when she stepped back to admire the one wall that had been completed, she decided the results were well worth her efforts. Thus inspired, she tackled the remainder of the room with considerably more enthusiasm.

"Good God!" Ancel exclaimed when he returned to the house for lunch. "What have you been painting with, a spray gun? You're a mess!"

"Thanks a lot! Never mind me, what about the room?"

He inspected her work. "You need more coverage here...and here. Lay it on thick. What's for lunch?"

Deflated, she could only mutter, "I've been busy. I haven't given a thought to lunch."

"That's all right. Didn't we get some sliced ham and cheese yesterday? I'll just have a sandwich. I don't want to waste a lot of time."

Jennie, also anxious to return to work, quickly prepared two sandwiches, which they devoured hurriedly and washed down with milk. She wondered at her suddenly voracious appetite. In Fort Worth she was deliberately abstemious, forever counting calories and watching her weight; now she seemed to be starving every time she turned around. *At this rate,* she thought, *I'll be out of shape before we get this damned place in shape!*

By four o'clock that afternoon the kitchen had been finished. In the whole of her life Jennie did not think she had seen anything more splendid, more beautiful! But now everything else about the room appeared drab and dingy. Once the brushes and the roller and the tray were cleaned and put away, Jennie made up a pail of sudsy water and began washing everything in sight. Refrigerator, stove, table, and floor all got a thorough going-over. Then she washed the windows. The more she did the more she felt like doing. When Ancel returned to the house at six o'clock he found her slumped at the kitchen table, battle-weary but exultant.

"Welcome to the cleanest room on the North American continent!" she said proudly.

"Looks nice," he observed blandly.

"Nice? Is that all you can say? It sparkles, it shines, it's beautiful! Look at these hands! These once-lovely hands have scrubbed every inch of this room. You could eat off that floor right now, and all you can say is that it looks nice!"

His amused eyes made a quick sweep of the room before settling on the lovely, weary creature in front of him. He raised his shoulders in a little shrug. "What do you want, Jennie? A six-page spread in *House Beautiful*?"

"Oh—oh—you!" She stood up and began stalking out of the room. "I'm going to take a bath."

"What's for supper?" he called after her.

She turned at the foot of the stairs. "Don't you ever think about anything but food?"

He had walked into the dining room and was leaning against the door frame, grinning. "You might be surprised at some of the things I think about, Jennie," he said with delightful wickedness, "but a working man needs sustenance. But never mind for tonight. You go on and take your bath and relax. I'll see to supper."

It occurred to Jennie that Ancel was carrying more than his share of the burden around the place, but she couldn't think about that tonight. Upstairs she drew her bath, then eased in her aching muscles, quite certain there wasn't a spot on her body that didn't hurt. She laid her head back, wanting nothing more than to stay in the deep, fragrant comfort of the water. Her eyelids grew heavy. Oh, she was tired, so tired.

In what seemed like only minutes but must have been much longer she was startled out of her stupor by heavy pounding on the bathroom door.

"Jennie! Jennie! Are you all right? Answer me!" It was Ancel, and his voice throbbed with alarm. She heard the doorknob rattle. "Damn it, why did you lock this door? Are you all right?"

"Huh?" she asked groggily. Then she straightened in the tub and shook her head. "Oh...yes. Yes...I'm fine."

"My God! You've been in there forever. I thought you had drowned. Are you sure you're all right?"

"Yes, Ancel, yes. I'm sure."

"Well, get out of there and let me see you!"

"Just—just a minute." Jennie climbed out of the tub, quickly toweled herself dry and slipped into a white terrycloth robe. Cinching it tightly about her waist, she opened the door.

"Thank God!" he cried, slumping against the wall. "I almost had a stroke when I came up here to see what in hell was taking you so long and found you still were in the bathroom. As tired as you are, I shouldn't have let you out of my sight."

"It might have been rather difficult for me to bathe under those circumstances," she reminded him.

"Come on. Supper will be ready in a minute."

"But I haven't dressed," she protested.

His eyes looked her up and down. "You're fine. Come on."

"Wait, let me pull the plug." She bent to let the water out of the tub, hung her towel neatly across the bar, and then like a docile child she followed Ancel down the stairs and into the kitchen.

He looked as fresh and clean as a spring morning, Jennie noted. He obviously had showered in the down-stairs bathroom, changed clothes, and had begun supper, his energies and spirits undaunted by a day of hard work in the warm sun, while she was a physical wreck who could barely stumble from room to room after a day's bout with a paintbrush.

A flush of admiration for her robust companion washed over her, along with a vow to do better. Tomorrow she would be up bright and early, would paint and scrub and still be alert and active enough to prepare their supper. But not tonight. Tonight she was just too tired to do anything.

Wearily she sank into one of the chairs at the kitchen table and watched Ancel spurt around the kitchen, moving from stove to refrigerator to cupboard and back to the stove. He was no neophyte at kitchen work, that she could see; he knew what he was doing, and his movements were sure and expert. Jennie's eyes drank in the clean lines of his superb lean body. He was a prime specimen of forceful, appealing masculinity at the very height of its power, and once again Jennie was awed by her awareness of him. Most men did not interest her sufficiently to arouse this kind of curiosity. But then, Ancel Gunter definitely was not most men.

Ancel took two cans of beer out of the refrigerator, popped open the tops and set one in front of Jennie. "Here, drink this. It'll do you good."

"Thanks," she said gratefully. "I'm sorry to be such a washout tonight. I promise, tomorrow night I'll fix supper."

"It doesn't matter who does the cooking, Jennie, as long as it gets done."

"It's just that I'm beat! I'm not used to this sort of thing."

"Yeah. That city living really softens you up."

Jennie took a long swallow of the ice-cold beer and watched him admiringly. "These steaks look more like roasts," Ancel observed. "They'd taste better cooked outdoors, but I forgot to bring a grill and charcoal from my place. There wasn't time for baked potatoes. I hope french fries will do."

"Fine. I'm sure everything will be wonderful," Jennie said, trying to stifle a lusty yawn. At the sound Ancel turned around and frowned at her.

"Lord, you're really zonked, aren't you?" He

slapped a huge piece of meat and a mound of potatoes on a plate, grabbed a bowl of salad and carried the food to the table. "Here you are, ma'am. Hope you can do justice to it."

Surprisingly she could and did. Among his other accomplishments, Ancel was a good cook. The steak was cooked to rare perfection, just the way she liked it, and the potatoes were deliciously crispy. When she had finished the meal, Jennie sighed contentedly and felt some of the weariness leave her.

"That was wonderful, Ancel. Some lucky girl is going to get a real bargain when she gets you."

One corner of his mouth twitched. "Yeah."

Jennie glanced around the room. "New curtains," she mused. "That's what it needs."

"Good idea," Ancel agreed.

"And the kitchen makes everything else look so drab. I can hardly wait to get the dining room painted."

"What'd I tell you? We'll have this place shipshape in no time."

Something occurred to Jennie just then. "Oh, Ancel, I forgot to call Mr. Walde today."

"Oh, didn't I tell you? I called him from my place this morning. I told him you were having some work done on The Croft and to keep it on the market. We'll spring the new price on him when the work is finished."

"You think of everything. What did he say?"

"He said Paul would be terribly disappointed."

"What did you say to that?"

"Tough," he said, spitting out the word, and Jennie laughed.

Seeing that Ancel had just finished his meal, Jennie stood and began clearing the table.

"Hey, you don't have to do that," he protested. "You're too tired."

"No, I firmly believe that the one who does the cooking shouldn't have to do the dishes too. And I'm getting my second wind. That really was a delicious meal."

She carried their plates to the sink and scraped the remains of the food into a plastic scrap bag. Twisting it shut, she walked to the back door to carry it to the garbage can. But when she stepped onto the porch a pair of glowing eyes shone brightly in the dark night. "*Oh!*" she cried in alarm. Dropping the bag, she scurried back into the safety of the kitchen. Once the screen door had been firmly latched, she felt courageous enough to look at their intruder.

The "beast" was a sad-faced little deer, but quite the strangest one Jennie had ever seen, and she was a native of deer country.

At the sound of her cry, Ancel had hurried to her side. "What's the matter, Jennie?"

Her hand went to her chest and she laughed nervously. "Nothing. I was frightened by something, but now I see it's only a deer." She pointed, and Ancel's eyes followed her gesturing finger. He chuckled when he saw the animal.

"Oh, Ancel, isn't he the cutest little fellow? But so odd! I don't think I've ever seen a deer like that."

"You probably have, you just don't remember. It's a velvet-horn buck," Ancel explained. "I haven't seen one in years."

Jennie peered intently through the screen door. The little animal seemed in no great hurry to get away from these "dangerous" humans. On the contrary, Jennie thought his plaintive little face was pleading to be allowed to stay. Then Jennie remembered the amazing docility of hill-country deer. She had seen them walk right up to a barbecue grill while a cookout was in progress.

"Look, Jennie," Ancel was saying. "See his antlers, how dwarfed and misshapen they are? And they're still coated with the skin covering called 'velvet.' A normal buck would have lost that a long time ago."

"A velvet-horn," she repeated. "Oh, he's so dear! But he looks more doelike than bucklike, doesn't he? And he's not a bit afraid of us."

"No, the velvet-horns are pretty much outcasts. The regular bucks won't let them get anywhere near the feeding grounds, particularly during mating season. But they manage to be well-fed in spite of that—due to nocturnal calls on local ranchers, no doubt."

"Will he eat those scraps I dropped?"

"Probably."

"Help yourself, Velvet," she called to the animal. "There'll be more tomorrow night if you feel like stopping by." She closed the door to give the deer some privacy and returned to the sink with Ancel.

"Where do the velvet-horns come from?" she asked him.

He shrugged. "No ones knows. They're a biological phenomenon but apparently not an important enough one to expend time and effort in studying them further. Large herds of them will roam these hills for years and then suddenly disappear. Killed off probably, since their meat is smoother and more tender than ordinary venison. They don't reproduce, so they tend to come in cycles. No one seems to know whether their condition is genetic or the result of accidents with barbwire fences."

"Do you suppose Velvet will keep coming back if I continue to put scraps out?"

"I don't know. Probably. You can try, if you like."

They finished washing the dishes and straightening the kitchen, then Ancel suggested sitting on the front porch for a while. Jennie turned off the kitchen light and followed him out of the house. The old porch swing, a relic from her childhood, squeakingly protested under the weight of their bodies, shattering the eloquent silence of the black night.

"Ah, such a lovely evening!" Jennie said, inhaling the pure, clean air.

"We need rain," Ancel commented.

"Ranchers *always* need rain," she reminded him with a smile.

"How true."

He was watching her, the light fluttering of her eyelashes, the tilt of her nose, the curve of her chin. His eyes moved over her, taking in the beauteous curve of her high, firm breasts under the white robe. She was dainty, incredibly feminine, with a small waist, small hips. If there was one ample thing about her it was those round breasts.

"You know something, Jennie. You're shaped exactly the way a girl should be shaped."

She colored deeply, wondering if the robe was indecent. She wasn't wearing anything under it. No one would know that, but still...

"Ah...thank you, Ancel," she said simply. It was a nice compliment, but somehow it disappointed her. She sensed that Ancel was a man who adored beauty in all things—cows, horses, the land, women. Particularly women. So she couldn't take this as a normal man-woman compliment. He merely was giving her his assessment of her physical attributes.

Ancel leaned back in the swing and stretched his long legs in front of him. "Would you like to know the first time I saw you, Jennie?"

"Sure," she said brightly.

"It was at the White Rock-Clear Springs Championship game nine years ago. You were prancing around in that short skirt, waving those green and white pompoms, urging the Fighting Tigers of White Rock High on to victory."

She chuckled at the memory. "As I recall, the Fighting Tigers didn't get the message that night. I believe they went down to inglorious defeat. Lord, that seems a hundred years ago!"

"When you first started showing up on Paul's arm, I remember thinking, *she's* going to marry *him*?"

Jennie stiffened. "I don't want to talk about Paul, Ancel," she said stonily.

"Suits me," he said. "I don't want to talk about him, either." He regarded her with inquiring eyes. "What do you want to do over the long haul, Jennie, say ten or fifteen years down the road? You really don't talk about yourself much."

"That's because there's so little to talk about."

"But you must have plans. There must be something you really want to do."

"Well..." She looked at him, hoping to ascertain if his interest was genuine or merely polite. She couldn't remember ever confiding in anyone but Rob Cameron, and it wasn't easy for her to do so now. But Ancel was so much like Rob in so many ways that it made Jennie's heart ache. "I—I've always hated telling anyone this because they seem to think it's silly, but... I'd like to write someday."

"That's not silly," he said quietly. "What do you want to write? Stories? Novels?"

"Yes."

"Good! I hope you're enormously successful."

"That's an unusual reaction," she said. "Most people don't take you seriously when you tell them you want to write. They seem to regard it as something frivolous and silly... sort of a hobby more than anything."

"Nothing's silly if you really want to do it, Jennie."

"What about you, Ancel? What do you hope the future holds for you?"

"I've got what I want," he said, looking the very picture of contentment. "This is what it's all about. My place in the sun."

How fortunate he was! Such simple things. But wasn't what she wanted simple things too? A bright, shining love to warm the good days and make the bad ones bearable. A home, children, and eventually, the time and maturity to write down all those jumbled thoughts in her head? Simple things really, but so damnably hard to come by.

"Tell me, Ancel, just what is there about these hills that makes you love them so? What's the magnetic pull?" she asked quietly and with interest.

"I don't know, honestly I don't," he replied. "God knows there are easier places to try to work. This isn't rich bottomland or grassy prairie or fields of waving grain or fertile delta. There are spots on my property that are so rocky and hilly there's no chance of plowing them, and when the drought years come, as they inevitably do, I wonder what in hell would make a man deliberately choose this kind of life for himself. But there are compensations. Here we still have the clearest springs left in America, and we have rambling trails that few human feet have trod. We have so much deer and game that a man could live off the land if he had to, and God knows we've got more cedar than anyone ever wanted or needed."

He paused to look at Jennie, and a hint of a smile played at his mouth. "Am I boring you? Are you sorry you asked?"

"Of course not," she said, her eyelids growing heavy. "I love hearing you talk."

"Well, I guess none of that really explains the hold this land has on me," he continued, staring absently into the black night. "I guess it gets all tangled up in a longing for self-sufficiency, and here a person can come as close to it as it's possible to do in this modern age. There's a wonderful privacy to this country, a timelessness. And a feeling among the people. Where else, in this day and age, can you find a place where people really care about their heritage? You know, Jennie, ninety percent of the people in White Rock can tell you the name of the ancestor who stepped off the boat in Galveston Bay in 1845. I know not many people care about that sort of thing anymore, but I find something immensely satisfying in it."

Ancel paused in his monologue to gauge his companion's reaction. Her head was leaning against the back of the porch swing, her hands lay limply in her lap, and she was asleep—sound asleep.

He chuckled softly. "Fascinating conversationalist, aren't I, Jennie?" He stood, then bent to scoop her up into his arms. "Come, little one, I think it's past your bedtime."

She barely stirred. Her eyes opened briefly, then one arm went around his neck, and she buried her head on his shoulder. A soft sigh escaped her lips.

"You smell as sweet and clean as a baby, and you weigh nothing at all," he whispered as he carried her into the house and up the stairs.

In the bedroom he gently laid her on the bed. Instinctively, in spite of her semiconscious state, she tightened her hold on him. He paused as his hands were about to release her, and Jennie was dimly aware that their faces were only inches apart, then touching. Slowly, he brought his mouth down on hers.

It was the tenderest kind of kiss, with just the right amount of pressure. Their mouths fused perfectly, softly, pliantly. Even though drowsy, Jennie clearly experienced a warm, rushing sensation and a surge of dizziness. She melted passively in his arms, feeling his firm yet gentle mouth on her cheeks, in her hair. She sighed, squirmed, then sighed again, wishing with all her heart that he would find her mouth with his once more.

Gently Ancel released her, and when he did the white robe fell from her shoulders, revealing the smooth swelling of those beauteous breasts. His hands moved over her, and his lips came down to gently touch the soft mounds. Then he closed the garment and pulled up the sheet to cover her.

She tried to open her eyes, but the lids were like lead. She tried to say his name, but the sound would not come. She thought she heard small sounds deep within his throat, but she could not be sure how much of this was real and how much was a dream. His voice came to her, as though from another room, low and guttural.

"Ah, Jennie, Jennie," it said. "What a lovely temptation you are." His big hands, surprisingly tender considering their size, moved slowly, lingeringly, down the length of her smooth, soft arms. "Another time," the faraway voice said huskily. "Another time, when you're wide awake."

She was aware that he had left the room. She wanted to call to him, but her languor would not permit it. Instead, she settled further into the soft mattress, and her head sank into the pillow. A breeze stirred the curtains at the open window, and fingers of moonlight played on the walls. An animal cried mournfully, crickets chirped. Jennie slipped into peaceful slumber, still feeling Ancel's kiss on her lips.

Chapter Five

"Do you think you can do without me today, Jennie?"
Ancel regretfully asked at breakfast the following morning. "I drove over to my place this morning while I was
waiting for you to wake up, and there are a few minor
emergencies that seem to require my attention."

Ancel had the most unfortunate, if unintentional,
knack for making Jennie feel like the world's laziest
slob. "Of course Ancel. I certainly don't want you to
feel tied to The Croft. Do whatever you have to do."

"I'm afraid it will take most of the day. I doubt I'll be
back before—oh, suppertime. Is that all right?"

"Well, of course it's all right. Don't rush. I'm going
to paint the dining room and, hopefully, get started on
the living room, so I'll be busy all day."

But the moment he'd left, Jennie felt oddly bereft.
Then she thought how foolish she was being. Even had
Ancel been at The Croft, she wouldn't have seen him
until lunchtime anyway, and then only for a few minutes. Besides, why did she care? They weren't going to
be together very long as it was. A week, ten days, two
weeks tops. Then she would hop on back to Fort Worth
and doubtlessly never see Ancel again.

She worked steadily and industriously throughout

the morning. Every muscle in her body ached from the previous day's labors, and she was determined to work some of that off. And if she needed any inspiration to stay with her task, all she had to do was look into the bright, sunny kitchen.

It was not yet eleven o'clock when she heard the crunch of tires in the driveway. Jennie smiled, glad that Ancel had finished his "emergencies" so quickly. She heard heavy footsteps on the front porch, but instead of seeing Ancel walk through the door she heard a knock, then another.

Frowning, she climbed down the step ladder and carefully laid her brush across the paint can. *Who on earth...?* she wondered. Ancel wouldn't knock, and only a few people knew she was here. She opened the door, and her heart gave a lurch.

"Oh, Paul," she said weakly.

"Good morning," he said in his deep baritone. "May I come in?"

Jennie hesitated, but only for an instant. "Of course," she said and stepped back to allow him to enter the room. She couldn't have been more surprised. Not once had it occurred to her that Paul might come to see her. Of course she was certain he wouldn't give up on the real estate deal, but she had imagined any future negotiations would have been with Jeremy Walde. She had thought—hoped—she wouldn't have to see Paul again.

It crossed her mind that she probably was the un-loveliest sight on earth. She hadn't bothered with makeup since she would look a fright by the time she finished painting anyway, and she once again was wearing that big shirt of Ancel's, thoroughly paint-flecked now.

Paul on the other hand looked bandbox fresh. He was dressed very casually in a sport shirt and slacks, but he looked as faultlessly attired as he did in his business suits.

His eyes made a quick sweep of his surroundings, then came to rest on her. "What are you doing, Jennie?" he asked, taking in her clothes.

"Painting," she replied. Why did her voice sound so wavering? She cleared her throat, furious at herself for feeling so flustered.

"Painting what?"

"The dining room."

One dark eyebrow arched. "Oh? Why?"

"Because it needs it."

Paul pulled on his chin, eyeing her speculatively. "Did Ancel talk you into this?"

"Why would Ancel care whether or not I painted my house?" she hedged.

"I don't know. But my brother has some very strange ideas, very strange indeed. May I sit down, Jennie?"

"Of course." Then she spied Ancel's bedroll, neatly tied and propped in the corner. Dear God, she didn't want Paul to know Ancel was staying here! She maneuvered her visitor around to a chair where his back would be to that corner, then she sat opposite him, her hands clenched together in her lap.

Paul smiled at her, but it was a curious smile without much warmth or mirth. "I've been thinking about our meeting Monday morning, Jennie, and I think I owe you an apology."

"Y-you do?"

"Yes. You're feeling nostalgic about your old family home. I should never have so callously announced I intended razing the place. It was terribly thoughtless of me, and I do apologize.''

"Not at all," Jennie said, relieved that her voice had returned to normal. "I'm glad you told me what your plans were."

"I've come up with an idea that might be agreeable to both of us," Paul then said, the corners of his mouth twitching. "Sell me all of The Croft but the house itself and the acre immediately surrounding it. Then you can keep the house on the market and make a little extra money from its sale."

Strange. Had he come up with something like this Monday morning, she would have pounced on it like a dog on a bone. But now....

"And you'd build the resort hotel right next door?" she asked.

"Oh, not right next door. There would be a long sweeping drive running up to the hotel, and the building itself would sit far back from the road. I'd probably want to build some sort of high fence to hide—er to give this house some privacy."

For the life of her Jennie couldn't understand why his grandiose plans seemed so distasteful to her. Why did she care?

"I'm sorry, Paul. I just don't want to sell my father's property to anyone but another rancher."

His mouth set in a tight line, but he stayed in control. "I see. You *have* been talking to my brother." He paused a moment and then said. "Ancel, I suppose, considers building a resort hotel 'raping' the land."

"Something like that," Jennie admitted. "I'm not too sure I don't agree with him. I tend to think there are some places that shouldn't change, and White Rock is one of them."

"What utter nonsense! I thought you were smarter than that, Jennie."

And what was she supposed to reply to that? *Well, I'm not? If I were the least bit smart I never would have let myself fall so insanely in love with you?* Damn! She wished he hadn't come. She had that awful out-of-control feeling again. She longed for Ancel's presence, to shore up her sagging defenses. Yet under no circumstances did she want Paul to know Ancel was staying at The Croft. There was nothing wrong with it; it was all perfectly innocent. But she didn't want Paul to know.

She chose to ignore his last remark. "Tell me, Paul, how is your wife? It's—er—Ellen, isn't it?" she asked pleasantly, knowing perfectly well what Paul's wife's name was.

He stared at her darkly. "Yes, it's Ellen. Why did you ask about her?"

Jennie's eyebrows raised. "Why wouldn't I? It seems a natural question."

"I—I thought perhaps Ancel had said something."

"Why, no, Paul, he's said nothing."

"Ellen's the same as always," he said, dismissing his wife. "So, tell me, Jennie, what you've been up to these—what has it been? Five years now?"

Bastard! she thought acidly. Summoning up her sweetest smile, she said, "Yes, it's been five years since Papa passed away." Then, as succinctly as possible, she gave him an account of her life since leaving White Rock, embellishing the facts slightly in order to make it sound more interesting than it actually had been. She stopped short of portraying herself as a free-swinging career girl who was steadily advancing up the corporate ladder, but neither did she mention her miniscule apartment nor her overworked budget. The account was, in fact, a delightful piece of fiction, and it was at times like this that Jennie thought she really might be a writer someday.

"So," Paul said disinterestedly, "you seem to be carving a niche for yourself in the world."

"Yes."

Paul lapsed into thought for a minute, then looked at her solemnly. "Jennie, could you spare me a few hours of your time?"

She frowned. "I beg your pardon?"

"I'd like you to come with me. I want to show you something. It won't take more than a couple of hours, and I'll treat you to lunch as a return favor."

What if Ancel comes back? was her immediate thought. He would be disappointed if she hadn't finished the painting. But then she chided herself for being absurd. So what if he did come back to find her gone? She didn't have to answer to Ancel or to anyone. She could go and come as she pleased, and she certainly didn't intend becoming a slave to a paintbrush. This was her vacation, for Pete's sake, not that anyone could tell!

She was conveniently ignoring the warning bells that were going off in her head. The man seated across from her had once had a devastating effect on her. But she told herself that that was all behind her now. She was older and had been around the track a few times. She suspected that whatever Paul wanted to show her had something to do with the sale of The Croft, so that made this business. Besides, she was curious.

"I have all the time in the world," Jennie said, "but you'll have to give me a few minutes to clean up my brushes and then to change clothes."

"Of course," Paul said. "Take all the time you need."

Thirty minutes later Jennie was seated beside Paul in his elegant Mercedes, and they were driving away from The Croft. She had changed into a blue and white print shirt, well-tailored white slacks and a pair of medium-heeled white sandals she had paid far too much for. But seated in the luxurious automobile, Jennie felt it only right that she be wearing something, anything, outrageously expensive.

It didn't take her long to realize that Paul intended taking her on a brief tour of the Highland Lakes, and she thought she knew the reason for it. It had been a long time since she had traveled lazily through the area, so she sat back and simply enjoyed the view.

The soft, gracious vista was more inspiring than spectacular—great distances rimmed by green-black woods and granite hills that meandered by the clear, deep Highland Lakes.

"Do the rock hounds still have a field day around here?" she asked Paul.

"Oh, yes," he assured her. "Absolutely."

She chuckled. "I remember once—I was still in high school, I think—when the city fathers got into a big flap with the citizens of some little town out near El Paso. Each was claiming to have the oldest rocks in Texas. I never saw so many people get so excited over nothing. Were the hill-country's rocks really a hundred million years old or only eighty million? What difference did it make?"

"I suppose to a geologist it would make a great deal of difference. In much the same way that community growth makes a difference to bankers and realtors and merchants—"

"And solitude and wilderness make a difference to ranchers and farmers," she concluded.

"Indeed," he said grimly.

One thing was clear to Jennie as they drove through the area: It had undergone tremendous growth during the five years she had been gone. The rock hounds and deer hunters, who had always been part of the scene, had been joined by fishermen, boating enthusiasts, and campers. Beautiful resorts had been built, and the number of private residences had quadrupled—everything from spruced-up mobile homes to stone-and-cedar mansions. What once had been sleepy little fishing villages now teemed with activity. This apparently was "the season."

Paul made little comment as he drove through the area, save to occasionally point out some particularly lavish structure or to mention that "our bank financed that restaurant." And Jennie said little, partly because she didn't know what to say.

It wasn't until Paul had reversed direction and they were driving back toward White Rock that he eased the car off the road, braked and switched off the engine. Then he turned to her, his eyes bright. "Well?" he asked.

"Well what?"

"What did you think of it?"

"It's...impressive. Very busy. Booming, from the looks of things."

"So, Jennie...what's wrong with that?"

She frowned. "I don't think I understand, Paul."

"What would be wrong with White Rock getting in on some of the action?"

Jennie didn't know. Nothing, she supposed. Except...White Rock was cattle country. Damn, there was more of Rob Cameron in her than she would have dreamed! "I—I don't know, Paul. I guess—I guess I just prefer to have White Rock stay as it is. Steady but unspectacular growth. That's the way Papa felt, and... it would appear that's the way I feel too.''

Paul uttered a foul epithet then, surprising her. She didn't remember his ever doing much swearing. Then he seemed to give himself a little shake, as though realizing that cursing wasn't the way to get what he wanted. He shot a smile in her direction and one hand moved to her shoulder. She shivered a little at the contact.

''Jennie,'' he murmured in a rich voice, ''why don't we go back to The Croft? I have some of the architect's drawings in my briefcase. You might change your mind, you know, when you see just what I have in mind....''

Now his hand had gone to the nape of her neck, and Jennie's eyes widened in horror as she saw that his head definitely was bending toward her. She gasped at the first contact with those cool male lips, shaken to the point of senselessness. For one awful minute she found herself responding to that kiss.

Then he lifted his head, and she saw it—the note of triumph in his expression—and the warning bells became a clanging racket. This man! No, no! Anyone but this man who had made such a fool of her. Paul Gunter was a dangerous opportunist—a dangerous, *married* opportunist—and five years ago he had hurt her more than she felt any human being had the power to hurt another. Had done it cruelly, too, in the bargain. She couldn't let him destroy her with his charm again!

Jennie didn't know if it was possible for one's entire life to pass before one's eyes in a split second, but she knew that at that moment she clearly relived her relationship with Paul. He had never been in love with her. He had been in love with her adoration of him. She had been good for his ego, but when something more compelling had come along, meaning Ellen and her millions, he had turned from her without even a backward glance. Jennie was thoroughly appalled at herself. "Take me home, Paul!" she demanded icily.

"Damn it, Jennie...!"

"*Now!*" Her voice sounded frantic, and small wonder. She was frantic. Frantic to get away from him. "I want to go back to the ranch now!"

His eyes were blazing, but he was struggling for control, that much she could see. He knew he couldn't get anywhere with her if she was frightened or angry. He inhaled deeply, then expelled his breath slowly and tried for something like a smile. "I promised you lunch."

"I don't want lunch! I'll eat something at the house. I—I have to finish my painting."

A long, hostile silence followed, and Jennie refused to look at him. Then she heard him sigh a disgusted sigh. He abruptly turned in the seat, switched on the key in the ignition and eased the car back onto the road.

"You didn't get a hell of a lot done today, Jennie," Ancel commented reproachfully as they were eating their evening meal.

If he only knew! She had raced into the house when Paul had dropped her off, praying Ancel wouldn't have returned, then had hurriedly changed back into her painting clothes and finished the dining room. She was almost exhausted, but she actually had little to show for a supposedly full day's work. "I'm sorry," she said contritely. "I guess... after yesterday I just... had a hard time getting cranked up today. I'll do better tomorrow."

"I didn't mean to sound accusing," Ancel said.

"I know, but you're right. I wasted an entire day, really." She had no idea why it was so important to her that Ancel not know she had been with Paul. She truly had had no business going off with him, and she supposed she didn't want Ancel to know how foolish she could sometimes be. But still, that was no reason for feeling like an unfaithful wife!

Ancel had been watching her intently all evening, thereby intensifying her guilt feelings. Jennie stood up and began clearing the dishes from the table, carrying them to the sink. Still she could feel his eyes on her. The more she tried for nonchalance, the more edgy she felt.

Finally he asked, "Is there something wrong, Jennie?"

"Goodness, no!" she said much too quickly. "Why do you ask that?"

"Beats me. You just don't seem yourself."

She uttered a nervous little laugh and began running water into the sink. "Maybe I'm just having trouble adjusting to my new life-style. Maybe all this fresh air and exercise have thrown my system out of whack."

"Maybe," he said noncommittally and sipped thoughtfully from his beer can.

With her back to him, Jennie hesitantly asked, "Ancel, have you and the other ranchers around here ever thought about forming a group to—well, to do what you can to see that pasturelands stay in the hands of stockmen and farmers?"

He chuckled. "Now, if that doesn't sound just like someone from the city. Organize! Form a committee! Damned if I can remember the last time a committee got anything done."

She turned around. "There's nothing wrong with people who have common interests banding together to protect those interests. Maybe all it would require is a pledge that none of you ever would sell your property to someone who didn't intend using it for agribusiness."

"Wouldn't work, Jennie."

"Why not?"

"Well, take a rancher and his wife. The kids are all grown, they're getting along in years, and the ranch is just getting to be too big a job for them. Besides, they want to move to Arizona or Florida or wherever. Oh, sure, they want to sell the old place to another rancher, but suppose another rancher doesn't come along? They're going to sell it to whoever the hell will buy it."

"But that's where the organization would come in. In a case like that, the organization would step in and buy it, hold onto it until it sold."

"Where's all the money going to come from?" he asked sensibly.

"Where does any organization get money? Dues, fund drives—bake sales at the church, for all I know! It was just a thought." She turned back to the sink, frowning.

There was a brief pause, then Ancel asked, "What brought all this on?"

She shrugged. "I guess...I was just thinking about all those developments to the south of us. It looks like people are going to be chest-to-chest down there before long."

"When was the last time you were down there?"

Jennie was glad he couldn't see her face. "I...ah... saw a little bit of it on the drive from Fort Worth...and I've been reading."

"Oh. Well, Jennie, as much as I'd like to, I don't guess I can fence in the hill country and keep everyone out."

"No, I guess not," she said, surprised that her voice sounded so sad. *Why do you care, Jennie?* a nagging inner voice kept asking over and over and over....

Chapter Six

Ancel's indefatigable energy was a wonder to Jennie. She never had considered herself a lazy person, far from it. In fact, she thought laziness in a woman was inexcusable. But Ancel left her gasping. He was the very picture of industry, a human dynamo. And no matter how many hours he put in, no matter how weary he appeared when he returned to the house at night, after a shower and supper he was as good as new.

They had been working at a nonstop pace, and Jennie's muscles no longer cried for mercy; on the contrary, she felt marvelous—brisk and full of vigor. The more she did, the more she felt like doing. And, oh, what they had accomplished! Gradually the changes came, and The Croft began to take on the appearance of a home, a place loved by those who resided in it.

On her fifth morning to awaken in the room of her childhood Jennie shot a glance in the direction of the bedside clock, then quickly struggled out of bed. She had yet to beat Ancel to the kitchen in the morning, but she had determined that this would be the day she would be the one to prepare breakfast.

But again she was too late. Ancel not only had eaten, he had left the house. From the back door she could see the tractor in the distance, Ancel's strong, lean frame atop it. The coffeepot had been left on, and her food was in a plate on top of the stove. Ancel must have been up for quite a while and had been loathe to wake her. She knew she should have been grateful for his consideration, and she was in a way, but mostly she was irritated at herself for being such a slugabed. Breakfast with Ancel was a most enjoyable way to start the day.

She ate the lukewarm ham and cold biscuits without interest, washed the few dishes she had used, and soon was upstairs in her bedroom, the one remaining room in need of paint. It was surprising what an expert she had become. With the mechanics of her task now so familiar she breezed through this final chore, and by noon she was back in the kitchen cleaning the painting paraphernalia.

She waited expectantly, glancing at the kitchen clock from time to time. Why wasn't Ancel in here yammering for lunch? He normally was starved by midday. She waited a bit longer, and still he did not appear. Several times she walked to the back door, hoping for the sight of him striding toward the house, but she saw nothing.

Her disappointment was ridiculous; she realized that. But unconsciously they had slipped into a day-to-day routine that Jennie found comforting. She simply had come to expect him for lunch.

Minutes passed. Finally unable to stand it a moment longer she left the house and walked to a rising behind the barn, raised one hand to shield her eyes from the brilliant midday sunshine, and peered into the distance.

It was a moment or two before she caught sight of him. The tractor had been halted in a clearing, and he was sitting on the seat, munching on something. Jennie then noticed the small brown sack resting on the seat beside him; apparently he had packed a lunch before leaving the house. His back was to her. He had removed his shirt to let the hot sun beat down on his bare skin, but there was no fear of sunburn, for he was as brown as toasted earth.

Since he did not know he was being observed, Jennie could allow herself the luxury of watching him with no need for lowered lashes and averted gazes. Sinking to the soft grass, she stared at him openly, mesmerized by the man's utter masculinity. It was a strange sensation, this pleasure she derived merely from looking at him.

Somewhere in the dim recession of her mind lay a vague remembrance of Ancel's mouth upon hers the night he had carried her to bed. But damn it! she couldn't remember it well, and Ancel had not alluded to it in any way, nor had anything of the sort happened again. How she wished that kiss were forever emblazoned on her memory! It might very well be the only one she ever received from him.

It *probably* would be the only one she ever received from him, for, truthfully, Ancel treated her in a disgustingly platonic manner. Jennie thought she understood. He had been badly burned once, and he wasn't about to let another woman have access to his heart. He was doing a good job; that pal-buddy-brother routine was as effective as a steel cage.

She watched as he quaffed something from a thermos, stoppered it, and placed it on the seat beside him. Then he stretched, slumped down in the seat, and turned his face skyward, tipping the big hat over his eyes as he did so. He seemed completely at peace with himself and his world.

Jennie accepted the fact that Ancel Gunter fascinated her, and she wondered if that sense of belonging was what made him so irresistible. Ancel was vastly different from the other men she knew. He was a man who apparently had worked out his life to his own satisfaction, despite what must have been disappointments, frustrations, and inequities, and he had done it while retaining a cheerful zest for living. Jennie admired him tremendously.

She had no idea how long she sat on the ground watching him, but she thought it must have been for quite some time, for she was jolted out of her daydream when Ancel suddenly sat up, raised his strong arms to the sky and stretched. He pushed the hat farther back on his head, then started up the tractor's engine and soon was lumbering off across the pasture. Somehow Jennie just knew he was whistling.

Oh God! she thought. *What am I doing? Hiding here and watching a man take a nap, feeling rejected because he prefers getting on with his work to having lunch with me. Idiocy! I mustn't attach too much importance to this visit. A few more days and I'll be gone from here, probably never to see him again.*

She returned to the house to heat up a can of soup and eat alone in morose silence. The rest of the afternoon was given over to an orgy of housecleaning. Once she had pronounced the place as clean as human effort could make it, she went upstairs to bathe and change.

The sun was low in the western sky before Ancel returned to the house, entering through the back door with his shirt slung over his bare shoulder. He found Jennie standing at the stove, dressed in a bright yellow print dress, her freshly shampooed curls shining atop her head, a welcoming smile on her face.

"Good Lord, Jennie! If you aren't a sight for a weary man's eyes. If I weren't so damned bushed I might...."

She turned to him expectantly. "Might what?"

"Attack you, I think. That is, if I still remember how."

Her smile faded somewhat when she saw how tired he looked. There was a limit to everything, even Ancel's energy. Jennie was swamped with chagrin. "Oh, Ancel, you shouldn't work so hard! It's too much. Maybe I should just hire someone to do all this. I won't have you killing yourself over my place."

"Killing myself?" He hooted derisively. "Hardly! Hard work is the best medicine in the world. It keeps the juices flowing. Feel that!" He thumped his rock-hard midsection, then grabbed her hand and placed it on his stomach. A tingling sensation swept through Jennie. "Not a superfluous ounce! Give me time for a shower and shave, and I'll be good as new. I might even remember how to attack." He winked at her and walked out of the kitchen.

Within moments Jennie heard the sound of the shower in the downstairs bathroom and Ancel's off-key baritone rising above the noise of the pelting water. And true to his word, when he appeared in the kitchen in a half hour he looked as fresh and rested as if he had just taken a two-hour nap.

"Sit down and let me get you a beer," Jennie said.

"Sounds good." He sniffed appreciatively. "What's that fantastic smell?"

"An old family recipe for baked pork chops. You'll love them."

"I'll bet."

It was a delicious meal, as Ancel said over and over, remarking with wonder on her culinary skills.

"Heavens, Ancel, I cook almost every day, and since I have to eat my own cooking, I've made myself learn to do it well. When I'm alone I do simple things, but when I have company, I pull out all the stops. I even took one of those gourmet cooking courses once and can pull off some pretty fancy razzle-dazzle in the kitchen when I've a mind to. I make croissants from scratch and a delicious spinach quiche. Would you like me to fix you one some evening?''

She paused and laughed. The look on Ancel's face clearly told her that he did not consider spinach quiche fit and proper nourishment.

"Do you like living alone, Jennie?" he asked.

"I think I do, most of the time. Do you?" Her eyes watched him closely.

"I really don't think about it much—" which really did not tell her anything very revealing.

Jennie burned with curiosity about this man, but he volunteered so little information about himself. She knew him for a man who liked living close to the land, a man like her father in that respect. But otherwise she knew little. She wished he would tell her about the woman who had left a permanent mark on him, the one who hadn't known he was alive, for Jennie honestly couldn't imagine what kind of woman would not be aware of Ancel every second he was near. "Certainly it must be preferable to living with the wrong person," she prodded. "That would be the ultimate loneliness."

He nodded. "True. But finding the right person, that's the stickler."

"And having that right person think you're right too," she added.

"Exactly!"

That apparently was all she was going to get out of him, so she changed the subject, and they talked about only general matters from then on.

They lingered long over their supper, and since it had been served later than was customary, it was well past eight o'clock when Jennie rose from the table and said, "You just sit. Have another beer and relax. I'll do the dishes tonight."

"I could get horribly spoiled by this kind of life," he told her, "and I certainly could get spoiled by your cooking."

"Thank you kindly, sir." She moved to the sink, scraped the remains of the meal into a scrap bag, and then carried it to the back porch. When she returned, Ancel was smiling at her.

"For your friend, the deer?" he asked.

"Of course. Velvet's been here every night this week."

"How do you know it's Velvet?"

"It is. I just know it is," she said firmly.

"Jennie, you shouldn't get too attached to a wild animal. Not in these woods. One gunshot and...." He spread his hands in a hopeless gesture.

She turned a horrified look on him, all the while knowing he was right.

"I can see you've been away from livestock too long," he told her when he saw the look. "It doesn't pay to be too softhearted with animals. Once I had the sweetest old cow on my place. She'd come up and eat right out of my hand. But she started producing puny calves, so...."

"So...what?"

"So she had to go the hamburger route."

"Oh, Ancel!" she cried, plunging her hands into the dishwater. "How did you stand it?"

He shrugged. "It's part of the job. There's really nothing about ranching that I mind—except maybe castration and the really grim obstetrics."

"You do all of that?"

"Of course. Who else? You ought to know that. You grew up with it."

"I know, but I've been away from it such a long time. It's been ages since I thought of beef as anything but those nice little packages in the supermarket."

There was a brief pause before he asked, "Did you ever miss it—the ranch, the country life?"

She thought about it a moment. "I honestly don't think I did. I always seemed to be so busy, first with school, then with my job."

"What about now? Will you miss it when you leave this time?"

Jennie turned back to the sink, uncertain of what her expression might reveal. Yes, she was very afraid she would miss The Croft this time . . . but not half so much as she would miss Ancel. Odd how much a part of her life he seemed to have become in just a few days. "Yes," she said, "I think I will," and she rinsed a soapy dish and placed it in the drainer on the counter.

It was not in Ancel's nature to sit idly by and watch someone work. He was on his feet and standing by her side, dish towel in hand.

"You don't have to do that," she protested.

"I know that. I want to."

When the last dish had been put in the cupboard, Ancel suggested sitting on the porch swing for a while. It had become something of an every-night ritual with them, one Jennie enjoyed. But she had misgivings to-night; Ancel looked wearier than she ever had seen him.

"You're so exhausted, Ancel," she said. "Perhaps you should go to bed. That's something else I'd forgotten about living close to the land—the day begins and ends with the sun. I'll just read for a bit."

"Well, it has been a busy day, and there are more in store for us, but good grief, Jennie, we've accomplished a lot! However, all work and no play.... Why don't we knock off early tomorrow? I'd like you to see my place."

"I'd love to, Ancel."

Then, as casually as though he had done it hundreds of times, Ancel put out his arms and drew her to him in a comforting hug. Jennie could not have been more surprised. He simply held her very tightly without attempting anything else. Encased in the warmth of his embrace, she was startled by the erratic beating of her heart. Her face was buried in the soft cotton of his shirt, and she could smell the pleasing aromas of soap and after-shave. Tentatively she slid her arms around his waist; her hands met at the small of his back. Pressed against his hard warmth, her palms tingled with the feel of him.

They stood together for several wordless moments; then he released her and held her away from him. She lifted her eyes, hoping he could not feel the trembling of her body, hoping her eyes registered none of her inner feelings.

"Sweet Jennie," he said in his low, resonant voice. "Have I told you how nice the house looks? I don't think I have. And the meal was superb. I can't remember when I had a better one. You're so damned decorative I wouldn't have dreamed you could be useful too. And you're right—I'm so tired I'm numb. I'll say goodnight now, and hopefully tomorrow I'll be a more pleasant companion. Sweet dreams." He then bent and placed a gentle kiss on the side of her mouth.

Jennie could not have been more rooted in place had he swept her up and kissed her passionately. In a way, she was more profoundly moved than she would have been by raw passion. The warm afterglow of his embrace stayed with her long after he left the room. Weakly she grabbed the counter for support, while her mind raced wildly in time with her heartbeat.

Ancel was unlike any man she had ever known. Now that she thought about it, it seemed to Jennie she could sort most men she had met into two categories. There were the deadly serious workaholics who had their hearts and minds set on some distant dream, who would choose their wives the way they chose their suits—to create an image. Or there were the light-hearted "good old boys"; there were just an awful lot of twenty-seven-year-old juvenile delinquents running loose. Both categories had one common denominator: They lunged at the first opportunity.

But Ancel? Never in her life had a man so inundated her with such warm, easy friendship. Jennie in no way considered herself a *femme fatale*, but men normally reacted to her in a more predictable manner.

Sighing, she went to lock the back door, then crossed the kitchen and turned off the light. Entering the living room, she saw that Ancel had discarded his shirt and spread his bedroll out on the sofa. Now he was sitting on it, taking off his boots. When he saw her he grinned, stood up and whipped off his belt.

For a fleeting second Jennie envisioned being held against the hard expanse of that broad chest, and she flushed, dismayed at her own bold thoughts. Then a wave of guilt washed over her. He looked so tired, yet was having to make do with the sofa, and there was a perfectly good, comfortable bed upstairs. Still, she wasn't sure of a proper way to broach the subject.

"Ancel," she said hesitantly, "I know how tired you

are. Why don't you take my bed tonight and let me sleep down here?''

He turned to her, a faintly mocking gleam in his eye. "Well, now, that sounds perfect. But there are two beds up there, Jennie. Why don't we each take one?"

Her eyes widened. "Well, I—ah—I—" she stammered.

Then he laughed. "Ah, Jennie, what a beautiful sight! A blushing, flustered woman. I haven't seen one in years. Thanks, but this sofa is fine...and I've slept in that old bedroll so many times it's like being in my mama's lap. Besides, I like being down here where I can keep one ear cocked."

Jennie felt foolish. "All right," she said primly. "Good night."

"Good night, Jennie," he said, and she could feel his amused eyes following her up the stairs.

In the bedroom she left the door open and undressed in the dark. It was early, but she did not feel like reading. The light welling up the stairway was switched off, and the house became very dark and quiet.

Jennie sighed and moved toward her bed. Certain that sleep would be a long time coming this night, she scrunched down under the covers and stared at the window across the room. The upper branches of the gnarled old live oaks dipped and swayed in the night wind, creating grotesque patterns on the wall. Suddenly a strong gust of north wind blew in, tossing the curtains violently.

A change in the wind's direction...the promise of rain? Rob Cameron would have said so. Jennie's lashes fluttered, then her lids closed. Perhaps she was more tired than she had realized, a by-product of all that hard work. Within moments she had fallen asleep.

The storm broke just after midnight. Jennie knew the time because the first thunderclap woke her, and she looked at the bedside table. Like every other weather quirk in the hills, a thunderstorm could be something to wonder at. Rain always was welcome, for it meant grass and crops; however, it never seemed to come in the form of gentle, life-giving moisture, but rather as the product of rolling, boiling storms that lasted for hours, often knocking down trees and power lines.

The wind howled mournfully. There was an earsplitting clap of thunder, and the heavens opened up to unleash silvery sheets of water. Jennie jumped out of bed and crossed the room to close the window, shivering in her scanty nightgown as the blast of nippy wind hit her. Then she stood and watched, transfixed, as the rain pounded against the windowpane.

A great fork of lightning lit up the room. Simultaneously there was a burst of thunder so loud it made her ears ring, then another blinding bolt of lightning she could feel in her fingertips. As the storm continued to rage its wild fury there was a deafening *crack*; the windowpane rattled, and the entire house shook.

She must have screamed, though she could not remember doing so, for suddenly Ancel was standing in the doorway, his expression one of grave alarm. "Jennie! Are you all right?"

The sight of Ancel clad in nothing but a pair of undershorts created a turbulence in Jennie that made the storm seem calm by comparison. "Yes—I—I'm all right. Dear God, Ancel! Did you hear that noise?"

Instantly he was across the room, by her side, staring out of the window. "Yeah, it sounded like it hit mighty close." He put both hands to the sides of his face and peered out into the raging night. "Good

Lord! Close isn't the word for it! Look, Jennie, look at that.''

Mindless of her skimpy attire, Jennie moved closer to him, and her gaze followed his gesturing finger. At first she could see nothing. But then another bolt of lightning lit up the yard, and she saw the ancient live oak, its trunk literally sliced in two, lying in the yard, its uppermost branches crushed against the side of the house.

"Another inch or two, and we would have had far more to do to this house than we had planned," he told her. "That's about as close as it can come without hitting you."

"Do—do you think it's a tornado?" she asked apprehensively.

"I don't think so," Ancel said calmly. "It's just a good old-fashioned summer thunderstorm."

"I'm frightened to death of tornados—I don't mind admitting it," she confessed. "One touched down nearby once when I was a kid, and Papa made Meg and me stay in that downstairs closet for what seemed like hours. I think that's why I still suffer from a touch of claustrophobia."

As though he could sense her fear, Ancel put a comforting arm around her almost bare shoulders. As his fingers touched her smooth flesh Jennie sucked in her breath. His touch was gentle and sensitive; his arms drew her to him, and the warmth of his body seeped into hers. Now she was being held against that bare, broad chest, and she clung to him. The throbbing of her breasts against his skin was an alien, disturbing sensation.

"You are frightened," he said, and she knew he could feel her trembling. But she wasn't prepared to say the trembling wasn't caused entirely by fright.

"Oh ...." She uttered a fluttery, embarrassed laugh.

"How silly . . . for a grown woman to panic over a thunderstorm."

"Not at all." There was no censure in his voice as he said, "I think I'd better stay up here. This storm might go on half the night."

"Ancel, I—"

"It will be all right, Jennie. I'll just spread my bedroll out on the other bed since there are no linens. And don't worry"—he grinned down at her—"I won't attempt to ravish you."

"It—it wouldn't have occurred to me that you would," she said, despising the unsteadiness of her voice.

Gently he turned her around and guided her to the bed, while she implored her brain to start functioning.

"Get in bed," he ordered, "and I'll be right back."

The thunder roared and the lightning flashed ferociously, but Jennie scarcely noticed. She slid between the sheets, mutely watching as he left the bedroom. Within moments he had returned, carrying his bedroll, which he nonchalantly tossed across the other bed. Then he threw down his pillow and climbed into the quilted bag. Smiling across the distance between them— only the size of a small lamp table—he said, "There! Safe as if you were in your daddy's arms. You aren't afraid now, are you?"

"No . . . no." She suppressed a giggle. "I'm not afraid now."

"And with me sleeping in this chastity belt, the entire town could walk in here and find us like this without considerable damage to your reputation."

"I doubt that, not in White Rock. Are you comfortable?"

"Very."

She lay quite still, totally conscious of the masculine presence in the other bed. She seriously doubted anyone would believe the two of them could share a bedroom with absolutely no physical contact between them. She would have a hard time believing it about anyone else, and she wondered if Ancel would be such a perfect gentleman if it were another woman sleeping in the bed next to his. She feared she would have to accept the fact that Ancel simply felt no sexual attraction toward her—a humbling realization.

She turned her head on the pillow to look at the finely chiseled features of his profile. He really was an incredibly good-looking man. Odd. She had always equated handsomeness in a man with dark, smoldering, mysterious looks, yet blond, sunny, cheerful Ancel had captured her attention in ways no other man ever had, not even Paul. Especially not Paul. She felt so comfortable with Ancel, so warm, so relaxed.

"Good night, Ancel," she said softly.

"Good night, Jennie."

She inhaled deeply, exhaled slowly and felt some of the tension go out of her. The storm raged angrily throughout most of the night, but Jennie slept as peacefully as a baby.

The morning dawned with washed air and earth. Ancel must have opened the window again some time after the storm had subsided, for the bedroom was bathed in the pure fragrance of rain-drenched pastures. Jennie snuggled under the covers, sighing happily, then turned to look at the other bed. Ancel was gone and so was his bedroll.

Damn that man! she thought. *He must be the one who wakes up the roosters!*

From below came the sound of activity and the irresistible aroma of coffee perking. She rolled out of bed, padded down the hall to the bathroom where she brushed her teeth, made up her face, and ran a comb through her hair. Returning to the bedroom, she dressed in white shorts and a checked cotton blouse, tied at the waist. Then she made up her bed and scurried downstairs to the kitchen.

Ancel was nowhere to be seen, but the coffee was piping hot. She was pouring a cup when she heard his voice coming, she thought, from the front yard. Carrying her cup with her, she investigated and found him sitting on the porch steps talking to a short, dark-haired man who looked up at her with surprise.

"Good morning, sleepyhead," Ancel greeted. "Jennie, I'd like you to meet my friend, Manolo Guerra. Manolo, Jennie Cameron."

Manolo executed a half bow. "Ah, Señorita Cameron. How nice to meet you. I knew your father." His admiring eyes made a thorough and blatant sweep of her, and a slow, wicked grin spread from ear to ear. He glanced from Jennie to Ancel and back to Jennie. Ancel appeared unconcerned, but there was no question in Jennie's mind about the thoughts churning in Manolo's mind.

"How do you do," she said with extreme politeness, feeling more than a little embarrassed. She had always envied women whose poise never failed them; she had the most unfortunate way of acting guilty even when perfectly innocent. "It's nice to meet you too."

"Manolo works at the feed store down the road," Ancel explained. "He was making deliveries out this way, saw me, and stopped. He has some bedding plants left that we can have if you want them."

"They're the end of the crop," Manolo said, "and some are getting a little leggy. But if you pinch them back I think they'll do all right."

Jennie glanced at the flats resting on the ground at Manolo's feet. There were some dwarf marigolds, periwinkles, a few salvia, and some rather bedraggled petunias, but they could be salvaged. Once she got the shrubbery beds weeded, the flowers would add a charming touch to the front of the house.

"Thank you, Manolo. They will look lovely." Addressing Ancel she asked, "Have you had breakfast?"

"Yes," he said. "I would have fixed yours too, but I didn't know how late you would sleep. You didn't exactly have a restful night."

This was uttered very drolly and might have sounded all right had it not been for that secretive grin on his face. Jennie's face flushed, and she shot him a scathing look. Ancel was no idiot; he knew that Manolo suspected a situation far more intimate than the one that actually existed, and he was enjoying it, fostering it. *Just like a man,* Jennie thought sourly, and she could have kicked him.

"You—you mean the storm, of course," she said feebly.

"Of course," Ancel replied.

Manolo's grin had turned into a knowing smirk, and Jennie felt herself at a distinct disadvantage with those two. She thought it best to let the entire matter drop. Trying to explain things would only magnify them. But then Ancel stood up, climbed the stairs to stand beside her, and he slipped a possessive arm around her waist, branding her his in front of his friend. Jennie stared up at him incredulously, but his expression was as placid as could be.

"Appreciate it, old friend," he said to Manolo. "Stop by next time you're out this way. If you'll give us some notice I'll have Jennie whip up a meal for you. She's a helluva cook. Went to one of those fancy gourmet cooking schools."

Jennie's mouth dropped open in stunned dismay.

"I'll do that, Ancel." Manolo then turned to Jennie and again made a courteous bow. "Señorita," he said simply.

Jennie nodded, at a loss for words, and watched as Manolo drove off in the feed store's truck. Ancel gave her waist a little squeeze, then turned and walked into the house with Jennie hard on his heels.

"Why did you do that?" she demanded.

He stopped and turned around, raising his eyebrows. "Do what?"

"Let that man think we're staying together."

He laughed. "We *are* staying together."

Jennie sighed, exasperated. "You know what I mean. He thinks it's—it's more than it actually is."

"Really? You think so?"

"Yes," she hissed. "I know so, and so do you, so you can cut the innocent act! What's more, you did it deliberately." She paused for dramatic emphasis, then in a voice dripping venom mimicked him. "'Stop by, old friend, and I'll have the little woman whip up something for you.' Oh, Ancel, how could you?"

He appeared genuinely contrite. "Hell, Jennie, I'm sorry."

"Ancel, you've got to be careful. I mean, the two of us staying here in this house together, alone! You and I know it's perfectly proper, but there are those who are going to talk."

He grinned, and her sense of exasperation heightened. "Aw, Jennie, what do you care? You can't worry about what other people are going to think. But if it'll make you feel better I'll explain the situation to Manolo next time I see him."

"What will you tell him?" she asked, wary.

"I'll tell him we're not sleeping together, what else?"

Surely he was teasing. Her hand went to her forehead. "Oh, Ancel, you can't say it like that! It will only make it sound worse. That man is going to go back to the feed store, and in thirty minutes it's going to be all over White Rock that you and I are staying here. I know this town."

He folded his arms across his chest, and she could see that he was fighting desperately to keep his amusement under control. "All right, you tell me what I should tell people, since all this seems to upset you so much."

Jennie bit her lip. "Well...say nothing if possible, but if you should have to say something...you might begin by explaining that we're very *old* friends and that you were worried about my staying here alone, so you offered...." She paused. "Oh, hell!" she sputtered. "There's nothing you can tell them because we *are* staying here together, and the more you say the more suspicious it will seem."

Ancel threw back his head and laughed lustily. Then he reached for her, and once again she was being held in those strong arms, her face crushed against his chest. Her coffee cup rattled noisily in the saucer. "Relax, sweet Jennie. Enjoy life." His hold on her loosened, and he held her at arm's length. "Besides, what if we were living together in the intimate sense? What if we were sleeping together? Who would care, even in

White Rock? It hardly would be front-page news. It happens every day to all sorts of people.''

"Not to me it doesn't! I've never slept with a man, and I would just as soon people didn't think I was doing so now," she fumed, head held high.

The look he gave her was one of fresh wonder. He reached out and patted the side of her head—an infuriating gesture had it come from anyone else, but coming from Ancel it was surprisingly warm and affectionate. "You can't do anything about gossip, Jennie, except ignore it. Now"—he bent and again placed a light kiss on the side of her mouth—"you do whatever you need to do in the house. I'm going out to make some repairs on Rob's old tractor. When I come back we'll go over to my place. I think we deserve a break."

And he walked through the dining room, through the kitchen and out the back door, whistling.

Jennie stared after him, as perplexed and confused as ever. Ancel's lighthearted approach to her was unlike anything she had ever experienced. She had become expert in handling those men who made overt sexual advances early in a relationship, but Ancel was something else entirely. She simply did not know how to react to him.

For one thing, she had no idea how he felt about her. She was pretty sure he liked her, but she was pretty sure Ancel liked almost everyone. He had commented upon her appearance more than once, so she knew he thought she was pretty, but he was a man, and all men liked to look at pretty young women. She wondered if he thought her special in any way; did he think she was prettier or smarter or more fun or anything?

Most of all she wondered why it mattered to her so much. She was fast losing sight of her mission, which

was to get The Croft in good enough condition to sell
for top dollar and then get back to Fort Worth, to
Women Now, to her life. That was what she wanted...
wasn't it?

Jennie sighed and began trying to occupy her thoughts
with her housework. Earlier in the week she had driven
into town to purchase curtains for the kitchen and had
ended up spending a horrendous sum on little "ex
tras"—sofa pillows, a lovely dried flower arrangement
for the center of the dining table, cannisters and place
mats for the kitchen, and bright hand towels for the
downstairs bath. She supposed it had been a foolish
waste of money, but everything looked so nice!

Lovingly she ran her hand over the mahogany dining
table that had belonged to her maternal grandmother,
suddenly saddened by the thought that she had never
known her mother or her mother's mother. The table,
now polished to a rich patina, was much too precious to
be left behind in the house. She had no use for it now,
but someday when she had a home of her own she
would want it, and perhaps one day she could give it to
her daughter. The table would go into storage. In fact,
there were a number of things in the house that should
go into storage. Rob's fireside chair for one. It wasn't
right to have no links with your ancestry.

The hours flew by, and Ancel was back in the house,
his shirt covered with axle grease. There was a frown
on his face. "The damned thing needs a good over-
haul," he muttered.

"What?"

"The tractor," he explained. "It needs a lot of work,
but I'll bet it will take weeks to get it in the shop."

"Ancel, Papa's tractor is not your responsibility."

He stared at her for a moment. "Yeah, I seem to

keep forgetting that. Do you want to go over to my place now?''

"Yes," she said enthusiastically. "Should I change?"

His eyes traveled the length of her. "I can't think why. You fill out those shorts just right. But I need a fresh shirt."

"Shall we take my car or your truck?"

"How about on foot?" he suggested. "I know a shortcut. It's not much of a walk at all."

"Sounds great!" she enthused. "I'll lock up."

The river was barely more than a creek where it traversed The Croft's land, flowing clear and bright between pink-rocked banks laden with cedar and oak. Jennie and Ancel walked slowly along the western perimeter of the ranch, through the tamer parts of Jennie's property where the tenacious brush had been kept at bay and the grass was thick and lush and plentiful.

It was lovely country, in the way that wild, untamed things can be lovely. Once away from the towns, once away from the clearings surrounding the little ranches dotting the landscape, the land had not changed perceptibly since the days when those first German settlers had sent the Comanches packing.

Ancel helped Jennie cross the creek at its narrowest point, not a difficult task since the smooth granite slabs protruding out of the water formed natural stepping-stones. Once on the other side they were on Ancel's property.

They came to a clearing, and ahead Jennie could see a cabin. She wasn't sure what she had expected Ancel's place to be—a shack or a hastily erected lean-to—but the structure she saw was a large log cabin that looked perfectly at home in its surroundings.

"Why, Ancel!" she exclaimed. "How nice!"

"Shades of Abe Lincoln and all that, but it's home."

He ushered her in through the back door, and Jennie saw that the cabin was a huge one-room affair with a small kitchen alcove at the rear and a sleeping loft above that. At one end of the big room, completely dominating the cabin, was a massive limestone fireplace. There was a door to the right leading, she assumed, to a bathroom. The furnishings were heavy and comfortable and thoroughly masculine. Why, Jennie wondered, do women invariably think that a man who lives alone surrounds himself with clutter and disarray? Ancel's cabin was cozy and pin-neat.

"Ancel, it's a wonderful place. Really it is! I'm impressed."

"I built it myself," he told her proudly. "Every square inch of it."

She shook her head in wonder. "Is there anything you can't do?"

He grinned. "I'm a lousy banker."

She laughed and walked to the kitchen window, pushed aside the curtains and stared out. From this vantage point she could see Ancel's grazing pastures in the distance and dozens of creamy-faced, cinnamon-colored Herefords ambling along, heads down, feasting on thick grass. Half a dozen mounted cowboys rode among them. It was a picture from her past. There had been a time when Cameron beef was highly prized at market, and soon perhaps The Croft would again be running cattle.

She crossed the big room to sit on a leather sofa and continue her inspection. Everything about Ancel's home spoke of a place well cared for by someone who loved it. Unaccountably, Jennie thought of her own apartment in Fort Worth, and she felt a twinge of sadness. Oh, she loved it too of course, but she really didn't spend all that much time in it, and it had always seemed rather transitory to her. Certainly it wasn't the place she yearned to put down roots. Suddenly that bothered her.

Then she thought of her life in the city, of her job, and her friends. She had expected to miss them more than she did. Furthermore, she doubted that they missed her all that much. They weren't that much a part of one another's lives. She sighed, wondering at her melancholic introspection. This wasn't like her at all.

Ancel had been watching her. Now he crossed the room to sit beside her and take one of her hands in his. She raised her eyes to meet his, and she experienced the strangest fluttery feeling in the pit of her stomach.

"What's the matter, Jennie?" he asked quietly.

She shook herself free of her dark mood. "Oh...I was just thinking about your building this place yourself...and thinking about Papa's building The Croft," she lied. "Tell me something, Ancel, what do you do when you aren't lending a helping hand to neighbors? What do you like to do for fun?" It occurred to her that she really knew very little about him except that he was generous with his time and didn't lunge at women. At least he didn't lunge at her.

"I work," he said simply. "My work is my fun."

"But surely you have diversions. What about a woman? Is there one in your life? If so, she must be very upset with you for spending so much time at The Croft."

"Nope. No woman."

No one could ever accuse Ancel Gunter of being a

chatterbox, especially when it came to talking about himself. "Surely there have been women in your life," she persisted, determined to probe his dark depths. "Tell me about some of them. Have there been many?"

He smiled wryly, then reached out to place one of his hands on the nape of her neck where it began tender massaging motions. His touch elicited an immediate response from her, and Jennie could distinctly hear her own heartbeat as it pounded frantically in her chest. "No," he said with a tender smile. "I lied to you about the way I spent all those years away from White Rock. Actually, I was a Trappist monk."

At his teasing, the tension quit her immediately, and she laughed merrily. "Aren't you ever serious about anything?"

Abruptly his unruffled expression vanished, to be replaced by a smoldering gaze that made her catch her breath. Such a strange look coming from that cheerful face. The strong outline of his mouth changed from mirth to solemnity; the green eyes darkened, and when he spoke his voice throbbed with vibrant intensity. "Jennie, there are some things I'm very serious about... and kissing you right now is one of them," he said and leaned toward her. Jennie sat frozen, paralyzed, and watched as his mouth came ever closer. Then it found hers and clung there. Jennie gasped at the first contact with those moist male lips.

She wondered if ever there had been a kiss that felt so good. She had read about kisses like this but had thought them merely creations of very active imaginations. A dizzying response washed over her, and she experienced so many tingling, unfamiliar sensations. The room was very bright, but Jennie shut her eyes

tightly to block out everything but the incredible joy of
Ancel's nearness and warmth.

His mouth moved against hers, lazily at first, savor-
ing and exploring; then the pressure increased, and the
kiss became one of delighted discovery. When at last
Ancel drew away from her she stared at him in wide-
eyed wonder. "Dear God, Ancel! Wh-what are we doing?"

"Kissing," he said huskily. "It's an old tribal cus-
tom. It wards off evil spirits."

And his arms went around her to draw her to him in an
all-encompassing embrace, his hands gently guiding her
into a reclining position. Liquid fire coursed through her
veins, and her body became spontaneous and giving. Up
went her arms to meet behind his neck; her lips parted
under his, inviting his sweet kiss to become more demanding. The intenseness of the passion he was un-
leashing in her was startling and frightening, but she
gave no thought to resistance. Being held so close to Ancel simply was too appealing to be denied. She became a
mindless creature, perfectly willing to lie in the comfort
of his strong arms and let his mouth, his tongue, his
hands do whatever they wished.

It was beautiful...and light-years removed from
anything in her previous experience. Jennie clung to
him as though frightened he might run from her if she
released her hold on him. It seemed only natural that
his tongue should probe her mouth, that his hand
should come up from her waist to gently cup and
fondle her breast.

His expert fingers worked at the buttons of her
blouse while his mouth kissed her eyes, her cheek, the
underside of her chin, then roamed the silken curve of
her throat to come at last to rest on the gentle swelling

of her breasts. His big gentle hand slipped inside her
blouse and pushed the bra strap off her shoulder.
When his mouth closed over one taut nipple she
thought he cried her name softly, but she couldn't be
sure, for she had lost all sense of reality.

No other man had come close to arousing these emotions in her; the burning ache spreading through her
loins was a totally new experience for her. She had been
very young and completely lacking in worldliness when
she had fallen in love with Paul Gunter, and theirs had
been a proper, chaste relationship. Later, her fear of being hurt again had precluded serious involvement with
another man. But this man—this tall, gorgeous, golden
man—had uncovered emotions she would not have
dreamed she possessed.

Now Ancel was settling his long, hard length against
her and molding her small round bottom to fit her into
the comfortable niche of his hips. Her mind reeled and
stumbled, cleared for a moment, then again became a
swirling chaos. When he thrust one leg between her
thighs, she thought she was strangling.

"Ancel, please..." she whispered. "No...I...."

"Oh, Jennie, Jennie," he muttered thickly. "Come
with me...to my bed in the loft. Love me...love
me...."

She gasped. "Ancel...I can't! Dear God, I've never...."

He was nuzzling her neck, raining kisses across her
cheek, nibbling on her earlobe. "I know, I know. Don't
be afraid. I won't hurt you. You'll see...come with me
now. I'll be gentle...."

She squirmed, further inflaming him. "Ancel...I
can't think...."

"Don't think! Only feel!"

The rush of intense hotness spreading through her rendered her senseless. "I...don't.... Please, just hold me for a minute. I can't...."

His response was to crush her to him and give her a hard, demanding kiss. Jennie wrapped her arms around him and willed her mind to clear. She wanted him—God, how she wanted him!—but she had to have time to think! She was not at all certain of her ability to handle a seduction. If only he would just hold her, give her time to *think,* instead of moving his hands over her breasts and thighs and sending all those delicious little tremors prickling at her spine.

Jennie waited expectantly, hopefully. Any moment she was sure he would tell her how he felt about her. In a second he would say something, anything, that would tell her he felt real affection for her, over and above the mere physical wanting. He wouldn't kiss her this way if he didn't care for her, would he? Would he?

She covered his neck with light kisses while his hands continued their exquisite movements. Caught up in this primordial passion, neither of them at first was aware of the resonant baritone voice that spoke to them from the doorway.

"My, my what a tender little scene!" Paul Gunter said contemptuously.

So complete was their absorption in each other that neither Jennie nor Ancel could immediately come to grips with the reality of a third presence in the room. They parted slightly and exchanged startled glances, but emerging from the depths of their emotions was not something easily nor quickly accomplished. The voice had thoroughly shattered the erotic eloquence of the moment, but their fever had not abated.

Finally it was Ancel who collected his wits enough to

look toward the doorway; what he saw brought a flash of anger to his eyes. He jumped to his feet, hands clenched into fists at his sides, and Jennie was left to straighten and compose herself as best she could.

"What in hell are you doing here?" Ancel demanded of his brother.

"I stopped by Jennie's place. There was no one there, so I thought I might find the two of you here since rumors are rife in town that you are—er—is cohabitating too old-fashioned a word these days?"

"Oh, for God's sakes!" Ancel fumed. "Didn't anyone ever teach you to knock?"

"I didn't think there was any need. Obviously I was wrong," Paul said imperiously, fastening a cold, accusing gaze on Jennie, who was trembling with embarrassment. "Why didn't you lock the door?"

"*I* didn't think there was any need," Ancel said angrily. "And obviously *I* was wrong."

Paul strode nonchalantly around the room, scrutinizing the rustic decor with undisguised disdain. "I drove out to invite Jennie to dinner at the house tomorrow night. We're having a few friends over, and I thought she might enjoy it." Paul's sardonic mouth twisted as he looked at his brother. "And of course you're invited too."

"Thanks," Ancel said grimly and went to sit beside Jennie on the sofa. Apparently sensing her acute discomfort, he gently took her hand in his and patted it reassuringly, though Jennie had the strangest suspicion the gesture was meant more for Paul's benefit than hers. Ancel wanted Paul to think he and Jennie shared a special kind of relationship. She could almost feel the animosity between the two brothers; it was like a fourth presence in the room.

"What do you say, Jennie?" Ancel asked her. "Do you want to go? It might be a nice change for you. You've done nothing but work since you came home."

"I...ah, yes I guess so...if you'll come with me."

"Of course. You don't think I'd let you go without me, do you?" He returned his attention to Paul. "We'll be there."

"You're a little overdue, you know," Paul remarked coldly.

Instant alarm crossed Ancel's face. "What's the matter? Has something happened? Is something wrong?"

"Something's always wrong," Paul said.

Again Ancel was on his feet, eyes ablaze. "Damn you—" he exploded.

Paul raised a hand. "Relax. You'll find nothing very unusual has happened." He then made a curt bow in their direction. "Tomorrow night then. Cocktails at seven, dinner at eight. We'll be expecting you." He glanced at Jennie for a moment, and she recoiled under his penetrating stare. Then he turned and left the cabin without another word to Ancel.

The brief exchange between the two brothers puzzled Jennie, who sensed some sort of family problem that was none of her business, yet she was very curious. Whatever it was had deeply disturbed Ancel, and Ancel did not seem the type who was easily upset.

When the door closed behind Paul, Ancel expelled his breath in a disgusted sigh and reached for Jennie, but she pulled away from him. How humiliating to have been caught in such a compromising situation! It must have appeared so—so sordid to their intruder. Even without being able to see herself, she knew she must look disheveled, and she tried not to dwell upon what might have happened had Paul not shown up. She had been alarmingly close to capitulation, and she still was not confident that her emotions were under control.

"Ancel, we really should get back to the house."

His hand began a sensitive wandering up her arm. "We've plenty of time. Let's not go yet. We haven't had lunch, and we were going to spend a lazy afternoon, together, remember?"

He leaned toward her, and Jennie knew that in an instant she would be back in his arms, probably in his bed, for his merest touch seemed to have the most peculiar effect on her. He possessed the ability to shatter all her resistance, but how could she go to bed with a man who had not once uttered the word *love* to her? It was unthinkable. With supreme effort she pulled away from him.

Hurt and disappointment showed clearly in his eyes. "Damn Paul!" he muttered. "Why did he have to pick this particular time to show his face? He hasn't been out here in months."

"I'm...I'm thinking perhaps it's a very good thing he did," she said weakly.

"Damn it, Jennie. I won't have this conscience nonsense!" Ancel snapped. "It was beautiful, you know it was, and it would have been even more beautiful if that bastard of a brother of mine hadn't—"

Abruptly Jennie stood up, nervously rubbing the palms of her hands on her shorts. "Let's go back to the house, Ancel."

"Why do you feel safer there than here?" he asked sensibly. "We'll still be alone."

She shrugged and could not look at him. "We've lived there almost a week, and...nothing's happened."

"I won't promise I won't attack."

"You didn't attack. We both . . . just got carried away."

"Look at me, Jennie. Are you upset because you were found in a compromising situation . . . or because it was Paul who did the finding?"

She whirled to face him squarely, and her beautiful dark eyes flashed with anger. "What's that supposed to mean?"

"Does he still do something for you?" Ancel asked bluntly.

Although Jennie was beginning to feel less and less fascination for Paul every time she saw him, something prevented her from letting Ancel know that. Perhaps she needed some protection against the devastating, all-consuming power Ancel himself seemed to have over her. As long as he thought she was still somewhat attracted to Paul, Jennie felt she had a bit of a power base of her own. She looked down at her hands and said nothing, leaving him to think what he wished.

"Don't shut me out, Jennie," Ancel said meltingly, and for a brief moment she felt her resolve start to crumble. "We were so close to something wonderful."

She shot him a nervous half-smile. "Don't be silly. I'm not shutting you out. How could I? We live together. And tomorrow we're going to have our first date. It will be a lovely evening."

"I hope so," he said, sighing. Then he too stood and took her by the hand, and together they walked back to The Croft.

Chapter Seven

Jennie was not so naive as to believe their relationship would not be subtly altered by the lovemaking, and she was right. There was nothing overt; Ancel was as charming and amiable as ever, but it seemed to her that his casualness now was a bit forced, that his gentle teasing had a sharp edge to it, and she longed desperately to be back in the sheltering warmth of his arms, yet deeply feared losing control with a man who treated her only as a friend.

Needing something to do to fill in the day's remaining hours, she announced, "The cupboard is becoming a bit bare. All we ever seem to do is eat. I think I'll run over to Friedrich's and restock."

"Good idea," Ancel said without interest and returned to his work, leaving Jennie to wonder if the closeness and camaraderie they once had shared was gone forever.

Shopping at Walt Friedrich's store was a trip to the past. The rather ramshackle building had been enlarged, but otherwise it had not changed since the days when Jennie had accompanied her father on his weekly shopping trip. Staples still were ladled out of crates and boxes and jars; fresh fruits and vegetables still came from local gardens, and customers were urged to poke, squeeze, smell, and sample before buying. The meat and poultry still were home-raised, freshly slaughtered, and never would know the likes of Styrofoam cartons and plastic wrap.

Everything was irresistible, and Jennie was horrified at the cash register's total. "Seventy dollars! And I was only buying for a few days!"

"Wanna put some of the stuff back?" the clerk asked.

"No, that's all right. I just hope none of it goes to waste," she said, fumbling in her handbag for the money.

She was following the bag boy to her car when she was accosted by two birdlike elderly women dressed in plain black dresses that came almost to their shoe tops. They were the Bumgarner sisters, Hilde and Ruta, who had taught fourth and fifth grades at Davy Crockett Elementary for as long as anyone under forty-five could remember. Their stern, pinched faces belied their gentle, compassionate natures, for they were two women who taught for the sheer love of children and the profession. Moreover, once a child had passed through their classes, that child was never forgotten. They greeted Jennie warmly.

"Oh, Jennifer, how wonderful to see you, dear!" Hilde Bumgarner exclaimed. "How is Margaret?"

"Meg is fine, thank you, ma'am. I'll tell her you asked about her. She'll be so pleased," Jennie said graciously.

"Ruta and I heard you were in town. Someone—I can't think who—saw you with that nice Gunter boy. Paul, I think."

"No, ma'am. It must have been Ancel." Jennie was

almost certain no one had seen her with Paul the day they drove down south.

The frail little schoolteacher shook her head emphatically. "No, I'm sure it was the tall blond one."

Jennie smiled. "Yes, ma'am...but that's Ancel."

"But Ancel is that lovely Ellen's husband," Hilde insisted.

At that moment Ruta Bumgarner tapped her sister on the arm. "Hilde dear, you have the boys mixed up. Paul is Ellen's husband."

"Ruta dear, you're the one who has things mixed up. I see Ellen with the tall blond one all the time. I'm sure he's her husband."

Jennie couldn't understand why this little argument between the two slightly senile women disturbed her so much. Driving home, she was aware of her trembling hands on the wheel and the dull ache in her throat. There was nothing wrong with Ancel's being seen with his sister-in-law, nothing at all. So why did it bother her?

At the house Jennie placed the grocery sacks on the kitchen table, and Ancel looked at them in horror. "Good grief, Jennie! Who's going to eat all this food?"

"I got a little carried away, didn't I? Can't you use anything that's left over?"

"I suppose so. Here, I'll help you put them away."

Moving from table to cupboard, Jennie said, "I saw the Bumgarner sisters at the grocery store."

Ancel chuckled. "Lord, are those two still around? They were old when I was in the fifth grade."

"They haven't changed a bit," she said, then in as offhand a tone as she could muster she added. "Funny...Hilde thought you were the Gunter boy who's married to Ellen."

"Really," he said in what seemed like a natural enough voice, but his back was to her, so she could not see the expression on his face. Her nagging worry was not eased.

The following day, Saturday, was spent much the same as all the other days—breakfast, work, lunch, more work—the only difference being that they quit earlier than usual in order to dress for dinner at the Gunter home.

At five o'clock Ancel left to go to his place to change. He had managed to stockpile a considerable amount of clothing at The Croft, but there was nothing suitable for a party. When Jennie descended the stairs at six fifteen, he was back, and there was nothing forced about the look he gave her.

"My God!" he gasped. "You're the loveliest sight I've ever seen! What happened to the little ragamuffin I left less than two hours ago?"

Jennie had dressed in the only garment she had with her that she considered suitable for the occasion—a coral-colored crepe with swirling skirt and a draped neckline that showed just the barest hint of cleavage. She loved the sensuous feel of the soft fabric as it swished about her stockinged legs.

"Thank you," she said. "You look pretty fantastic yourself."

And he did. It made her heart lurch just to look at him. He was wearing a faultless tan gabardine suit, and there was nothing of the country cowboy image about this Ancel Gunter. It amazed her that he could wear such clothes with such aplomb. This Ancel Gunter would have been right at home in any drawing room in the world.

He was fussing with his necktie and running a forefinger around his shirt collar. "Inventing the necktie should have been a penitentiary offense," he grumbled.

Jennie laughed. "Shall we go?"

He tucked her hand into the curve of his arm. "Do you want to take your car or my truck?"

Jennie glanced at the battered pickup and wrinkled her nose. "Let's go in my car."

"Too bad," he said, grinning wickedly. "Dad just loves having my pickup parked in front of his palace."

The Gunter home was far and away White Rock's most impressive private residence. It was a dazzling white, two-storied, Mediterranean castle with lots of grillwork at the windows and a walled-in courtyard, surrounded by meticulously manicured grounds. The whole was enclosed by an iron fence that kept out sightseers but afforded them a splendid view of the mansion beyond.

A white-coated butler showed them into the huge tiled foyer with its magnificent mahogany-railed stairway rising before them. On their left was the library with its floor-to-ceiling, book-crammed shelves; on their right was the richly appointed reception room. "A few friends," turned out to be a sizable crowd of about fifty people, yet the house did not seem crowded, so spacious were all the rooms.

Jennie shot Ancel a surreptitious glance, wondering at the emotions stirring within him. Paul in this lavish mansion and Ancel in his log cabin in the hills. Ancel would have had to be inhuman not to feel the inequities of the situation, yet his outward appearance was as poised and cheerful as ever.

"Ah, Jennifer, my dear! How nice to see you again!"

A booming masculine voice reached her ears, and she turned to see Ernst Gunter, the family patriarch, striding toward her. Ernst was what most people referred to as distinguished looking. Nearing the age of sixty, the elder Gunter still was a handsome man, physically fit, tall, firm-waisted and straight-shouldered. Jennie realized she was looking at Ancel twenty-odd years down the road, for he favored his father to a striking degree.

"Mr. Gunter, how are you? It's very nice to see you too," Jennie said demurely, offering him her hand and accepting the way the man's keen eyes took in her appearance. Ernst Gunter had not wanted Paul to marry little Jennifer Cameron from that old ranch outside of town—Jennie had been only too aware of that—but now that she no longer posed a threat to his personal dynasty, Ernst could afford the luxury of being gracious and openly admiring.

"Your father would be proud of you," Ernst told her, his tone implying that he and Jennie's father had somehow been friends. Jennie seethed a bit inside. Ernst wouldn't have given Rob the time of day except when Rob needed to borrow some money from the bank.

With alertness Jennie noted the change of attitude as Ernst turned his attention to his younger son. The warmth left his expression and was replaced by—what? Disapproval? Disappointment? Though Ernst amiably slapped Ancel's back, the gesture seemed less than heartfelt.

"How are things going, Ancel," he asked without interest.

"Fine, Dad, just fine," Ancel said, his bland tone matching his father's. The obvious lack of genuine affection between father and son was incomprehensible to Jennie, who had unreservedly adored Rob Cameron. She moved possessively closer to Ancel, and he looked down at her with a sad smile.

"That's good," Ernst said vacantly. "Well, you two young people mix and mingle and have a good time. I'll see you again before the evening is over. Awfully nice seeing you, Jennifer," he repeated and was gone, caught up in the milling crowd.

Ancel led Jennie to a table laden with a staggering array of hors d'oeuvres, which they sampled and nibbled, and then they moved to the bar where Ancel ordered a Scotch and water and Jennie opted for vodka and tonic.

The bar, of course, was a popular spot, and Ancel was acquainted with most of the guests, all of whom were introduced to Jennie, but she despaired of remembering names. None of the guests was familiar to her, but that was not surprising; Rob hadn't moved in the Gunters' social circle, and the young people of her generation normally fled White Rock at the first opportunity.

She stood beside Ancel, watching the crowd with detachment. Parties such as this were her least favorite form of entertainment. She heard snatches of conversation in German, but there was none of the joyous *gemütlichkeit* that she associated with German parties. This was a sedate, affluent group, and the atmosphere reflected it.

As though reading her mind, Ancel slid one arm around her waist and said, "I'm suffocating! Let's go find some breathing room."

The library was far less crowded; only a few couples were seated in the big comfortable chairs, conversing in hushed tones. Ancel guided Jennie to the stone fireplace and pointed out the portrait hanging above it. The woman who stared down at them was stunningly beautiful, very dark, almost exotic. Paul Gunter resembled this woman as much as Ancel resembled Ernst Gunter.

"Your mother," Jennie said simply.

"Yes."

"She was so lovely."

"She was the prettiest thing you've ever seen, Jennie, and it was only after you got to know her well that you realized how truly beautiful she was."

"I only met her a few times," Jennie told him, recalling how Ernst's hostility toward her had precluded her visiting the Gunter mansion more often.

"She would have loved you had she known you well. For all her problems, and she had many, she never lost her sweetness. The world was a nicer place when she was in it. I miss her every day of my life."

The poignancy of Ancel's words clutched at Jennie's heart; her eyes misted, and she swallowed with some difficulty. "Ancel, that's a beautiful sentiment."

"I'm sure she's better off now. She was so alive, so full of joy and vivacity. Or at least she was...before Dad took it all out of her."

Jennie laid her hand on his arm, trying to communicate to him her sympathy. "Oh, Ancel, surely you don't mean that."

Bitterness raged in every word as he said, "You don't know this house the way I do, Jennie. It's a very stimulating life they lead here. The bank until three o'clock, except for Wednesdays when they leave at noon for an afternoon of golf at the club. Cocktails are served in the library at five sharp, and if you happen to be in residence at the time, the cocktail hour is a command performance. Dinner at seven, then brandy and cigars in the library. Women are tolerated but expected to remain silent. Creative thought or innovative ideas are out! The conversation always centers around banking and finance. If anyone in this house has ever read a book, seen a painting or attended a play or movie that impressed him, I have yet to hear about it. Of course, Dad and Paul take business trips to their banks in Dallas and Houston and Amarillo, but they hurry back here the moment they can. In cities they tend to get lost in the shuffle, but in White Rock the Gunters are royalty.''

Jennie didn't know what to say to him. This was a side of Ancel she had never seen before. Naturally she understood how he could be a little bitter, a little jealous, but his voice positively dripped with venom. It did not fit the Ancel she knew.

Ancel's hand made a wide sweep to indicate their surroundings. ''See these people? I promise you that everyone here tonight, with the exception of you and me, is in some form or fashion important to Gunter State Bank, and they're drawn together not by mutual interests but by a common affluence. They worship at the feet of the god of gold, and none believes more devoutly than Paul and Dad.''

Jennie groped for the right words to say to him, but she was spared the necessity of making an appropriate remark, for at that moment an alluring feminine voice called across the room. ''Ancel!'' the voice said, and Jennie turned to see Ellen Barton Gunter standing on the threshold.

Jennie had seen the woman only once before, at Rob Cameron's funeral, when Ellen had been the brand-new bride of Paul Gunter. At that time the wound had been fresh and so painful that she had been able to give her only the briefest of glances. Now, however, time had worked its wondrous healing, and Jennie's eyes made a thorough sweep of Mrs. Paul Gunter.

"Ravishing" and "beguiling" were the first words that popped into her head; mere "beautiful" did not seem to do the woman justice. She was tall, very slender, graceful and delicate. Her golden hair was twisted into a French knot that allowed small tendrils to escape and frame a face that looked as though it had been carved of ivory. She wore a flowing tomato-red creation that on a less striking woman would have been overpowering, but on Ellen Gunter it appeared almost understated. Everything about Paul's wife pointed to elegant perfection.

Except... Ellen obviously was terribly agitated about something. She clutched at the door frame as though she was seeking support, and her eyes darted about in a wild and frightened manner. Her attention was riveted on Ancel; if she even noticed Jennie she showed no sign.

"Ancel...oh, Ancel," Ellen said breathlessly, and she rushed toward him, grabbing for his arm and virtually collapsing against him. "Thank God you're here! I was so afraid you wouldn't come. Where in God's name have you been?"

Jennie frowned in puzzlement, but Ancel appeared to take Ellen's behavior in stride, as though it was the most perfectly normal thing in the world. "Ellen, dear," he said softly and calmly, "I want you to meet—"

Ellen cut him off. "Ancel, please come with me. I must talk to you," she said pathetically.

"Ellen, I have a friend with me," Ancel said patiently, using the tone adults often use with very young children.

"No, no!" Ellen's voice was barely audible, and she was shaking her head over and over. "I don't want to meet anyone. Please... you must come with me."

Ancel sighed with resignation and turned to Jennie apologetically. "Jennie, I'm sorry. Do you mind? I hate this... but I really should...."

Jennie shook her head and did her best to still her trembling chin. Of course she minded, but what could she say? "No, Ancel, I don't mind. Go on. I'll be fine."

"Are you sure? I hate to strand you like this."

Jennie turned her gaze on Ellen Gunter, but the woman seemed in a daze and totally oblivious to anyone but Ancel. She was being incredibly rude in not acknowledging Jennie's presence, but her entire behavior was so peculiar, so irrational, that Jennie suspected she could not be judged by normal standards.

"I'm sure, Ancel," Jennie said, giving him what she hoped was her nicest smile. "Go on... please."

He squeezed her hand and winked at her. "I'll be back the second I can," he said, then allowed Ellen to lead him out of the room.

Regretfully, Jennie watched them leave. There was something going on in this house that she didn't understand and probably never would. An aura of pathos surrounded Ellen Gunter, but there was no denying that she was an incredibly lovely woman. Jennie thought she could well understand why a man like Paul would be attracted to her. Any man, for that matter.

My, my Jennifer, her inner voice taunted. *Aren't you being magnanimous! Five years ago you seethed with jealousy. Five years ago you wanted to scratch the woman's eyes out!*

Well, she supposed jealousy had been an under-

Harlequin reaches
into the hearts and minds
of women across America
to bring you

Harlequin American Romance.™

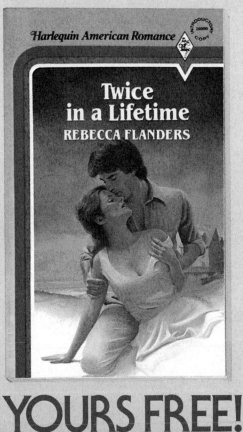

YOURS FREE!

standable emotion, given her youth and inexperience. Certainly it was far more understandable than the petulance she now was feeling at having Ancel so precipitously removed from her side. She was left in the awkward position of being the only one at the party with no one to talk to.

Feeling conspicuous standing alone in front of the fireplace, she decided to go nibble on some more tidbits. She left the library, crossed the foyer, and was about to enter the crowded reception room when a throaty masculine voice spoke to her from behind.

"Miss Cameron, I believe."

She turned to face Paul Gunter. Her eyes took him in all at once. She knew no man who constantly dressed with such flawless good taste. Paul, she thought, always looked like an advertisement for men's fashions. If only he had been able to muster some human warmth. . . .

"Oh, hello, Paul. It's a lovely party."

"Is it? I've been looking for you. Are you alone?"

"I was with Ancel, but . . . your wife wanted to speak to him for a moment."

"Ellen always wants to speak to Ancel." The small frown on Paul's face passed quickly. "Do you want another drink?"

"No, thank you."

Paul placed his hand under her elbow and began propelling her through the crowd. "Come," he said. "Let's go out into the garden. It's impossible to carry on a decent conversation in this melee."

She wanted to protest, for she did not want to talk to Paul, not alone. She couldn't be sure she didn't still possess some residual fascination with him. But there was no chance for her to decline. She allowed him to steer her through the dining room, out onto the veranda, and from there across the lawn, deserted in the early summer evening.

They walked idly for a time, commenting upon the weather, the condition of the grounds, the heady aromas from the flower gardens. Finally he directed the conversation into more personal channels.

"Jennie, I have something I would like to say to you. I don't know precisely the best way to go about this, but I want to apologize for—for a lot of things. For presuming too much in the car the other day. But primarily I want to apologize for the way I terminated our engagement."

"You mean the letter, of course," she said. "It was rather blunt, but it got the job done, and it hardly was unexpected. Quite a few of my 'friends' had taken the time and trouble to write to tell me about the beautiful girl from Galveston who was a guest in the Gunter home."

Paul winced. "Yes, Dad invited her. Ellen's father was a client of our Houston bank. I...didn't expect it to get out of hand, Jennie, and I certainly never meant to go behind your back. Ellen stayed with us a very long time, and...it just happened."

Jennie smiled inwardly. Yes, she could imagine Ernst Gunter's careful campaign, throwing Paul and the beautiful Ellen together while Jennie was safely away at college, pressing his son on to an advantageous marriage. "Of course," she said expressionlessly. "Besides, we weren't engaged in the strictest sense of the word. There was no ring or anything like that."

"I just want you to know I was embarrassed...and not mature enough at the time to handle it properly. I couldn't take a face-to-face confrontation with you, for fear my convictions would waver, I suppose."

"And that really would have screwed up things, wouldn't it?" she said tartly, enjoying his discomfort.

Paul looked startled "I've regretted it, if that makes you feel any better."

She raised one eyebrow, then in a cool and poised voice said, "Paul, I feel wonderful. I have for a long time. You needn't explain anything or apologize for anything because, you see, it simply doesn't matter anymore."

And the most amazing thing was that it didn't. Suddenly she felt very detached from this man who had possessed the power to twist and tug at her heart, then to shatter it completely. In a sharp flash of insight she thought she finally could see him as he really was—cold, aloof, imperious. Oh, why had she persisted in clinging to memories of him? Now it seemed such a foolish waste of time, so childish.

Was that it? she wondered. Had she simply grown up? Or had these days spent in the company of a man like Ancel—a man who was so warm and open and generous—enabled her finally to look at Paul fully and honestly?

Whatever the reason, Jennie felt a great burden quit her, and for one crazy minute she thought she was going to laugh out loud.

Paul had folded his arms across his chest and was staring down at her. "How's the redecoration project coming along?"

"Fine. The house looks wonderful."

"Have you given any more thought to my offer, Jennie?"

"Not really," she said truthfully.

"I'm sure we can come to terms on the price, and I do want the place, very much."

"It's not the money, Paul. I simply don't want to sell The Croft to someone who doesn't intend homesteading and raising livestock."

"That's patently ridiculous!" Paul snorted. "What do you care what the new owner does with the place?"

"I care, that's all."

"Who put that nonsense in your pretty little head? Ancel? It sounds like some of his foolishness."

She glared at him with contempt. "It's not foolish to care about the land. My father did, passionately. Ancel has a lot of that in him, and I, for one, find it very refreshing to meet a man who's interested in something other than the pursuit of the almighty dollar."

She spat out the words, hoping they hit their mark, but Paul merely stood, looking at her with an amused expression that she found infuriating. "Besides," she went on, "Ancel and I have done a lot of work on the ranch this past week, and The Croft has come to mean more to me than—than I thought it did."

"Are you sure it's the old family homestead that's come to mean so much to you?"

Not only had she been relieved of her attachment to him, but Jennie was beginning to actively dislike this man whom she had wasted so much time loving. "I beg your pardon," she said icily.

"I'm speaking of Ancel, of course."

"Ancel is my friend."

"Come, come, Jennie. I'm not blind. There was nothing *friendly* about what I saw in Ancel's cabin yesterday afternoon."

His gall was astonishing! Jennie leveled her frostiest stare on him. "That is personal, and, therefore, none of your damned business!"

"Do yourself a favor and take some good advice, Jennie. Don't get too—er—involved with my brother. Ancel is one of those free spirits who never will settle down. Dad and I have despaired of having him amount to anything. With all his advantages, he's turned out to be nothing but a hayseed. He's been a big disappointment to us."

Not only was Paul's manner offensive, his assessment of his brother was appalling to Jennie. Bristling, she turned to reverse her direction and return to the house, but Paul moved quickly to detain her. One arm stayed her flight.

"Don't go just yet, Jennie. I thought perhaps you and I could meet later, after the party. Surely you can get rid of Ancel. I—I realized when I saw you again just how much—how much you meant to me. My marriage has been a dreadful mistake, and I'd like to talk to you."

Jennie could not have been more horrified. "No!" she said between clenched teeth. "I make a practice of never having anything to do with a married man, and you are a married man."

A sardonic smile twisted his mouth. "In name only, my dear. Ask your friend Ancel... who also happens to be my wife's dear *friend*."

Jennie's mouth flew open. Paul's implication was quite clear, and a violent pain ripped through her. No, no! How dare Paul suggest that Ancel and Ellen.... She refused to listen to another word.

Trembling, she pulled herself free of Paul's grasp and marched resolutely toward the house. Climbing the steps of the veranda, she was startled to be met by an implacable Ancel, standing with arms akimbo, his jaw set stubbornly and his green eyes menacing.

"Where in hell have you been?" he demanded sharply.

Taken aback, Jennie could only mumble, "For a walk."

At that moment Paul appeared from the shadows. Ancel looked at Jennie, then at his brother, and back to Jennie. "I see," he said quietly, but the fire in his eyes burned brightly.

Jennie moved closer to him. "No, Ancel," she muttered softly. "No, you don't see at all. Now"—she extended one smooth arm toward him—"please don't leave me again for the remainder of the evening."

"Don't worry, Jennie. I don't intend to," he said and shot his brother a withering glare.

At dinner, however, Jennie found herself seated at the opposite end of the long banquet table from Ancel. His attention was focused only on Ellen Gunter, at whose right he sat, and Jennie was forced to watch Ellen on the receiving end of all those dazzling smiles, all that conspicuous charm. Ancel's concern for the woman was obvious, and as the evening wore on, Jennie thought she perceived the reason for his solicitude. Noticing the too-bright eyes, the forced laughter, the slightly slurred speech, she realized that Ellen Gunter was getting quietly, deliberately drunk.

She handled it well, Jennie had to give her that. Ellen apparently was one of those people who could consume an enormous amount of liquor and remain in control, but there could be no mistaking her condition. She ate sparingly, but she drank glass after glass of wine. A hovering servant kept the tulip-shaped goblet constantly replenished.

Paul and Ernst ignored her, and the other guests,

most of whom hardly were more sober than Ellen was, seemingly did not notice. Only Ancel was attentive; his eyes anxiously darted to Ellen from time to time, and he appeared poised to spring into action should the woman require assistance.

Jennie watched them, resenting the fact that she was being so thoroughly ignored by Ancel. Paul's words kept coming back to her, but she thrust them aside. She was not the suspicious type; she always chose to think the best of others, and she did not believe Ancel capable of lusting after his brother's wife. Still, a painful lump lodged in her throat, choking her and making eating difficult.

Somehow the evening got itself over and done with, and Jennie felt exhausted when she rose from the table, tired of feigning rapt attention at the small talk swirling around her. Moreover, while Paul and Ernst saw to their departing guests, it was Ancel who accompanied a very unsteady Ellen to her room upstairs, leaving Jennie to wait in the foyer for what seemed an interminable length of time.

She was near tears, and chastising herself for being so, when Ancel at last joined her. Worse, in the privacy of the automobile on the drive home, Ancel steeped himself in silence, and Jennie's dark mood deepened. She had been a prize idiot to let him come to mean so much to her. He was hurting her without knowing he was, and she had no one but herself to blame for that.

Choking back tears, she tried to concentrate on watching the dark countryside glide by the window. A white-gold full moon shone through the lacelike branches of the trees, and a million stars glittered. She rolled down the car window to sniff deeply of the thick, humus aroma of the woods.

At this movement Ancel turned to look at her. "Have a good time?" he asked.

She turned. "What? Oh...oh, not really," she confessed. "I'm not much of a party type person."

"Neither am I." Abruptly he slowed the car and turned right. Jennie saw that they now were traveling eastward on a once familiar road.

"Would you like to see Enchanted Rock again?" Ancel asked.

Her eyes brightened. "Enchanted Rock! Oh, Ancel, I almost had forgotten about it."

Of all the remarkably smooth domes scattered throughout the hills, by far the best known and best loved was the one called Enchanted Rock, so named by the Indians because they thought spirits lived at its top. Bald and brooding, it loomed high over the surrounding ranchland. Climbing Enchanted Rock was no great feat—Jennie had done it dozens of times—and at its summit, on a night such as this, with nothing but wind and sky and stars, one could experience something of the feeling of the world the Comanches had known.

Ancel parked the car nearby and they got out. Then, choosing a particularly large, smooth rock, he spread his coat in cavalier fashion and invited her to sit next to him. Jennie breathed deeply of the fresh evening air. The sounds of the woods came to them, but otherwise all was completely still.

"Oh!" she said with a contented sigh. "I think this must be one of the few absolutely peaceful places left on earth."

"There are a few places left," he said solemnly, almost wistfully. "but not many. I've seen parts of Canada and Alaska that I liked very much, but there aren't many places. Trouble is, people always seem to find them...and then they aren't quiet and peaceful any-more." He turned his head to look at her seriously. "I can't even imagine living in the city. How can you notice anything if you live in the city?"

She smiled. "Oh, we notice plenty."

"For instance?"

"Well...which lanes on which freeways are closed for construction. Which combination of one-way streets will take you to your parking garage...."

Ancel groaned in horror. "See what I mean? Damned shame what people do to a place. You know, Jennie, a few years back I thought I had found Shangri-la. A nice little town in western Canada. Great place. A few thousand friendly folks living close to the land, renting out boats to tourists. I gave some thought to settling down there for a while." He paused, and his face grew grave. "That town's gone forever now."

"Oh, Ancel! What happened?" she cried, alarmed, expecting to hear of some natural calamity.

"Oil was discovered nearby," he said morosely. "Now there are twenty-odd thousand people, a couple of supermarkets, and you can't rent a damned boat because everybody's opening a fried chicken place or what have you."

Jennie wanted desperately to laugh, but she saw he couldn't have felt worse about that town. "Well," she said weakly, "maybe everyone's happy."

"If they are, they're fools."

"Do you know the one place I've always wanted to go?" she asked brightly, trying to lighten the mood.

"Australia?"

Jennie's eyes widened. "How on earth could you possibly have known that?"

He shrugged. "All Texans want to go to Australia.

It's supposed to be what Texas was like before people moved in and started ruining it."

"Well, you're right. I've always wanted to go to Australia. So did Papa. I even went so far as to talk to a travel agent about it once. I wasn't encouraged, believe me. I figured if I started saving money that day and didn't let up, I might get there on my fiftieth birthday."

Ancel then lapsed into deep thought for a few moments. At a loss for anything to say to him, Jennie waited. When at last he spoke she was startled by the sharp edge to his voice. "What were you and Paul doing in the bushes?" he asked harshly, and somehow Jennie knew it was the question he had been wanting to ask ever since they left the Gunter house.

She gasped. "We weren't 'in the bushes' as you so crudely put it. We merely took a walk in the garden."

"What did he want?" he demanded.

"What makes you think he wanted something?" she asked, hoping, praying, he was jealous.

"I know Paul."

"He wanted to apologize for the rather ungentlemanly way he ended our engagement."

Ancel gave a derisive hoot.

"And he said he was sure we could come to terms on the sale of The Croft...and he asked me if I would meet him after the party—"

"That bastard!"

"—and he warned me not to get too involved with you—and..."

"And what?"

Something checked her tongue then. She quickly decided not to mention Paul's implication that an intimate relationship existed between Ancel and Ellen. Ancel might be in the mood for unburdening his soul, and Jennie knew she was not prepared to handle a full confession, if indeed one would be forthcoming. She realized this was sticking her head in the sand, but she needed time to sort and catalogue all her confusing feelings about Ancel Gunter.

"Nothing," she said with finality. "That was all."

Ancel pounded one knee with his fist. "Damn him!" he said viciously. "Who in hell does he think he is? And what did you have to say to all that?"

"I told him there was no need to apologize for anything. And I told him that money isn't the issue as far as The Croft is concerned. And, naturally, I refused to meet him after the party."

Ancel's eyes narrowed. "When he warned you about me—what did you have to say to that?"

She met his direct gaze without faltering. "I told him it was none of his damned business."

Ancel laughed lustily and with one swooping move gathered her into his arms and pulled her onto his lap.

It was meant to be a frolicsome gesture, but the love-making in his cabin the previous afternoon had erased the possibility that their touching, hugging, and kissing could ever again be casual. His merest touch aroused an aching longing in Jennie, a longing for total submission to this splendid man. And that was very unfortunate for her. She had no good reason to suspect that he felt any serious affection for her; what had transpired between them in his cabin might very well have been nothing but a pass, the normal reaction of a vigorous young man toward a pretty young woman.

Moreover, she now was worried that Ancel was emotionally involved with his sister-in-law. She shouldn't attach much importance to the confused mutterings of an old woman, and she tended to discredit anything

Paul said, but she had seen Ancel with Ellen tonight, and she was astute enough to realize that their relationship was a special one. It might be purely platonic, but then again....

Still, she couldn't seem to behave prudently where Ancel was concerned. As his strong arms pulled her to him, she settled her hips into the comfort of his lap, and dear God! every love scene she had ever read in novels now made sense to her. She wanted to cling, to press, to cleave. Her mouth was in his hair, one arm was thrown around his shoulders. With her free hand she loosened the knot of his tie and unbuttoned his shirt halfway down so that she could feel the satisfying warmth of that broad expanse of chest.

He turned his head, his bright eyes now dark with emotion. His lips settled on the smooth hollow of her throat, while his hand began sensitively moving down the soft folds of her dress, coming to rest at its hem. With agonizing slowness it slipped beneath the fabric and then began a journey upward.

A strangled sob caught in Jennie's throat. A shudder swept through her. The enormity of her passion now was more than she could handle. His gentle hand was burning her stocking-clad thighs. She bent her head, parted her lips and begged to be kissed.

He obliged, and her nostrils drank in the stimulating male fragrance of him—spicy, musky, sense-drugging. There was nothing soft nor tender about the way his mouth claimed hers; it was raw, potent, savage, a kiss that bruised her lips, yet Jennie wanted it never to end. She was caught in a whirlpool of hot, sensual desire, powerless to escape. She moved her mouth under his in a silent invitation for more and more of his kisses.

When at last he brought his mouth away from hers,

his voice was so choked with emotion it barely was recognizable. "Let's go home," he said in an agonized whisper. "There's no need for us to make love in the woods like a couple of high-school kids."

Home! Home with Ancel! Home to that house where no one would interrupt them! A satisfying, terrifying thought. Jennie was not sure her legs would carry her to the car, so weak and unstable were they. She clung to Ancel for support, and when she was seated beside him in the automobile she was trembling with her need for him.

And he knows it, too, she thought, watching him. *He knows I want him. Oh, I am wanton, wicked! I'm going to bed with this man, and I have no idea how he feels about me, but I'm not going to be able to stop this. I don't even want to stop this!*

Chapter Eight

Ancel unlocked the front door and stepped aside to allow Jennie to enter the house. A welcoming lamp had been left on, and the interior smelled of soap and wax and polish. A warm flush of elation rushed through Jennie as her eyes took in the familiar surroundings. It was nothing but a plain, old-fashioned hill-country ranch house, but her labors had transformed it into a pleasant, comfortable, cozy haven.

Behind her Ancel locked the door, and she turned to him. He opened his arms, and wordlessly she went into them, clinging to him for a long moment. He was balm, warmth, and comfort, and as his big hands caressed her gently, she settled her body against his, molding, melting, fitting into the curve that seemed made only for her. Then he released her and crossed the room to turn off the light. At the foot of the stairs they joined hands and silently went up the stairway together.

Beside him Jennie moved like a sleepwalker, only dimly aware of her movements. *What should I be feeling?* she wondered. *Joy, anticipation, panic—or a combination of all three?* She was going to bed with a man for the first time in her life, and nothing about her was functioning right.

Neither of them thought to turn on a light when they entered the bedroom. Brilliant moonlight filtered in through the window, affording all the illumination necessary. Ancel walked to the bed and pulled down the bedspread with one quick motion, while Jennie stood numbly watching. Then he came to stand in front of her, and his hands began a sensual sweep of her shoulders and arms.

"Jennie...sweet Jennie," he said in a throaty whisper that sent tingling shivers up and down her spine.

His swift, sure fingers worked with the zipper in the back of her dress, and the garment was pushed from her shoulders to fall in a heap on the floor at her feet, leaving her to stand before him in her slip. Her arms went up to meet behind his neck, while his mouth came down hard on hers. Groaning as though in agony, he moved his hands to cup her small round bottom, and he lifted her, carrying her to the bed.

"Get out of the rest of that stuff," he ordered as he pulled his shirt free of his trousers and unbuttoned it.

Trembling from expectancy and apprehension, Jennie could not comply; she could only lie, mute and wide-eyed, and watch as his lean, taut body was exposed to her. She thought she would faint from wanting him. When he had stripped down to his undershorts, he threw himself down on the bed, almost crushing her, and began kissing her with an expertise that brought her to new heights of exquisite pleasure.

"I told you to take off the rest of that stuff," he teased softly, while his lips and tongue continued their tantalizing wanderings. "I guess I'm going to have to do it for you."

"Oh, God! Ancel...I don't know what's happening to me," she cried, all the while clinging to him and returning his kisses with abandon.

"Here, sweet...let me." His hands pushed the slip straps away from her shoulders, exposing her creamy smooth breasts, for she wore no bra. His face came down on their cushioned softness; he parted his lips and closed them over one very hard nipple. His mouth on this erotic zone brought a cry of ecstasy from Jennie.

All this latent sensuality, so long dormant, now flowered and bloomed. Jennie's mind reeled and stumbled. So this then was what it felt like to be a real woman! Never before had she experienced anything approaching the passion of this moment. And never again with anyone else, for he was the one, the only one. She had been waiting for him so long. Her newly awakened body squirmed restlessly under his, coming into firm contact with his hardness and further inflaming him. His hands moved intimately over her body, exploring, as her fingers dug into the corded muscles of his back, and his mouth continued its movements at her breast.

If only he would utter the word *love* she would have screamed for joy, for she now knew that she cared for Ancel Gunter more than she would have dreamed she could care for anyone. In the short span of a week he had invaded her heart and mind, and in a few moment's time it was likely that he would also invade her body. She would have liked to remain the way they were forever, locked together in this frantic embrace while his hands and mouth and tongue covered every inch of her. The fire inside her was raging out of control.

Say it, she silently implored him. *Please say it, and you won't have to take me. I'll give myself to you.*

He raised his hand from her breast like a satisfied infant and smiled down at her. His compelling eyes reflected all the eloquence and turbulence of the moment. "Oh, Jennie...Jennie, if you only knew darling. I wish I could tell you, but the words won't come. I..."

Say it, damn it, say it!

"...I want you," he finished, his voice throbbing.

Bitter disappointment welled inside Jennie. Want? Of course he wanted her. She could *feel* his wanting. But for all her very up-to-date ways, Jennifer Cameron was not sophisticated enough to accept raw sex without love. Sex was not entertainment; sex was the ultimate expression of love. It had to be that way, it had to be.

Ancel was speaking against her mouth. "Here, darling...let me help you with your slip, and I suppose you're wearing panty hose. Then you finish undressing me."

Apparently he felt her resistance, for he pulled away from her slightly. "You're frightened," he said.

"No...yes...oh, I don't know," she cried, on the verge of a deluge of tears. *He could lie a little,* she thought irrationally. *Men do it all the time. Is it so awfully difficult for him to say that one little word?*

"Don't be, don't be. I'll be gentle, I promise. I'd never hurt you." His mouth resumed its erotic journey over her body. "Jennie, Jennie...I want you to realize what we're doing, to want it as badly as I do. I won't have any attacks of remorse afterwards. I'll make it good for you, you'll see."

"Oh, Ancel...how can I think with you doing all these things to me?"

"You know that if it happens tonight, it'll happen

every night we're together—every afternoon and morning, too, for all I know. I don't want to go back to that damned sofa, and I don't think I could get enough of you in a lifetime. Tell me you want me."

With her mouth against his ear she whispered, "You tell me, Ancel."

"Tell you what, my sweet?"

"Tell me...what you feel for me."

His voice was low and husky. "I told you, Jennie...I want you. And you want me too, don't you?"

Hot tears splashed out of Jennie's eyes. So there it was. He couldn't say he loved her because it wasn't true, and she had a feeling Ancel was a man who didn't lie, not even to attain physical pleasure.

"*No!*" She screamed it in her hurt and frustration.

His body stiffened in her arms. Slowly he raised his head, a disbelieving expression clouding his face. His breathing was heavy and labored; his chest heaved against her breasts. "Forgive me, but I don't believe that."

"It's...true," she sobbed.

"Then you're an amazingly good actress," he said coldly. "You should have told me that before things went so far. It would have saved us both a great deal of trouble."

"Oh, Ancel, please try to understand. I tried, really I did...and I thought I could, but...it has to be more than two sets of glands calling to one another."

He appeared shocked, but his passion-induced frenzy was not easily overcome. His labored breathing continued for a moment, but his hands and mouth stopped their sensuous wanderings, and his eyes grew increasingly vacant and remote. Finally he pushed himself up and away from her.

"I see," he said. "I see." He stood up, gathered his clothes together and walked to the door. "I won't bother you again," he said stiffly and was gone.

Jennie could hear his footsteps on the stairway, then the sounds he made as he moved about the living room below. The tears were coming in a rush, and she did nothing to stem their flow. She had been right, of course, to withhold her love from a man who was not in love with her, but the emptiness she felt after their parting could not be denied. For one brief instant she thought of calling him back, and confronting him with, "I think I'm in love with you, Ancel." He would have to say something then, would be forced to tell her if he felt more for her than mere physical desire.

But that would have been shameful and humiliating. A violent pain ripped through her, and she thought her heart was withering inside her chest.

Ancel was gone when she awoke the next morning. No coffee had been made, there were no signs that he had eaten breakfast, and a subsequent perusal of the grounds clearly showed that he was nowhere about. Well, it was Sunday morning after all; perhaps he had gone to Mass at St. Helena's. She remembered that the Gunters often did. It would have been nice if he had asked her to accompany him, but then she hardly could expect Ancel to treat her in his formerly friendly fashion, not after last night.

It occurred to her that he might not want to see her again, that he might consider her something of a welcher, leading him on to great expectations only to renege at the last moment. A scarlet flush diffused her face, and the ache around her heart deepened. She wasn't at all sure she could face him again.

Lethargically, she made coffee and toast, choked them down, and then went out into the fresh morning, determined to weed the shrubbery beds and get the bedding plants in, sensing that physical labor was the most effective way to block out mental anguish.

Surprisingly, the morning passed quickly. It was noon when Jennie straightened and arched her back, then surveyed the fruits of her labors. The recent rain had done wonders. The lawn's color had brightened and intensified, and the shrubbery beds now were neat and free of weeds. The bedding plants, for all their scraggliness, had good roots and would be in bloom in a week or so. The homestead was a beautiful place. If Rob Cameron could have seen it, he would have been very pleased.

Jennie stepped back and looked at her home through misty eyes. Her work here was about finished. She might be able to stay busy for another day or two, three if she really stretched it, but then it would be over. Never to see it again! The ancient live oaks, the cedar brakes, the barn and corral and the north pasture beyond. The lovely green and golden days of a hill-country summer. Never to live at The Croft again! And no one on earth, except herself, would ever know how painful that would be.

It was then that she heard the familiar sound of Ancel's dilapidated pickup chugging through the main gate. Jennie turned, brushing a stray curl with a muddy glove and struggling with her self-control, pondering what she would say to him.

She needn't have worried. Buoyant, carefree, casual Ancel was back, in as radiantly good spirits as ever.

"Good morning...or is it afternoon?" he called cheerfully as he climbed out of the truck and approached her, smiling. "I had some things to do over at my place. I drove up the road a bit and got us some hamburgers. Not much of a Sunday dinner, but"—he produced a small paper sack—"I hope that's all right with you."

"Yes—yes, of course," she stammered.

"I'll get a couple of beers out of the refrigerator, and we can eat out here on the porch. Great morning, isn't it!" He clomped up the steps and into the house, whistling.

He's the damnedest man I ever met! she thought in bewilderment.

They munched on hamburgers and french fries while Ancel chattered away about gossip he had heard at the café where he'd purchased their lunch. Jennie barely heard what he was saying, but she watched every flicker of his eyes, every curve of his mouth, every movement he made. He was so incredibly good-looking, so splendid in every way, so expert in touching her and kissing her in all the right places, and she longed for him with an intensity that threatened to suffocate her.

Dear God, how many weeks, months, years would it take her to forget how he had aroused her? She was kidding herself; it wasn't The Croft she couldn't bear to leave. Oh, she loved the place all right, but the pain of never seeing home again would be far, far easier to bear than the pain of never seeing Ancel Gunter again.

Why, she wondered, couldn't she be just a little more adept at the art of seducing a man? Not his body— there was no great art to that—but his heart and mind and soul. How did a woman go about making a man fall desperately, hopelessly in love with her?

She knew there was no pat answer for that one. It

was either there or it wasn't, and for Ancel it wasn't there. That awful, mystifying, magnetic attraction he held for her simply did not exist in reverse, and there was nothing she could do about it. Nothing. Her sense of depression returned, stronger than ever. "Ancel...I'd like to say something if I may. About last night, I—"

He held up his hand to interrupt her. "No, Jennie, you don't have to say a word. I thought about it a lot last night, and I think I understand. You're an honest woman, and I admire that. It's forgotten."

Forgotten? How she wished *she* could forget. For all his open and lighthearted manner, Ancel sometimes could be enigmatic, a bit unknowable. But certainly Jennie felt enormous relief that he apparently wasn't angry, that he apparently meant for them to remain on friendly terms. It wasn't exactly what she wanted, but it was something. It would have to be enough.

His eyes were almost dispassionate as they rested on her; then he blithely turned his attention to the work she had done that morning. "Say, Jennie, the yard looks great! What'd I tell you? You'll be on your way back to Fort Worth in no time."

His words sliced through her like a knife. When she said nothing, he looked at her. "That's what you want, isn't it?"

Her trembling fingers clutched at the can of beer she was holding, and she forced a measure of brightness into her voice. "Yes...yes, of course it is. In fact, I—I was thinking about calling my boss tomorrow to tell her I'll be back early. There doesn't seem to be much left for me...to do."

The food she was eating stuck in her throat. He could not have been more explicit—he expected her to leave soon. She wrapped her hamburger in her napkin and placed it in the sack. She couldn't eat another bite.

She spent the remainder of the day working in the yard, her inner torment seeming to increase her physical efficiency. From time to time she caught brief glimpses of Ancel hurrying about the ranch—puttering he called it. Nothing escaped his attentive eye. In less than a week the two of them had got The Croft ready for habitation, human and animal, but it was Ancel who was chiefly responsible for the homestead's immaculate appearance.

At five o'clock Jennie went inside to bathe and change and begin supper preparations. She was standing in the middle of the kitchen, trying to decide whether to fry chicken or pan-broil steaks when Ancel walked through. She inquired about his preference.

He stopped short. "Oh, damn it, Jennie, I forgot to tell you I'm going out to dinner tonight. I'm sorry—I should have told you. It's a party at the country club—a birthday party for an old family friend whom I happen to like a great deal."

Swallowing her acute disappointment, she gave him a cheery smile. "No problem," she said lightly. "I haven't started anything yet, and you've helped me make up my mind. I'm certainly not going to fry chicken for one person."

Petulance rose inside her and could not be put down. It was silly to feel so downright churlish just because Ancel was going out to dinner without her. He had his own life to live, and she had taken a disproportionate share of his time for a week. Doubtlessly he was eager to get on with his social activities. She imagined a man like Ancel would have a lot of friends.

Grow up, Jennie! her nagging inner voice scolded. *He's made his feelings for you crystal clear. Accept it!*

He came into the kitchen before he left, and he looked so handsome in his dark business suit that Jennie could have cried. She had to bite her tongue to keep from asking where he was going, with whom, what time he would be home.

Home? Inwardly she laughed a bitter laugh. This wasn't Ancel's home. It wasn't hers either, not really. Ancel's home was his log cabin in the woods; hers was her apartment in Fort Worth. They were poles apart. Why did she have so much trouble remembering that?

"Lock the doors when I leave," he ordered.

"I will."

"I don't know how late I'll be. Don't wait up."

"I won't."

The closing of the front door was a melancholy sound. Jennie prepared her supper and ate without tasting the food. She cleaned the kitchen, put out the bag of table scraps for Velvet; then she wandered aimlessly through the rooms of the house, straightening, rearranging, trying to stay busy so that time would not pass so slowly. Finally she sat on the sofa and tried to immerse herself in a paperback novel that had promised to be the kind of story she normally found entertaining, but tonight the heroine's problems seemed miniscule compared to the ones Jennie was grappling with.

But in the end she simply gave in to her despondency. The print swam before her eyes. She placed the book on the lamp table, realizing she wasn't giving the author half a chance. Her eyes burned from unshed tears, and her head throbbed dully. She had been such an imbecile, such a stupid, moronic fool! She, who had assiduously avoided emotional entanglements, had let a man enter her heart and mind and make a mess of both. And she hadn't even realized it was happening to her until it was too late.

So once again, sensible, stable Jennifer Cameron would leave White Rock an emotional cripple, longing for a man she couldn't have.

Twice she walked into the kitchen to stare at the wall clock, wondering if it were broken. She lost count of how many times she pulled aside the living room curtains, hoping for the sight of headlights moving up the deserted road. The little house seemed cavernous without Ancel to fill it up.

At nine o'clock she could stand the solitude no more and went upstairs to get ready for bed, knowing all the while she would never be able to sleep until Ancel came home. She was in the bathroom, clad in her white terrycloth robe, brushing her teeth, when the doorbell's ring made her jump.

Ancel! she thought. *He must have forgotten to carry a key.* Wrapping the robe tightly around her and securing it at the waist, she hurried down the stairs, elated and relieved. At least he was home. Maybe he would feel like talking. Now she could relax.

Her welcoming smile faded when she opened the door, for it was not Ancel standing on the other side. "Oh...Paul," she said weakly.

A faint smile touched the corners of his mouth. "Not a very warm welcome, I must say."

"I'm sorry, but I thought you were Ancel."

"Hardly. May I come in?" He did not wait for her answer but stepped across the threshold.

"Ancel should be back any moment," Jennie said quickly, closing the door behind him.

"So...he's still staying here."

"Yes," Jennie said, "he's still staying here. I don't know what I would have done without him."

"Hmm. Well, I doubt you can continue counting on him. I saw him at the club only moments ago, totally occupied with soothing my wife. Ellen seems to require a great deal of soothing these days. I doubt he'll be home soon. So you see, I didn't come to see Ancel."

Jennie's face colored deeply, and the pain in the region of her heart returned. So Ancel was with Ellen Gunter, and not only did Paul not seem to mind, he was behaving as though that was the most normal thing in the world.

"You...you wanted to see me?"

"Yes. May I sit down?"

"Oh...of course. Please." She indicated an arm chair, and when he was seated, she sat opposite him. "What did you want to see me about, Paul?"

But for the moment his attention was focused on the living room. "You've really done wonders with this place, Jennie. It looks the way it used to when I was a frequent visitor. In fact, it looks better."

Jennie did not particularly want to be reminded of the days when Paul was a familiar face around the house. "Thank you," she said demurely.

"I should think that someone who wanted a nice place in the country would pay a handsome price for the house now." Then he looked at her squarely. "And I'm willing to pay a handsome price for the land surrounding it—although perhaps not quite so much as that ridiculous figure Ancel is parrying about. Really, Jennie, I think it's a bit much."

Jennie set her chin defiantly. "Ancel would disagree with you. He says The Croft is worth every penny we're asking for it."

Paul's look was full of scorn. "Ancel places a great deal of value on brushland. However, I would like to talk to you about buying this property, Jennie. Talk seriously. I'm certain we can come to terms."

Her fingers played nervously with the ends of the robe's tie belt. She suspected Paul of seizing the opportunity to come to see her when he knew Ancel would not be around to shore up her conviction. "I won't sell this place for the purpose you have in mind, Paul."

"Why do you care, Jennie? You're a career girl now—you told me so yourself. Once you get back to Fort Worth you'll forget this place ever existed, so what difference does it make?"

"My father built this place with his own hands!"

"Come, come, Jennie. Rob Cameron was a sensible man. He never intended for this ranch to stand for all time. He certainly would understand that you and your sister could never run it."

"I'm not too sure about that," she said briskly. "But it goes beyond just my property, my feelings. I know how Ancel and some of the other ranchers around here feel about your plans. I know how my father would have felt. He loved these old hills, and I owe him a little loyalty."

Paul snorted derisively. "What absurdity!"

"I don't think it's absurd at all," she said determinedly.

"This whole area is changing, Jennie. In ten, fifteen years the ranchland will be gone."

"I hate the thought of that," she snapped. "My God, Paul! Surely there can be a few places left in the world free of asphalt and neon lights."

"More of Ancel's influence, I suppose," he said caustically. "The man is an anachronism. He would have been far happier to have been born a century ago."

"He would be flattered."

"I didn't mean that as a compliment."

Jennie's enormous dark eyes flashed. "I find Ancel very refreshing. There's something warm and human about a man with emotional ties to the land. Most are interested only in money." It was a cutting remark, and she meant it to be.

Paul's gray eyes narrowed with suspicion. "What about your emotional ties, Jennie? Surely you aren't serious about Ancel."

"If I were it would be none of your business...as, I believe, I told you last night."

His ill-disguised amusement was infuriating. "Gone forever is the sweet little girl I used to know."

"You're right," she said bitterly. "And you're more responsible for her demise than anyone."

"I apologized for that. If I had it to do over again, I would marry you, Jennie."

And, dear God, once she would have married him! Now the thought of being married to this cold calculator of a man made her shudder. "That's being very disloyal to your wife, Paul."

"My wife!" he said cruelly. "My dear, deluded, demented wife! She's such a pathetic creature. Every time life gets to be too much for her she runs to Ancel, whom she considers a gentleman. Actually, I suppose they're well suited for one another. Certainly neither of them is suited for the real world. My wife is a fool, and Ancel is a fool, and fools do not have an easy time of it. Small wonder that they feel they must escape. Ancel's escape is his bucolic existence. Ellen's is..." He paused and shrugged, as though none of this truly interested him. "Who knows what Ellen's is?"

Jennie settled back in her chair and stared at him, unable to believe that she once had thought him so special. He was being positively vicious. And he wasn't even as good-looking as she had once thought. Ancel was superior to him in every way. She didn't blame Ellen for turning to Ancel for solace. It didn't lessen the hurt...but at least she understood.

Paul grasped his knees and sighed. "All right, Jennie. You've turned into a stubborn woman. I'll pay whatever you want for this place."

"It's no longer for sale," she said quietly.

A dark eyebrow shot up. "Since when?" he demanded.

"Since this minute."

Even she was surprised that the words had come out, but even more surprising was the fact that she meant what she had said. She did not want to sell The Croft. She had thought it no longer was home, but she had been wrong. It was home, and she didn't want anyone else to have it. Her mind had gone no further than that. She didn't know what she would do with it; she didn't know what she intended doing about her life in Fort Worth, and she had no idea how she would come to grips with living so close to Ancel. All she knew or cared to know at the moment was that she would not, could not, sell The Croft, and that she probably had begun marching toward that decision with that first swipe of paint on the kitchen wall.

Paul's amused look bothered her. "This is very interesting," he said. "May I ask what you plan to do with it?"

"I'm...I'm not sure."

"You're not being sensible, Jennie."

"Probably not...and being a good, sensible girl was

always my forte, wasn't it? But it's curiously pleasing to do something a bit rash for a change, something I want to do instead of always doing the *right* thing. I don't want to sell this place, Paul, and I didn't even realize it until right now. I suppose it has something to do with the work I've done on it. Papa used to tell me, 'Jennie girl, if you build something yourself, you'll never take it for granted,' and he was right."

Paul's voice was clipped. "It's impossible for you to run The Croft. You realize that, I hope. For one thing, it takes a great deal of money. There's not a rancher in these hills who wouldn't go under if it weren't for our bank."

Jennie's eyes flashed. "Are you hinting that Gunter State Bank wouldn't finance my operation should I need a loan?"

"I didn't say that."

"No, but that's what you meant!"

"We don't finance foolishness." Paul rubbed his chin thoughtfully. "You know, Jennie, I don't think the ranch has a thing to do with your decision. I think you want to stay here to be near Ancel—and if that's the case, my dear, you're courting disaster. Ancel's values and ideals are misplaced. He'll only break your heart. He has...er...other priorities, shall we say. You'll get hurt."

"Well, I've been down that road before!" she flung at him. His words had sent the blood rushing hotly through her veins. "I'm a big girl now and much better equipped to handle life's little disappointments."

"I doubt that, my dear. In spite of what you think, you're still a babe in the woods. Real life chews up and spits out little girls like you. Emotional and economic upheavals would destroy you. You'll wind up thoroughly disillusioned and considerably poorer than you are today. You cannot run this ranch, Jennie. Sell it to me, be done with it, and go on back where you belong."

Abruptly she stood up, rage surging and boiling inside her. This was her house! She had not invited him here. She didn't have to sit and listen to Paul's speculations, intimations and out-and-out threats. He saw too much that she preferred to keep hidden deep inside. "I'll make coffee," she muttered, needing something to do.

But Paul was on his feet, stepping in front of her. His hands gripped her arms. "Don't always run from me, Jennie. I don't mean to frighten you, but I do wish you would try to be sensible. We once meant a great deal to each other...."

"Once!" she emphasized. "Past tense, Paul."

"It could happen again. Believe me when I say that my marriage is not destined to last forever."

Aghast that he would say such a thing, Jennie raised her eyes to his just as he bent his head and kissed her mouth. She stood in his embrace, dumbfounded, not responding to him in any way but too dazed to pull herself free. He was trying to work his old magic charm on her, she knew, but he was wasting his time. The kiss meant nothing, felt like nothing. It was like kissing a windowpane.

At that moment the front door burst open, and Ancel's angry voice cut through the silence. "Damn it, Jennie, I thought I told you to lock—"

He stopped in his tracks and stared at Jennie and Paul, a stupefied expression crossing his face.

Embarrassed, Jennie disentangled her arms from Paul's grip. "Oh, Ancel, I—"

But Ancel looked straight through her; his eyes were only on his brother. "I didn't see a car outside," he said. "What in hell are you doing here?"

"I parked my car around at the side of the house," Paul said, smiling an ugly smile. "I came to see Jennie. This is her house, remember? I didn't think I needed your permission to drop by. The last time I saw you, you were slathering over my wife, I believe. Did she get home safely?"

"Yes, no thanks to you!" Ancel spat out.

Jennie's hand moved to her chest. She had harbored a nebulous hope that Paul had been lying when he said Ancel was with Ellen. Now she knew it was true.

Stinging tears welled in her eyes as she looked from brother to brother, alarmed by the animosity between them. Their acrimony was almost a tangible thing. Ancel's hands were clenched into fists at his sides, and the green eyes that normally were so kind and full of humor now blazed with anger.

He raised one arm, thrusting out a forefinger and aiming it at Paul. "I want to talk to you about Ellen," he said.

Then he turned to Jennie for the first time, as though only now aware of her presence, and she wondered if the hurt ever would end. "Jennie, do you mind if I speak to Paul alone?" he asked in the coldest voice she ever had heard.

Jennie shuddered involuntarily. She was being summarily dismissed from her own living room, but under the circumstances she was only too glad to leave these two smoldering men. "No, of course not," she said, then turned and fled up the stairs.

In her bedroom she flung herself across the bed and clutched at the pillow. From below came the incoherent cacophony of savagely angry voices. She heard her own name once or twice, and Ellen's a dozen times, but she could make out nothing of what they were saying. Only one thing was certain: Both men were furious!

A serious family feud was far outside her experience. She and Meg and Rob had lived together in this tranquil setting in relative peace and harmony, and she had assumed most families lived that way. Ancel's alienation from his family, his rancor toward them had to have a source, and Jennie's insight told her that it went further than Ellen Gunter. Ancel did not seem the sort who hated without good reason.

She did not know how long the brothers raged and stormed at one another—a long time she thought—and she wondered what her own actions would be should they decide to go at each other with their fists. But finally, mercifully, she heard the slamming of the front door, the sound of an automobile engine turning over, and the screech of tires in the driveway.

Jennie turned to lie on her back, and she sucked in her breath; her mind was a confused jumble of thoughts, none of them pleasant, all of them serving to stir up the stew of emotions churning inside her. Ancel and Paul had been quarreling about Ellen...and it had been a quarrel of gigantic proportions. Tonight Jennie hardly had existed as far as Ancel was concerned, and that was a bitter pill to swallow.

Rigidly she lay listening. After the frightful din of the shouting match, the house seemed deathly quiet. From below came the sounds of restless movements, and she longed to go down to talk to Ancel, to listen to what he had to say even if he said words she could not bear to hear. Instead, she moved off the bed and crossed the room to stand at the open window and stare out at the homestead grounds, pristine in the summer moonlight.

Purple night shadows lay over all. Such wild, beautiful, unyielding land! Small wonder that the people who lived and worked there became as obdurate as their surroundings. Jennie watched, enthralled, and it seemed she had never been away from it. Perhaps it was true that hill people only thought they owned the land; actually, the land owned them.

Jennie's heart skipped a beat, then seemed to stop as she heard the heavy *thud-thud* of footsteps on the stairs. Turning, she saw Ancel standing in the doorway. His coat and tie had been discarded, and his white dress shirt had been pulled free of his trousers and unbuttoned, as though he had been in the process of undressing when he decided to come to her.

"Jennie, I want to talk to you," he said without preamble.

"I want..." He paused, and his eyes narrowed as they swept over her. "Are you wearing anything under that robe?"

She glanced down at the terrycloth wrapper. "Well... no. I was getting ready for bed when the doorbell rang. I thought it was you, that you had forgotten your key."

"How long had Paul been here when I got home."

"Not long. Why?"

"Did you invite him over?"

Jennie's face flushed hotly. "Now, just a damned minute, Ancel! I resent—"

"Never mind. Come over here." He walked to the bed, sat on its edge and patted the spot beside him.

Jennie crossed the room and sat down. Gritting her

teeth, she said, "How could you possibly think I would invite Paul to this house and then meet him dressed like this?"

"How? I come home to find him pawing you—"

"He wasn't pawing me. He grabbed me and kissed me, that's all. Had you not shown up at that precise moment I might very well have slapped his face. It was nothing. I know what it must have looked like, but believe me, you didn't see what you thought you saw."

He stared at her for a moment; Jennie had the feeling he was trying to gauge the truthfulness of her words. Then he said, "I'm going to ask you a personal question, Jennie. Will you tell me the truth?"

"Of course, Ancel. I'll try."

"Are you still in love with him?"

She expelled her breath. "Oh, good grief, no!"

"Sure?"

"Positive."

She thought the look he gave her was one of relief, and her heart turned over. Impulsively, she reached out and took his hand and was enormously comforted when he squeezed it hard.

"I never know when to believe Paul," Ancel said, "but during our 'discussions' tonight he told me you're taking The Croft off the market, that you want to keep it for yourself. Is that true?"

"Yes."

With his free hand he brushed at the curls framing her face, then stroked her cheek sensitively. "It's impossible, Jennie," he said softly. "You know that as well as I do."

"No, it isn't," she said. "I'm staying."

"Sweet Jennie, it is patently impossible for a mere

slip of a woman to take a place like this and rebuild it from scratch. It would be a Herculean task for a group of experienced cowhands."

"I'll do it," she said stubbornly.

"You can't."

"I can."

Ancel sighed a long exasperated sigh. "Look, be reasonable, realistic. How are you going to do it? Do you have any idea how many farmers and ranchers go under every year? I've stopped going to those auctions because it just damned near breaks my heart. Now, do you honestly think you're going to come in here, plant crops, and stock the place with cattle and sheep and goats and chickens?"

She was annoyed; Ancel was not taking her any more seriously than Paul had. "Yes," she said firmly. "If that's what I have to do, I'll do it. I've always believed a person can do anything that *has* to be done."

"That's very admirable and, I suppose, true... but this is not something that has to be done. It's a whimsical, spur-of-the-moment decision made—for whatever reason I cannot imagine."

"It's not whimsy!" she insisted, staring at the floor. She refused to look at him. There was within her a powerful desire to blurt out her love for him; if she looked at him she might give in to that desire and make a fool of herself in the doing.

"Jennie, Jennie... you can't do it. Even if it were physically possible, which it assuredly isn't, what about money? Do you have any idea what it costs to stock a ranch?"

"I have my trust fund. I'll use that."

"What am I going to do with you?"

"You don't have to *do* anything with me, Ancel,"

she said miserably. "I'm sorry if you don't like the idea, but I'm staying. I'll have to go back to Fort Worth for a few weeks, of course, but I'm coming back. I'm going to live here, and you just might as well get used to the idea."

A long moment of silence passed, and then Ancel said, "Sell the place to me."

"Wh-what?" Now she did look at him, and she saw that he couldn't have been more serious.

"Sell it to me, Jennie. You know I'll take good care of it."

She shot him a wary glance. "Why haven't you offered to buy it before?"

"I had my reasons."

"You really must want to get rid of me." It was a petulant and childish statement, Jennie realized, and she had no idea why she had uttered it. Perhaps she had hoped he would protest. If so, she was badly disappointed.

"I want to keep The Croft in the right sort of hands, it's as simple as that," he said tiredly.

"I see. Well, you're the one who came up with the rather staggering appraisal of what this place is worth. I suppose you have that kind of money lying around unused. Paul isn't going to loan it to you, that's for sure."

"Suppose you let me worry about that."

She stared at him pensively for a moment. "No, Ancel. Sorry. I'm not waiting for the best offer or the right offer. I don't want to sell this ranch! I meant what I told Paul. This is my home, and I've come back to claim it. I—I want to belong. I don't know if I can explain it to you or not, because I'm not too sure I understand it myself, but . . . I guess it all comes down to wanting to put down roots. You told me that these old hills get to be part of you, and maybe you're right. All I know is, I can't sell The Croft! I don't want to end up like Gloria Travis!"

Of course he had no idea what Gloria Travis's circumstances were, and of course he didn't understand how Jennie felt. She suspected he didn't care. The look he was giving her was totally lacking in comprehension.

"You're not being sensible, Jennie," he said helplessly.

"Where does it say I have to be sensible all my life? I've made up my mind, and wild horses couldn't drag me away from here. You'll have to get used to the idea, Ancel," she added wearily. "I'm going to be your neighbor whether you like it or not!"

Ancel lapsed into silence, frowning slightly. Then he rose from the bed and walked out of the room without another word. Jennie stared after him, thinking that the hardest part of all this would be living so close to him while longing for him with such intensity. She pounded her thighs with her fists in a gesture of frustration and futility, a resigned weariness settling on her. Shrugging off the robe, she slipped her nightgown over her head, then slid between the sheets to wait for sleep that refused to come. The tick-ticking of the bedside clock was the only sound to be heard in the hushed house.

At some point during that fitful night Jennie decided she needed some expert advice. Not that Ancel's judgment couldn't be relied upon; it could. But it wasn't what she wanted to hear. She would go to an objective third party whose verdict would be uncontestable.

"Where are you off to this morning?" Ancel asked over breakfast, eyeing her dress and high-heeled shoes.

"I'm going into town to see Otto Standen," she told him.

"Good idea. Maybe you'll listen to him," he said in a maddeningly gentle tone.

Otto Standen was, and had been for as long as anyone could remember, the president of the Central Texas Breeders and Feeders Association. In that part of the world it was a much respected and influential position. Otto had been a friend of Rob Cameron's, and Jennie expected she would receive the same sort of advice Rob would have given her.

The offices of the Breeders and Feeders Association were housed in a rather nondescript building on a side street leading off Flach Avenue. The furnishings were, to say the least, spartan and utilitarian—worn leather chairs, Otto's massive wooden desk, rows of battered filing cabinets, brass spittoons. The place reeked of stale tobacco.

Otto greeted her with enthusiasm, embracing her warmly. Then he waited for her to be seated before sitting behind his desk and propping his feet upon it.

He was as German as knockwurst and kraut, and given different clothing and an alpine setting he would have looked every inch a Bavarian dairy farmer. However, Otto was a fifth-generation Texan, as attested to by his faded denims, scuffed boots and string tie, and though he spoke German almost exclusively in his own home, when he addressed Jennie it was in pure Texanese, uttered in a laconic drawl.

"Well now, Jennie, you say you want to get The Croft going again, and I think I can sympathize with that. I know how Rob felt about the place, and I've hated seeing it laying idle all these years." He reached for a note pad and a pencil. "So you want to know what it'll take in terms of money. Well, let's see...." He began scribbling and talking, mostly to himself. "There's the cost of a good bull and maybe four or five cows. Then seed for the forage crops and grain for supplemental feed...."

The list seemed to go on forever. Finally, Otto stopped scribbling and reached for an ancient adding machine. Totalling his figures, he scrawled the accounting across the bottom of the paper and shoved it over the desk to Jennie. "There you are. If the rains come when they're supposed to, and if we don't have a flood or another goddanged drought, I figure you could have The Croft running pretty good in about ten years."

Jennie blinked once, then twice as she stared at the five figures at the bottom of the page. "Ten—ten *years?*" she stammered.

Otto nodded and gave her a small smile. "If everything goes all right," he further qualified.

"Oh, my God!" she almost whispered.

"Jennie," Otto said softly in a fatherly tone, "if I didn't tell you the God's truth, I wouldn't help you at all."

Jennie thanked him and left the office with a renewed sense of frustration.

There's got to be a way, she thought in desperation as she parked her car at the side of the house. *There's got to be! I can't leave this place! I'll just lock it up, go on back to Fort Worth and slave over a hot typewriter until I've saved enough money.*

The figure Otto had presented her then came to mind, and she shuddered. She wouldn't have dreamed it would cost so much. On top of that, what about all the work she and Ancel had done on The Croft? Now it was spotless, beautiful. What would it look like by the time she had saved enough money, if she ever did? Sighing a long struggling sigh, she got out of the car and walked around to the front of the house.

Ancel was sprawled on the porch swing, looking so relaxed and self-satisfied that Jennie cheerfully could have choked him. When he saw her he sat upright and gave her an expectant look.

"Well?" he asked.

"Well what?" she replied sourly.

"What did Otto have to say?"

"Just exactly what you hoped he'd say," she said icily and stalked into the house.

He followed her, reaching and grabbing her shoulders to turn her to face him. "No, sweet Jennie. Not what I hoped. What I knew he *had* to say. There's a difference."

She forced herself to raise her eyes to him. "It doesn't make any difference, you know. I'm not leaving."

He gave her a little shake. "God! If you aren't the most stubborn woman I've ever met!"

"You'll find I can be *very* stubborn. I'm not leaving, Ancel," she repeated and shook herself free of his grip. "I'll think of something.... I'll think of something."

For the remainder of the day Jennie's mind conjured up and discarded dozens of ideas, most of them ridiculous, none of them workable. So immersed in her thoughts was she that she didn't realize the day had slipped away from her. She was jolted back to reality when Ancel wandered in from the pastures, inquiring about supper.

"Oh," she said, glancing about helplessly as though

she never before had had to get a meal together. "I'll fix something."

Somehow she managed to get a decent supper for them, something nourishing but uninspired. She didn't even notice that Ancel was every bit as preoccupied as she was, and their conversation that evening was limited to remarks like, "May I have the salt, please?" When the meal was over, Jennie implored him to leave her to do the dishes alone. As though sensing her need for solitude he did not argue, merely left the kitchen and went out onto the front porch. Jennie watched him go with relief. Ancel's presence was a distraction; for once she had to forget, if possible, the agonizing torment of wanting him. She needed time to think.

She couldn't afford this place, and she damned sure couldn't run it alone. It came down to that. She could try to find tenants, if such a breed still existed, but where would they live? She didn't want to share her home with strangers. She could move into the house, let the land lie idle while she worked and waited for enough money—but how much time could she devote to the ranch if she had a nine-to-five job, assuming she could find one in White Rock? Besides, that was a criminal waste of good pasture land. Everywhere her thoughts turned they ran into a brick wall.

By the time Jennie retired that night she had a splitting headache. Worse, Ancel had been so deep in his own thoughts that he barely had spoken to her. She wanted to reach out to him, to ask him to comfort her, but even had he complied, the entire thing would have been a charade. His feelings for her weren't that deep, and she had to accept that, had to get on with her own life. Whatever happened to all that good common sense that had served her in such good stead on so many occasions? It seemed to have abandoned her completely.

Tossing and turning, Jennie was wide awake an hour after she went to bed. She was contemplating turning on the bedside lamp and giving the paperback novel another try when she heard the sound of Ancel's heavy tread on the stairway. She caught her breath. It was beginning to look like another long night.

"Jennie," Ancel called softly.

"Yes," she answered immediately.

"I can't sleep. I want to talk to you."

She sat up, looking at the golden head silhouetted in the doorway. "I can't sleep either...so talk away."

He crossed the room to sit on the edge of the bed. Grasping one of her hands, he lifted it to his lips and gently kissed her fingertips, a simple act that left her as shaken as his more passionate overtures had.

"Jennie," he said huskily and with some difficulty, "I've been thinking, and I've come up with an idea."

"An idea? About what?"

"Look, you can't run The Croft, no matter what you think. But you love it and want to stay here, and I certainly can empathize with that. So, if you're serious, really serious about staying, I think I might have come up with the perfect solution to all this."

"And that is?"

"Jennie .you're just going to have to marry me."

Chapter Nine

Jennie bolted upright in bed. She could not have been more stunned if he had slapped her. "Wh-what did you say?"

"I said, you're just going to have to marry me. Now, don't say anything yet. Just listen to me and think about this. It makes such good sense. We could combine our holdings and turn this into a hill-country showplace. Search these hills for twenty years, and you'll not come up with a better rancher than I am, as immodest as that sounds. I could easily work both our places with the help of a few more hired hands, and we could remodel this house, put in that fancy modern kitchen you were talking about. And, Jennie, I think if I wanted to write, I could write a lot better out here in the peace and quiet of the hills than I could in a noisy, crowded city. Think about it! Picture it in your mind!"

His eyes were bright and his voice animated as he spoke, but when he searched her face for some response and found none, his tone became more subdued. "Anyway," he said lamely, "I wish you would give it some thought. We'd make a great team. We're a lot alike."

For a moment she could only stare at him, dazed. Then her body sagged. She didn't know whether to laugh or cry. "Oh, Ancel!" she wailed.

He frowned. "Does the thought upset you that much?"

Jennie pulled her knees up under the sheet and hugged them. "You're without a doubt the damnedest man I ever met! You—you just don't understand. You just don't!" She no longer attempted to stem the flood of tears, and they came in a deluge.

"Hey...hey." Ancel put his arms around her shoulders and buried his face in the thick curls atop her head. "I didn't mean to make you cry. Please...don't, Jennie. I'm sorry if I upset you. I didn't dream this would be so disturbing, but if the thought of marrying me is going to make you cry...hell, darling, I'm sorry."

She raised her glistening face and wiped at the tears with the back of her hand. "It's not that at all, Ancel. I'm enormously flattered that a good man like you would entertain thoughts of marrying me, but...a woman dreams of a marriage proposal all her life, and she expects—hopes—it will be at least a little bit romantic. You're making this sound like a—corporate merger."

Ancel sighed and seemed to be searching for the right words. "I might have known I would botch this, but if it's a knight in shining armor you're looking for, I'll admit to being a bad bargain. However, I'll get down on my knees if you'd like."

She managed a small smile. "You would look perfectly silly on your knees."

"I'm not too proud to get down on them if it will do some good," he told her softly. "I'm just asking you to think about it, Jennie. I think we have a lot going for us. For one thing, we like each other, and that's a helluva good start. For another, there's a strong sexual attraction between us... whether you want to admit it or not. I'm not saying that's the most important thing in the world, but I can't imagine marriage without it, can you?''

Jennie simply stared at him, flabbergasted, and wondered what he would think if he knew just how strong a sexual attraction he held for her. Ancel waited, and when she said nothing, he continued in a low and throbbing voice. "Furthermore, we both have emotional ties to this land. I doubt that you even realize yet just how deep yours are... and that's a powerful mutual bond. I've seen some lousy marriages in my day, and I vowed never to enter into one, but I think ours would be a good one. So I'm asking you... will you marry me?''

Jennie did not reply, for she had lapsed into deep thought. Odd, she mused silently, at times she felt as though she had known Ancel all her life, and yet she still really knew very little about him. Never in a million years would she have dreamed he would propose marriage. She never would have allowed her dreams to progress that far.

But as startling as his actions were, they were no more incredible than the fact that she seriously was contemplating an answer in the affirmative. Oh, she knew it was impossible for her to take the homestead and turn it into a working ranch. She had realized that all along, even without Paul's and Ancel's warnings; Otto's "God's truth" had been the frosting on the cake. Her decision not to sell The Croft had been a rash one, not rooted in thought. Even without the money problem, which was formidable, rebuilding the ranch would require knowledge and physical strength that she simply did not possess.

But dear God, she did so want to stay in this peaceful, timeless place! She knew as well as she knew her own name that her future was here. To live at The Croft forever, with Ancel! To work together and grow together and raise a family together—the prospect was irresistible. But beyond that was her sure knowledge that she had grown to love him so much she did not care to contemplate life without him.

With a start Jennie realized that Ancel had left the bedroom; her heart constricted sharply. A sense of compelling urgency overtook her. "Ancel!" she called loudly, a little frantically. "Ancel!"

He was back in an instant, taking the stairs three at a time and bounding across the room to sit beside her.

"I had decided I wasn't going to get an answer tonight," he told her in a choked, expectant voice.

He was so close, making mincemeat of her brains again. She lifted her arms to him. "I wonder if you know what you're doing, Ancel. I wonder if—could you honestly promise to cleave only unto me until death do us part?"

He gathered her to him, and she melted into his arms. "If you could," he murmured as his mouth began to wander over her face. It wasn't exactly the answer she had been seeking, but it was a step in the right direction.

"Think, please think of everything you would have to give up," she implored him, and Ellen Gunter came fleetingly to mind.

"I'd prefer to dwell upon what I would be getting," he said, and his mouth came down gently on hers; their lips fused together like fragments joining to make a whole. Every part of her came alive, and this was, she now knew, the source of the fascination he held for her: With Ancel she finally felt complete as a human being. As his kiss became more urgent, she parted her lips and wound her arms around him, giving herself up to her demanding need for him. Deep shudders racked her body.

When at last they parted, Jennie's tremors would not subside, and she clung to him for comfort and strength. There was a plaintive quality to her voice as she asked the question most important to her.

"What about love, Ancel?"

"Love?" he asked, as though he never before had heard the word.

"Yes, you know—moon and June, hearts and flowers. The kind of thing that normally sends people scurrying to the altar."

His hands came up to hold her face, and as he gazed down into her dark, fluid eyes, his expression was unreadable, something so twisted and agonized that she found it impossible to guess at the thoughts lurking beneath it. "It will come, Jennie," he said softly. "Just be patient, darling. It will come."

Once again his mouth possessed hers, so fiercely he seemed determined to draw all of her inside him. A muffled cry was stifled and stuck in her throat. Oh, he was so brutally honest! He wouldn't lie to her even when a tiny lie would have been kinder than the truth. He was telling her he would have to learn to love her.

But as his hands and mouth worked their wondrous magic and the familiar fire spread through her body, Jennie felt the old primordial urge for him, felt the changes in her body as her passion for him surfaced. Yes, they already had this powerful sexual attraction. It was a force so overwhelming it staggered Jennie. Ancel wanted her, of that much she was sure. Perhaps he even needed her, much as she needed him. Love would come later. Was that enough? She supposed it would have to be.

With her lips against his cheek, she spoke to him. "Let's pretend a little, shall we?"

"What?" he gasped.

"Pretend. Love me, Ancel.... Love me."

He emitted a tormented groan as he pushed her down so that her head was on the pillow, and his hands began a sensual sweep of the length of her body, while his mouth and tongue wandered over her face, moved to her throat, then lingered on the velvety mounds of her breasts and their erect nipples. Jennie sank further into the deep comfort of the mattress and let the lean hardness of his body crush her. If only she could make his skin tingle, burn, hum and sing the way hers was.

Her trembling fingers began fumbling with the buttons of his shirt, then her hand slipped inside to caress the warmth of his broad chest. Strange, guttural sounds were coming from his throat, and his breath rasped in her ear. With the feel and taste and smell of him washing over her, Jennie wanted him so badly she would take him any way she could get him. If that meant marrying him with the sure knowledge that she would have to teach him to love her, that was the way it would be. Sane, sensible Jennifer Cameron was gone forever. She was wildly, irrationally, passionately in love with this man, and she intended never letting him get away from her.

His big strong hands practiced an exquisite kind of torture on her inflamed body, raising her to new heights of desire. She responded to his demanding kisses with abandon and ardor, and her hands stroked and fondled him until he had reached a fevered pitch of excitement.

He raised his golden head and looked down at her, his eyes mirroring her own emotional impatience. "God, Jennie! You must be the softest, sweetest creature on earth! Here I am ravishing you...and you haven't even said you will marry me."

"Surely you know the answer is yes," she said, smiling against his mouth, reveling in the feel of him. "Otherwise I would not be tumbling in this bed with you like a wanton vixen."

He laughed quietly. "Ah, my beautiful wanton vixen! I can't seem to keep my hands off you. I hope you'll never regret casting your lot with me."

"I won't...provided, of course, you do this every day."

He nestled his face against her smooth silken shoulder. "Every day, sweetheart? Isn't that expecting quite a lot of me."

"Not at all," she said with a sly smile. "Every day."

She felt his mouth move against her skin. "Well, I promise to look for a high-potency vitamin...."

"You won't need one," she said and put her hand to his face to lift it up for her kiss.

The kiss seemed to go on forever, a beautiful thing of hungry lips and tongues. Jennie felt she was drowning, then surfacing, only to once again be swept away by a tidal wave of passion. When they parted breathlessly, Ancel clutched one of her hands.

"Tell me what you like, Jennie. Better still...take my hand and show me."

Jennie gulped and blinked back tears. "I—I don't know what I like, Ancel. I—I've never been this far before. I don't know. Don't you know?"

His body tensed in her arms, and a sound came out of his throat, an incoherent sound that might have been a strangled chuckle, although Jennie could not imagine a less likely time for chuckling. "It's different for every woman, Jennie," he said quietly. A minute passed, and though they remained locked together, Ancel was so motionless he might have been paralyzed.

Then, to Jennie's complete astonishment, he rolled off her with a moan and sank beside her. Never had her arms felt so empty.

She reached to bring him back. "Don't leave me," she begged.

"Oh, Jennie, I don't want to, but—damn it, honey, I have to."

Jennie couldn't understand any of it. "But...why?"

"Because if I stay you know what's going to happen. Do you want that?"

She hesitated, but only for a second. "I—I think so," she said, not without some trepidation. "Yes. Yes, I want it very much."

He rolled off the bed and stood up. His shirt was hanging loose and was unbuttoned; he wore no belt or shoes, but otherwise he was fully dressed, while she was clad in the skimpiest of nightwear, and even that was rumpled and half-off her body. Modestly she covered herself with the sheet, just as though he never before had seen her naked breasts.

"Well, I don't think you do. My sweet, you are still a virgin, and any woman who has waited that long expects to wait until her wedding night. I want to give you that wedding night."

"Don't tell me what I want!" she spit out, hurt and frustrated. "I suppose I should be grateful for your consideration, but I've managed to guard my virginity all these years. I think I can safely decide when the time is right to make love."

"Jennie, Jennie," he said softly, smiling down at her as though she was an irascible child. "Hush, darling."

She pounded the mattress with her fist. "How do you *do* that?"

He frowned. "Do what?"

"Rein in like that. *I* can't."

He walked around the bed and came to kneel on the floor beside her and place a gentle kiss on her trembling lips. "Good. I don't ever want you to learn."

"You beast! You want to leave me wanting!"

"Yes," he hissed. "Yes. It will make the final realization so much sweeter. I want you to want me, Jennie... always. I want it to be perfect for us, from beginning to end. I intend giving you a wedding night you'll want to write a poem about."

He leaned forward again, but when her arms reached for him, he clutched them and firmly laid them at her sides. "Don't do that, or I won't be able to leave. Tomorrow is the beginning of our life together. We have so many things to discuss, not the least of which is our wedding day, but we've made enough monumental decisions for one night. Sweet dreams, sweet Jennie."

Another soft kiss, then he got to his feet, and she watched as he left the room. With nothing but quiet and darkness about her, Jennie succumbed to her feelings of want and need. She sucked in her breath and exhaled very slowly in an attempt to let some of the sensual tension go out of her.

He's the damnedest man I ever met! she thought for the hundredth time. Dear God, how could he just walk away from her like that? It didn't make sense, it just didn't!

Everything, simply everything had changed. When Jennie awoke the next morning it was to a bright, shimmering new world. The aroma of coffee wafting up the stairway galvanized her into action. She dressed hastily, then fled down the stairs to find Ancel, as usual, at the kitchen stove. She paused in the doorway to drink in the sight of him. His back was to her, and he had not heard her approaching, for her bare feet had moved soundlessly through the room.

"Remember when I told you that some girl was going to be lucky when she got you?" she asked softly. "I wouldn't have dared dream that the lucky girl would be me."

At the sound of her voice he turned, his smile dazzling, and gone forever was the casualness of their morning greetings. He held out his arms to her, and she went into them, and he held her.

She no longer cared why, under what circumstances he was to be hers. He was going to be her husband, and suddenly life was filled with allure, abandon, freedom, and satisfaction. How good it was to be young and alive and in this place, to be so conscious of another's touch! It seemed to Jennie that Ancel was everything— strength, shelter, comfort.

"Haven't changed your mind, have you?" he asked, holding her tightly against his chest.

"Not at all," she assured him.

"Sleep well?"

"Yes. But I would have slept better had you been beside me."

"I doubt that, pet. I doubt we would have slept at all."

Pet? It wasn't her favorite endearment, conjuring up as it did visions of someone who was meant to be played with and then set aside when real, meaningful work had to be done. She did not intend to become merely the soft, warm, decorative part of Ancel's life. She wanted to be everything to this man—his helpmate, his sounding board, his buffer, his cushion against life's disappointments. How she loved him! She loved him enough for both of them—and she would teach him to love her. She would. She had to!

Over bacon and eggs they talked, about the immediate and about the future. "Jennie, sweetheart," Ancel said earnestly, "I hope you've given this plenty of thought. There's a helluva lot to being a rancher's wife. I don't want to give you the impression that I'm sentencing you to a life of drudgery, but running a ranch, even with plenty of help, will make an office job seem like *Romper Room*."

"Oh, Ancel, I know that! I grew up on this ranch, and when Meg and I got old enough to be of real use, Papa didn't spare us one bit. I want to be part of everything, the good and the bad. I don't want you sparing me anything. I want to be your full-time partner."

"Okay, partner." He grinned, took one of her hands and began idly playing with its fingers. "There's a lot to do right now, not the least of which is tearing down part of the fence I spent last week putting up," he said with a chuckle. "For the time being we'll let my livestock graze on both sections, until calving and lambing time and until we can make a trip to the market in Fort Worth. I might need to hire a couple of extra hands to take care of the new territory." He brought her hand to his mouth and kissed her fingertips, causing Jennie to shiver with delight.

"Now...about a wedding date," Ancel went on. "Soon, or do you want to wait a bit?"

"Soon," Jennie said boldly. "But I still have to go back to Fort Worth. I hope Gloria won't require me to work two more weeks, but she certainly has that right. Come with me, Ancel...please. I can't stand the thought of being away from you for two whole weeks."

"I can't, sweetheart. I'd like to, but there's just too much I have to do here, too much I've neglected. I'll get caught up on everything while you're gone, and the day you come back, we'll be married."

Bitterly disappointed, she swallowed hard. "I'll miss you."

"I'll miss you, too, Jennie," he said, but without the emotion she would have liked to hear in his voice. In spite of the summer morning's warmth, she felt a sudden chill. He wasn't being very convincing. He wouldn't miss her half as much as she was going to miss him.

Resignation settled upon her. This, she supposed, was the way it would be for a time. She cared for him so much more than he cared for her; she would have to get used to wanting more than he was prepared to give, at least for the time being. The thought put a bit of a damper on her soaring spirits.

When Ancel stood and began clearing away their breakfast dishes, Jennie aimlessly walked to the back door and peered out, thinking how peaceful and serene the countryside was in the fresh early morning. It had been her father's favorite time of the day. How wonderful it was going to be to awaken each morning and call the day her own, for no matter how much work there would be to do, it would be accomplished away from schedules and deadlines and time clocks and rush-hour traffic jams.

In the midst of these delightful contemplations, Jennie's eyes fell to the floor of the back porch, and she let out a little cry.

Turning quickly, Ancel asked, "What's the matter?"

"Oh, Ancel, Velvet didn't come last night." She stood and stared at the bag of scraps lying on the porch, untouched. Her eyes were wide in mute appeal. "He didn't come. That's the first time. Something's happened to him."

Ancel crossed the room and drew her to him in a comforting embrace. "Aw, Jennie, I shouldn't have let you get so attached to that animal. Sweetheart, something was bound to happen sooner or later." His lips brushed the hair at her temple. "God, don't cry!"

"It's not even deer season!" she raged.

"Since when did that make any difference?"

"I know I'm being silly," she said, sniffling noisily. "It's just that—that I had come to look forward to seeing him every night."

Ancel took her by the shoulders and looked down at her fondly, a bit indulgently. "You are definitely the sort of person who needs a pet. As soon as we're married, we'll get a dog. How would you like that?"

She smiled at him with grateful, loving eyes. "Thank you, darling. That will be nice."

He brushed at a stray curl, then kept the palm of his hand pressed against her cheek. "Do you know that's the first time you've called me 'darling'?"

"Really? I've thought of you as 'darling' many times."

A flame of desire swept through them simultaneously. Jennie trembled in his arms and laughed lightly, a bit nervously. For a moment she thought he might... But then he bent, gave her a light kiss and playfully slapped her on the bottom, and the tender moment passed. "Now, let's get these dishes done and be about our chores," he said, suddenly very business-like. Jennie sighed as he released her and turned back to the sink. She seemed to be existing in a permanent state of sexual arousal, while Ancel—well, Ancel was not an easy one to figure out.

While they did the dishes he chatted away happily, full of enthusiastic plans, and Jennie responded as she thought she should, but her mind kept straying to the sad-eyed little deer who wouldn't be coming to visit any longer. She hoped whoever had bagged the poor outcast velvet-horn choked on his venison steaks.

Then something crossed her mind. Something Otto Standen had told her. "Ancel, how long will it take for this ranch to start paying its way?"

He gave it some thought. "Oh, I don't know.... A couple of years, I suppose. It depends on too many va-garies, chiefly the weather. At least we're not starting from scratch."

"A couple of years!" she repeated. "That sounds like an awfully long time to start making money. You'll have to forgive me, but I'm a twice-a-month paycheck sort of person. What do we do in the meantime?"

"We'll manage," he said casually. "Don't worry about money, Jennie."

"I've always worried about money. I couldn't stop now even if I wanted to. Does your place make money?"

"Sometimes...a little. Usually I'm happy if I break even."

"And that doesn't bother you?" she asked incredu-lously.

"Of course not," he replied. "I've only had the place

in operation a few years, Jennie. The money will start coming in one of these days. Anyway, money couldn't buy the satisfaction I get from doing the kind of work I want to do."

Jennie envied him, but there was no way she could understand such a lighthearted approach to one's livelihood. She had been a budget addict for too long. And apparently her worried expression told Ancel what she was thinking, for he said, "Honey, you have to remember that we won't need cash for nearly as many things as city folks do. Most of our food will be raised right here, for instance. And we won't need to keep a couple of cars constantly replenished with gas for the battle of the freeway. Life will be simpler for you . . . and, I hope, nicer."

It did sound simple and nice, and she had discovered something during the past week—she felt loose and free, far more so than she had since childhood. "Something else just occurred to me, Ancel. Half of The Croft belongs to Meg."

"I know."

"I'm going to have to buy her half from her."

"Of course."

"I'm sure she'll let me pay it out, but still, we'll have to budget like crazy."

He laughed. "I'm terrible with a budget. I'll gladly turn that over to you. But when it comes to getting things done around here, I'm superb. The trick is to make a list of everything that needs to be done and then to establish priorities. Just start in with number one and work your way down the list. And I think number one priority should be this kitchen. You'll be spending a lot of time in it, and I want it to be first class."

"That alone will take a small fortune!" she cried in

dismay. "Together we won't have half the money we need to get this ranch running. My trust fund is not a large one."

Unaccountably, Ancel shot her a hard glance. "That trust fund isn't to be touched unless it's for something personal, something you want. Understand?"

"Ancel, marriage is a fifty-fifty deal. Anything I have is yours too. I won't have it any other way."

"Except for your trust. That was Rob's legacy to you, and I don't want any of it. Use it to buy yourself a bauble occasionally."

"A bauble indeed! You're being unreasonable," she insisted stubbornly.

His green eyes twinkled merrily. "You'll find I can be—very—if the situation demands it."

"We'll need every cent we can scrape up."

Ancel dried his hands on a dish towel, then turned to take her by the shoulders. "Jennie, let me worry about that. Are you afraid I can't take care of you?"

"Oh, Ancel, no! Of course not!"

"Good, because I can. I'll always take good care of you, Jennie. You have nothing to worry about. I assure you, sweetheart, you'll always be number one priority on the list."

"Well, all right," she said, giving up. "I'll talk to you about it later, when we're married and I feel more like arguing with you." She wiped the last dish and placed it in the cupboard. Folding the towel and hanging it neatly across the bar, she asked, "May I have the key to your cabin?"

"Sure. Why?"

"I'm going over to call the telephone company about installing a phone here. Then I'll call Mr. Walde and tell him to take the house off the market. And I have to

call my boss in Fort Worth. I don't want to wait until I
go back to spring this on her. Gloria's been awfully
good to me, and I want her to know my plans. Then I'll
call Meg...especially Meg." Jennie's enormous eyes
grew luminous. "This is going to be quite a surprise for
her."

"Jen!" Meg's voice gushed over the telephone. "Don't
tell me you're still in White Rock!"

"Yes, and I'll be here until the weekend."

"God, you must be about to die of boredom. Whatever could be forcing you to stay in that dump so long?"

"I'll tell you in a minute, but first, how was the
yachting trip?"

"Oh..." Meg's voice dripped with disillusionment.
"Not as much fun as I had imagined it would be. All
that time and trouble—I spent a small fortune on new
clothes—and as it turned out it was for nothing. The
Petersons really are quite snobbish, and frankly I think
that's a bit pretentious of them, considering the fact
that they're strictly nouveau riche. And my God, they
consume an enormous amount of liquor! There were
dozens of other people on board, so Steve didn't have
too much time alone with Gregory Peterson. The entire week was a waste of time. I was glad to get home to
my own friends, who are far more civilized. Really,
Jen, some very wealthy people can be absolutely
boors!"

Jennie was glad her sister couldn't see the wry smile
crossing her face. So Meg finally was learning that
wealth did not always equal good taste and manners. To
Jennie's notion, Meg's week hadn't been a waste at all.
"I'm sure that's true," was all she said.

"Now, tell me, Jen, what's going on with the house? I do hope our buyer came through."

There was a brief pause before Jennie said, "I'm not going to sell it, Meg."

"Not going to sell?" Meg sounded incredulous. "Why on earth not?"

"I—I want to keep it for myself. I'm going to move back to White Rock."

A startled gasp came over the line. "Oh, my God! Why? Honestly, Jen, this doesn't sound like you at all. You were as anxious to flee the old homestead as I was. And pray what are you going to do with the old place— shovel hay and manure?"

Jennie laughed. "A bit more than that, Meg. Actually, I'm getting married."

The silence on the other end of the line lasted so long that Jennie was beginning to suspect the connection had been broken. Finally, however, Meg's astonished voice was heard. "*Married?* To someone in *White Rock?*"

"Yes. Ancel Gunter. Do you remember him?"

"Mmm. The bankers, right? Weren't you and his brother kind of sweet on each other at one time?"

"That was a very long time ago, Meg. And Ancel isn't with the bank. He owns the property adjacent to The Croft. We're going to combine our holdings. Ancel has so many plans for the place, and I'm so excited about it. One day we hope to turn The Croft into a real showplace."

"I see," Meg said, and her suspicious tone was not lost on Jennie, who chose to ignore it. She hadn't expected Meg to understand.

"Meg, naturally we want to buy your half of the

ranch, and we need to talk about that. Ancel thinks the place is worth about—"

Meg interrupted. "Oh, pooh! Who cares about that? Jen, are you sure about this—really sure?"

"Absolutely, Meg."

"But—you didn't even know the man a week ago. And now you're going to turn into a rancher's wife—feed the chickens, slop the hogs, and worry about the weather—and give up that perfectly splendid job in Fort Worth to boot. That this could be happening to my sister . . . ."

Jennie sighed, then patiently explained, "Meg, that 'perfectly splendid' job was really nothing more than a nine-to-five rat race."

"It sounded so glamorous to me."

Jennie smiled. "Why is it that every woman who doesn't work thinks all jobs are glamorous? Few are, Meg. Most are just a lot of work for very little pay. I've found something that's so much more. I want to be Ancel's wife, so if Ancel is a rancher, then I want to be a rancher's wife."

"But marriage is such a serious undertaking."

"I know, Meg. Why do you think I've waited such a long time?"

It was Meg's turn to sigh, and she did so dramatically. "That's what has me worried. You've always been so sensible."

Jennie clenched her teeth. "If one more person says that word to me—"

"It's just so damned sudden. Do you—well, do you *love* him?"

Jennie chuckled into the receiver. Meg said the word *love* as though she was afraid of being heard uttering an obscenity. "Yes, Meg, I do. Very much."

"Then tell me something about him. I vaguely remember him from years ago, but he was four or five years ahead of me in school. How come he's still single? Has he been married, divorced, widowed?"

As succinctly as possible Jennie gave an accounting of Ancel's attributes, tempering her own less-than-objective description slightly so as to make him more believable, and she was acutely puzzled over Meg's lack of enthusiastic response.

"I must say, Meg, you might try to be happy for me," she scolded a bit irritably.

"Are you happy, Jen?"

"Gloriously. I'm drunk with happiness."

"Then forgive my jaded outlook. I see supposedly perfect marriages crashing down about me every day. I'm beginning to think Steve and I are the only happily married couple I know. And I'm always suspicious of men's motives in marriage, particularly when they stand to gain a great deal in material possessions. As I recall, the Gunters always had a sharp eye out for a dollar."

"Not Ancel," Jennie insisted. "He's not associated with the rest of the family. He's strictly a hill-country rancher, like Papa. In fact, Ancel reminds me of Papa in a lot of ways."

"Oh, *gawwd!* And I suppose he'll want you to cook his meals, keep his house, relieve his periodic urges, and keep his kids away from him until they're old enough to behave in a civilized manner."

"Meg! That's a horrible thing to say to a bride-to-be!"

"Yes, I guess it is," Meg said with a sigh. "Sorry. I do suppose I'm invited to the wedding. When and where is it to be? Why don't you come to San Antonio and let me throw a real shindig for you?"

"No way, Meg! Ancel would run from that like a frightened rabbit. When our plans are firmed up, I'll call you."

"Jen, I..." Meg's worried voice trailed off.

"What is it, Meg?"

There was a long pause, then another heavy sigh. "Nothing. I'll be waiting to hear from you. Good-bye."

It dismayed Jennie that her sister had misgivings about the marriage, but the more she thought about it the more she understood. Throughout adolescence, whenever the sisters had talked about boys and the nature of life and love, Jennie had staunchly insisted that she would never marry except for love. Of course, at the time, her ideas about what constituted love had been rather fuzzy, but always she had been certain she would be madly in love with the man she married, and she never had given much thought to what he would look like or the size of his bank account.

But Meg... As far back as Jennie could remember, her sister had declared her intention of marrying a rich man, and Meg's campaign to capture wealthy Stephen Curtis would have done credit to a four-star general. Jennie assumed Meg loved Steve; they seemed happy enough, and there was no question that Steve absolutely adored his wife. But of one thing Jennie was certain: At no time was love one of Meg's prerequisites for marriage. So how could her sister understand how Jennie could throw over all traces of her former life in order to live with a man she plainly was insane about?

Still, Meg was all the family Jennie had, and she would have been so much happier had her sister shown a little more enthusiasm.

Later that afternoon, Jennie was putting out the lawn

sprinkler when a sleek Mercedes pulled through the main gate, and in a swirl of Halston and diamonds, Margaret Cameron Curtis descended on her with a shrieking swoop.

The two women would have had a hard time denying their kinship. They favored each other to a striking degree, although there was a soft femininity about Jennie, even when dressed in jeans, that was missing in her very sophisticated older sister.

"Meg!" Jennie cried in delight. "What on earth are you doing here?"

Meg embraced her sister, kissing the air beside her cheek. "Are you serious? I had to come up and get a good look at my future brother-in-law. Besides, I *have* to talk to you, Jen. It's only an hour's drive from home. I told Steve I would be back before dinner."

"So soon? You aren't going to stay the night?"

"Oh, I can't, Jen. Steve and I are going to a party tonight. I'll be *exhausted!*"

Jennie frowned. "What could possibly be so urgent? Why didn't you wait until you had more time?"

But Meg was paying no attention to her, concentrating instead on the homestead's immaculate appearance. "My goodness, everything looks nice! Better than it did when we lived here. You've been a busy girl."

"Ancel and I have worked like beavers on the place," Jennie said proudly. "There's nothing that man can't do."

Now Meg's glance came to rest on her sister, and the look she gave Jennie was very un-Meg-like, serious and thoughtful. "I'm beginning to wish I had forgotten the yachting trip and had come up here to take care of all this myself."

"Why?" Jennie asked. "I'm certainly glad you

didn't. I wouldn't have gotten to know Ancel if you had."

"Exactly," Meg said obscurely. Then she flashed a forced smile. "Now—where is the groom-to-be? He might as well pass inspection."

A disturbing sensation was churning in Jennie's stomach. "Come inside, Meg. I'll fix you something cool to drink, and then I'll get Ancel."

When Meg was seated comfortably in the living room, Jennie poured a tall glass of lemonade for her, then excused herself to look for Ancel. She found him at the horse corral where he was mending the fence. Shirtless, his bronze skin glistened with sweat. Momentarily forgetting her mission, Jennie hoisted herself up on the fence and watched him for a minute, her heart swelling with love. Then she came back to the present and called to him.

"Hey!"

He turned, and his face broke into that dazzling smile. "Hey, yourself!" he called back.

"My sister's here. She wants to meet you."

"Oh?" He put down his hammer and grabbed his shirt off the railing, then crossed the corral and expertly scaled the fence. Grabbing Jennie around the waist, he pulled her off her perch. "She wants to give me the once-over more than likely," he chuckled.

"Probably."

Ancel slipped into his shirt and buttoned it, then stuffed it into the waistband of his jeans. "How do I look?"

"Hot, sweaty, tired, and dirty," she told him truthfully.

He laughed. "That ought to make a good impression."

"Actually, you look fairly gorgeous."

Arm in arm they walked toward the house, but as they stepped up onto the back porch, Jennie suddenly stopped and slipped her arms around his waist to give him a ferocious hug. Ancel held her for a moment, then stepped away from her slightly and looked down at her quizzically.

"What was that for?"

"Does it have to be for something? Can't I hug my future husband anytime I feel like it?"

"Of course." He bent and placed a very thorough, moist kiss on her lips. "Are you all right, Jennie?"

She nodded her head, unable to understand why she didn't feel all right at all. Meg's visit disturbed her, but for what reason she couldn't imagine. She hugged Ancel again, this time even more insistently, then together they went into the house.

For the next half hour or so Jennie watched in amusement as Meg was treated to a full dose of Ancel's formidable charm. It oozed from his pores. By the time he excused himself to return to fence-mending, Meg was positively simpering.

"Well, what did you think of him?" Jennie asked her sister when they were alone again.

"Oh, my! A smooth one. I expected a real hayseed, but..." A fresh and alarming thought then crossed Meg's mind. "Good Lord, Jen! Are the two of you staying in this house together... *alone?*"

"Yes," Jennie said primly.

"Good heavens! How... *modern!*"

"It's not like that, Meg," Jennie said quietly, and it occurred to her that the only reason it wasn't "like that" was because Ancel hadn't let it be.

"Far be it from me to pry. You're a grown woman

now, and I suppose the sexual revolution has even reached White Rock by now," Meg said, dismissing it. She settled back on the sofa and looked at Jennie solemnly. "Jen, I don't know how these things get around, but not an hour after you called this morning I received another phone call. This time it was from Paul Gunter. You can imagine how surprised I was."

Jennie's throat tightened, and her eyes narrowed. "What did he want?"

Meg studied the beautifully manicured hands in her lap. "He had some things to tell me that he said he thought I should know."

"I hope you hung up on him!" Jennie said frostily.

"Jen, if even half of what Paul told me is the truth, you're making a dreadful mistake in marrying Ancel. I don't want to hurt you, but I *am* concerned."

Jennie did not have to wonder how Paul knew she and Ancel were going to get married. She could well imagine it; her first phone call that morning had gone to Jeremy Walde, and she had told the realtor to take The Croft off the market because she and Ancel were going to live there. She knew as surely as if she had been sitting in Jeremy's office at the time that his next call would have gone to Paul Gunter.

"I see," she said. "May I ask just exactly what Paul told you?"

"Oh, Jen..." Meg's voice was all helpless and fluttery; Jennie could see that her sister truly was upset. "I don't know how to tell you this, but...Paul says that the only reason Ancel is marrying you is to get The Croft, and that the only reason he wants the place is to keep Paul from having it. Jen, Paul told me he had made a reasonable offer on the place. Why on earth didn't you sell it to him and be done with it?"

"One, I didn't consider the offer a reasonable one. Two, I don't care if he offered me twice what the ranch is worth. I still wouldn't sell it to him."

"But why?"

"Because he wants to tear down the house and the outbuildings, to bulldoze the place and put in a—a resort hotel!"

Meg shrugged. "So, who cares?"

"I care, that's who!" Jennie exclaimed. "Papa would turn over in his grave."

"Is *that* why you're staying here? Out of some misguided sense of loyalty to Papa?"

"No, that's not the only reason, Meg, although I must admit I've thought about Papa more during this past week than I have in years. I don't expect you to understand this, but when I got here I felt—oh, I don't know—I felt a sense of coming home again, of being back where I belong. I just don't want to sell The Croft. I don't!"

Meg threw up her hands. "Don't you see, Jen, you're on a nostalgia binge. You'll forget all about this the moment you get back to Fort Worth and to your job."

Jennie smiled ruefully. Her second phone call that morning had been to Gloria Travis, and she wasn't sure she had a job. It seemed that Connie, her young assistant, had worked out beyond Gloria's wildest expectations, and that Jennie, while missed, was not indispensable.

"It goes well beyond that, Meg," Jennie said softly. "You forget—there's the small matter of my upcoming marriage."

Meg looked away and bit her lip. "Ah, yes. God, I paced the floor for an hour after Paul called. Jen, did you mention your feelings about The Croft to Ancel before or after he proposed?''

Jennie frowned, trying to remember. ''Before, I think. Why?''

''And by chance did he point out the impossibility of your running the ranch? Then did he just happen to mention that *he* could run it? That it would be a good idea for the two of you to get married and combine your acreage and—''

Jennie clenched her teeth together. ''I won't listen to this, Meg!''

''Oh, Jen!'' Meg cried in exasperation. ''Haven't you heard anything I've said?''

''I heard. But all your information comes from Paul, and I wouldn't believe Paul Gunter if he said the sky was blue. He wants The Croft himself, and he would do anything, say anything, to get it. The man has a dollar sign for a mind and heart.''

Meg leaned forward and touched Jennie on the hand, an uncommonly intimate gesture between the two sisters. ''Jen, I wish you wouldn't rush into this. Go on back to Fort Worth and think about it awhile. If it's right, it will be right in a month or so.''

''No!'' Jennie almost shouted.

''Dear God, I had hoped you wouldn't force me to tell you this, but... Paul also hinted at something else. He intimated that you aren't the only woman in Ancel's life—''

''See what I mean? Can you imagine the gall? Hints and intimations! I refuse to listen!''

''—that he is deeply involved with and committed to another woman, a *married* woman. Oh, Jen, I don't want you to get hurt. You must give yourself more time to think about this, to get to know Ancel better. Paul says—''

"Paul says! I don't give a damn what Paul Gunter says."

"But, Jen, just suppose he's right."

"I don't care!" Jennie cried, near tears.

Meg looked startled. "You don't mean that."

"Yes, I do." Jennie was on her feet, pacing nervously, hugging herself and briskly rubbing her arms. "I know that sounds ridiculous, but I mean it, Meg. Oh, I *care,* of course. I want to be the only woman in Ancel's life. But even if I'm not, I will be someday, I'm sure of it. I'll take that chance. I'll take him any way I can get him. I've waited for him so long. Paul can go to hell!"

Meg sat back, stunned. "Why, you've suspected all this before, haven't you? This isn't a startling revelation at all."

Jennie lowered her eyes and said nothing while Meg continued to stare at her. Then, at last, Meg stood and smoothed at the skirt of her very expensive dress.

"Whew! You're the last person in the world I would have thought would fall so hard. I don't know how to argue with that kind of thing. If I thought Steve ever even looked at another woman I'd shoot him in the leg! I just don't know what to say, Jen. I can't believe you fell for charm and looks alone. He must be one hell of a man."

"He is."

Meg stared at her thoughtfully for a moment. "Well, all I can say is, I hope all this turns out all right."

Jennie turned. Meg looked so downright distraught that Jennie's heart went out to her sister. The solicitude was unexpected, uncharacteristic, and, therefore, Jennie felt it was sincere.

"Please don't worry, Meg," she said quietly. "Ancel and I are very close, really we are, and if there's another woman—remember, I said *if*—she won't be around once we're married. I know Ancel. Maybe I'm second choice, but as I said, I don't care. I really don't, just as long as he's going to belong to me."

Meg's worst worries clearly had not been assuaged, but there seemed to be nothing she could do about that. Faced with a determined Jennie who would not be swayed, she gave up. Promising to return for the wedding, she drove off in a cloud of dust, a worried expression still clouding her normally placid face.

Jennie watched the Mercedes disappear down the country road, her stomach churning and boiling. Paul had his nerve, calling her sister and making all those dreadful accusations! She ought to march out back and tell Ancel about all this. He'd put Paul in his place. He'd be furious! She ought to let Ancel know the terrible things Paul was saying about him.

But she knew she wasn't going to say a word to him.

Chapter Ten

"You seem awfully preoccupied tonight, Jennie," Ancel told her that evening as they sat on the porch swing after supper. He had been in his usual good spirits throughout the meal that she had prepared with extraordinary care, and had not appeared to notice that she was edgy and nervous and had a great deal of difficulty eating a respectable amount of food.

"Do I?" she asked with a curious inflection in her voice. "I can't think why."

"Does it have something to do with your sister's visit this afternoon?"

"No," she lied.

"Is it because of Velvet?" Now his voice became soft and tender, and his hand moved to slowly stroke the nape of her neck. She grew all warm and pliant, as she always did when he touched her, and she longed to tell him all the horrible things Paul had said, to hear his protestations, perhaps to hear a few endearments designed to make her relax and feel secure.

"No," she said in a thick voice. "No. I wish he would come walking out of the woods right now, but that's foolish. He's a wild animal, and terrible things happen to wild animals every minute of every day. No, I'm not thinking of Velvet."

"Then...what is it?"

Cautiously Jennie slid her hand along the length of his strong hard thigh, letting it come to rest on his knee.

"Ancel, I..." She swallowed hard several times, unable to find the words she wanted to say to him. Her deep and instinctive desire to blurt out everything, to get to the bottom of this even if the truth hurt, was sparring with something else entirely—the wish to remain ignorant. If she forced Ancel to confess his affection for someone else, if indeed that was what he would do, her pride would demand that she call off their wedding, and then she would never get the chance to teach him to love her.

And dear God, she did want him so! No one had ever meant so much. She was quite prepared to believe no one ever would mean this much again. If she lost Ancel—the vision of a lonely, middle-aged, career woman in an immaculate beige and white apartment swam before her eyes.

All this inner conflict was tying her stomach in knots; she was tense and nerve-whipped, and there was no hiding it from Ancel. He was watching her with a mixture of confusion and concern. His arms reached out to draw her to him.

"Hey, come on. What in the world is the matter with you? It must have to do with your sister's visit, Jennie. I'm not stupid. You were as happy as a lark before she came. Now, tell me what happened. Doesn't Meg approve of me?"

Locked in the warmth of his embrace she felt like a lost child who had just been returned safely home. "Ancel," she whispered against his neck, "I don't want to go back to Fort Worth."

His arms tightened about her. "I thought you said you had to go."

"I do, but I don't want to go without you."

"That's ridiculous, darling. Why? It's only for a couple of weeks, and when you get back, we'll be together for the rest of our lives."

Only a couple of weeks! A lifetime! An eternity! All sorts of things could happen in a couple of weeks. Look what had happened to her in only one!

"If I go back to Fort Worth alone... I'll lose you."

He held her away from him slightly, and a frown furrowed his brow. "That's the most absurd thing I've ever heard! Why would you say such a thing? You couldn't run me off with a shotgun. The only way you can lose me, Jennie, is to tell me to get lost."

"Please come with me."

"I can't, Jennie. I would if I could, but I can't. There are things I have to do. If I don't get busy and do some things around my place, I'm not going to have a ranch. That's the bad thing about not training a good foreman— I have to stick close. But, then, I never particularly wanted to go anywhere, so I didn't anticipate the need for a foreman. I didn't anticipate any of this." He drew her close again and began nuzzling her neck, nibbling at her earlobe. "Oh, but it's so nice! You smell good... you taste good."

He was trying to lighten her mood, to make her feel better, but he was not succeeding. She wound herself tightly about him, like a coiled snake, trying to hold him close enough to drive out the demons plaguing her. Closing her eyes, parting her lips, she began to kiss his face, his neck, his throat, the V of bare skin where his shirt was unbuttoned. A very real and desperate need was overtaking her—the need to make him belong to her in such a profound way that he never could bear to be without her. "Then make love to me," she said in a plaintive voice, loving him so much she no longer had any choice.

"Jennie, sweetheart. My God!" Each word throbbed vibrantly. "You're driving me out of my mind!"

Her hands began a sensitive exploration of him. She undid two more buttons of his shirt, then with great deliberation she slipped her hands inside to rub him provocatively. The palms of her hands burned against his flesh as she stroked and massaged, kneaded and caressed, first the back of his neck, then his powerful shoulders, and on down across his chest and the flat male nipples. She heard him suck in his breath.

"Make love to me, right now," she commanded. "Upstairs. And none of that reining-in. Finish it. And then when I'm gone, think about it every night."

Her voice was low and tremulous, but she knew from the way his body had tensed, from the heavy pounding of his heartbeat under her palm, that he had heard every word. She took one of his big gentle hands and placed it on her breast so that he could feel the heaving of her chest.

At first the hand remained motionless; Ancel was staring at her with an expression of awe, as though he never before had touched her so intimately. Then slowly his hand lifted the creamy mound and began fondling, kneading. "Jennie," he breathed.

"Just make love to me," she commanded again. "I may not be experienced, but I can satisfy you. I know I can. You teach me...."

His hand on her breast was trembling so violently that Jennie placed hers over it to still it. Ancel didn't move for what seemed forever. She waited, her breath suspended. Then he stood, bringing her with him, and scooped her up into his arms. He kicked open the slightly ajar front door, then pushed it closed with the heel of his boot. Stooping, he spoke sharply. "Lock it!"

The arm around his shoulders shot out, and her fingers groped for the lock. Then, without bothering to switch off the table lamp, he marched to the stairs and carried her to her bedroom. Jennie's heart was beating senselessly. She settled her body into the cradle his arms made for her, amazed at her own abandon.

Inside the bedroom, Ancel set her on her feet and told her to undress and put on her nightgown.

"I don't need a nightgown," she insisted.

"Yes, you do."

"Then you put it on for me."

He complied almost roughly, seemingly trying to avert his gaze from her trembling, naked body. She slipped the flimsy nightie over her head, then moved to the bed where he quickly jerked back the covers. "Get in," he ordered, as though she was a naughty child being sent to bed with her supper.

Her mouth fell open, and stinging tears rolled out of her eyes, but she did as she was told. Once between the sheets she lifted her dark, fluid gaze to him in perplexed astonishment. "Ancel, I..." she began, at a loss to understand his attitude.

All at once she saw his body sag, and a low moan escaped his lips. He threw himself down beside her, on top of the sheet, and pulled her into his arms, holding her so tightly she was having trouble breathing. "Oh, Jennie, my God! Not this way, darling. Not because you're upset or frightened or worried. I want our first time to be...so...perfect."

Jennie lay as still as death. She felt humiliated, shamed, thoroughly rebuffed. She had offered herself

to him, had begged him to make love to her, and he
was refusing. Again!

"You—you certainly are a man in rigid control of his
emotions," she said bitterly.

Ancel propped himself up on one elbow and stared
down at her. "Good Lord! Is that what you think? I
assure you, darling, that's not the case. If you could
feel me, you'd know better. I—Jennie, don't!" He
roughly snatched her hand away and held it.

"I—I must be some kind of masochist," she cried
angrily. "I keep inviting you into this bed only to be
rebuffed. What is it, Ancel? Is it me? Is it? Don't I turn
you on?"

He groaned and collapsed against her once more,
burying his face in her satiny smooth shoulder. "Oh,
sweetheart, of course you turn me on. I'm not doing any
better job of this than I did my proposal. I'm afraid
you've acquired the world's least adept lover. I want you—
you can't imagine how I want you! But not when you're
harboring all these fears, whatever they are. You're upset about something, and sex won't cure that. And I
damned sure don't need sex in order to remember you
when you're gone. If I were to make love to you now it
would be taking advantage of you, and that I won't do.
When it happens between us for the first time I want it to
be so free and beautiful, with nothing but contentment
afterwards. And tonight isn't the night."

His hand stroked her face, and his thumb brushed at
the wet tears on her cheeks. "But I do think you need
something tonight, Jennie. Comfort perhaps, not sex.
So I'm going to stay here with you. Just like this. I'll
sleep here on top of the covers with my clothes on."

Curiously, she relaxed then, melting into the comforting warmth of his encircling arms, and though her

erratic heartbeat continued its frantic hammering, a flush of satisfaction washed over her. Ancel simply held her, placing light kisses on top of her head and murmuring endearing words of encouragement to her while she nestled against him. There was something so quietly blissful about having him simply hold her. She loved the texture of his skin, the salty-sweet flavor of his tongue, the spicy scent of him.

"Ancel, will you be able to sleep? This bed isn't very wide."

"I'll sleep like a baby."

Her forefinger traced the strong outline of his lower lip. "We seem to spend a great deal of time in bed together, considering the fact that we haven't..."

He smiled and nibbled at the finger. "That's going to change soon, thank God! Have I ever told you how soft and smooth and warm you are? And you smell as sweet and clean as a baby."

"Shouldn't you at least take off your boots and belt?"

"I will...later. Just relax, sweet Jennie, and don't worry about anything. I'll always take good care of you. Sleep, sweetheart, and we'll talk in the morning."

"Kiss me first."

He did, giving her a warm, melting kiss that awoke no erotic desires, only the tranquil feeling of peace and sufficiency. It was enough.

They were aroused out of their slumbers the following morning by a heavy pounding on the front door. Ancel struggled out of bed, rumpled and a little bleary-eyed. "Stay here, Jennie," he said, "and I'll see to it. And get rid of whoever it is *fast.*"

Jennie snuggled happily beneath the sheets and

waited for him to return. When he did, instead of lying down beside her again, as she had hoped he would, he sat on the edge of the bed and sighed. Groping on the floor for his boots, he said, "Two of the hands didn't show up for work today. The rest are going to need my help. Will you be all right, darling?"

"Of course," she said. "But I wish you didn't have to leave. Will you be back for supper?"

"Yes, but I don't know what time it will be. Don't wait on me if you get hungry."

"Oh, I'll wait. I want to."

He smiled. "We already sound like an old married couple." He leaned down to kiss her lightly on the cheek, but her arms slid up to hold him to her briefly. He stroked her arms gently. "Feeling better this morning?" he asked.

"Much better."

"That's good. I wish I had time to talk to you, sweetheart, but it will have to wait until tonight."

The day stretched languorously ahead of her. Once Ancel left, she slept for another half hour, then dressed slowly, breakfasted on toast and coffee, and busied herself about the house, for there always seemed plenty to do. Her household chores suddenly had taken on new importance. This was going to be her home, hers and Ancel's, for the rest of her life. Mentally she made note of the things in the Fort Worth apartment that she would want here. Her big four-poster bed, of course, and several other particularly lovely things she had managed to acquire over the years. She was going to create a home Ancel could be proud of. Happily she allowed herself the luxury of wallowing in her thoughts.

By mid-afternoon, time was beginning to weigh

heavily on Jennie's hands. She paused in her labors long enough to prepare a pot of beef stew and set it simmering on the stove's back burner. It was something that could be eaten whenever Ancel was ready for it.

By five o'clock she was growing fidgety and restive, glancing at the kitchen clock every fifteen minutes or so. She prepared a salad and put it in the refrigerator, then set the table. When Ancel had not appeared by six o'clock, she turned off the heat under the stew and waited impatiently for a few more minutes.

Finally she decided she would just walk over to Ancel's place and see what was keeping him. It wasn't much of a walk, it was a lovely late afternoon, and she wanted to get out of the house. Besides, she missed Ancel.

The lowering sun was washing the green earth in a golden glow, bringing a soft gentleness to the land. Leaving the clearing surrounding her ranch, she thought it strange that she never had noticed how much of The Croft's land still was wilderness. How formidable and impenetrable it must have appeared to those first settlers a century and a half earlier! Fortunately, all those generations of human inhabitants had done little damage.

Every few yards Jennie stopped and took careful note of her surroundings. Once she had known every rock and tree in these woods, but that had been a very long time ago, and should she miss Ancel at the cabin, she would have to find her way back home alone.

Her sneaker-clad feet moved soundlessly through the dense covering of brush and cedar. The floor of the woods was as soft as a thick carpet, covered as it was by centuries of rotting leaves. The air was thick with the pungent scent of cedar and oak. She came to the opening in the fence that Ancel had shown her earlier, the spot where the river was at its most shallow and the huge granite slabs formed a natural bridge. Crossing gingerly, she felt a light-headed elation as the clear, sparkling water splashed at her feet. Back to her beginnings, when the woods had seemed as comfortable and familiar as had the old stone ranch house.

Once across the water it was a mere matter of negotiating a thick stand of cedar and oak before she was in the clearing surrounding Ancel's cabin. In the distance, to the west, she could see several cowboys still mounted and riding among the herd, their day's work done only with the setting of the sun. None of them resembled Ancel, so Jennie continued on toward the log cabin, since she noticed that Ancel's battered pickup was parked alongside it. Arriving at the back of the structure, she quietly opened the kitchen door and stepped inside.

The place looked deserted. She stood in the alcove for a moment, trying to decide whether to wait for Ancel's return or just to go on back home. No doubt he was still far afield and would quit working only when he no longer had light to see by.

It was then that she heard the voices. At first they were unrecognizable, and Jennie wasn't sure from where they were coming, but after a few seconds she realized that the voices belonged to Ancel... and to Ellen Gunter. Moreover, they were coming from the sleeping loft above the kitchen.

Jennie's heart lurched, then began to race wildly. She should leave, she knew. Leave before she heard an intelligible word. To do anything else was eavesdropping, pure and simple, so she was asking for trouble. She should leave or call out. But she couldn't seem to make herself move. She stood rooted in place as though paralyzed, her mouth achingly dry, and listened to the conversation coming from above.

Ellen obviously had been crying; her voice came in halting spurts and carried with it a mournful pathos. "Ancel... I don't know what you expect me to do! My God, how am I to survive? I thought I could depend on you. I've trusted you. You've been everything. When I heard the news I wanted to die! You said you'd never desert me—and now this."

"Ellen," Ancel said in his most soothing voice, "I'm damned sorry you had to hear about it that way. I hoped I could be the one to tell you. But, dear girl, you're being unreasonable. We've been through this over and over again. I'm not deserting you."

"You're getting married! What do you call that? I still don't believe it. To someone you've known such a short time."

"That has nothing to do with you."

"Oh, Ancel," Ellen whimpered. "I'm trying to understand. You're always accusing me of not trying, but I do try, honestly I do. This week has been pure hell for me."

"I know, dear. I know... and I'm sorry. But, Ellen, you simply cannot come here anymore, at least not for a while. How did you know I would be here today?"

"I didn't. I—I've driven by every day, hoping to find you here, but you never seem to be anymore."

"No, I'm staying at The Croft with Jennie."

At this Ellen began to cry softly. "And that's where you'll be from now on, isn't it?"

"Yes," Ancel said quietly. "For the most part, yes."

"I can't make it, Ancel. Without you I simply cannot make it."

"Of course you can!" Ancel's voice was uncommonly brusque. "I've explained to you that I have no intention of deserting you."

"But you're going to have a wife. It can never be the same again. I'll just have to wait until you have time for me. Oh, Ancel, I'm so frightened. Paul frightens me. If I didn't know you, I think I would have killed myself long ago."

"Don't talk like that!" Ancel almost roared. "Listen to me, Ellen. Pull yourself together. I've got to be getting back. Jennie is expecting me."

"See! That's the way it will be from now on," Ellen sobbed.

"For God's sakes! Stop crying and listen to me!"

"Then hold me. I've got to have something to hold onto!"

There was a long, silent pause, and Jennie could only stare at the kitchen floor in numb shock as she imagined Ancel's strong arms comforting Ellen Gunter as they had comforted her the night before. For what seemed forever neither Ancel nor Ellen spoke. Jennie could hear nothing but the frantic pounding of her own heartbeat. Finally, Ancel's voice came to her, and when it did Jennie's world stopped.

"Ellen, Jennie is leaving for Fort Worth this weekend. She'll be gone two weeks. I promise—you'll have my undivided attention while she's gone."

"But, Ancel," Ellen whined pathetically, "what about afterwards—after you're married? What then?"

Ancel sounded as though he was nearing the end of his patience. "I don't know, Ellen. We'll just have to work that out as best we can. I'll have to be a full-time husband to Jennie—certainly she deserves that. I can't be running every time you telephone...."

Jennie's head began to throb painfully. The wild, unbelievable reality of it all! It was too much! She had heard her future husband tell his lover that they would have to work out their meetings after he had married Jennie! If anyone on earth had tried to tell her this about Ancel she would not have believed it, but she had heard it with her own two ears.

She turned and fled out of the cabin as quietly as she had entered. Once out in the day's fading sunlight, she stood for a moment—stunned, sweating, angry—clutching the back porch railing for support. She felt sick to her stomach, actually physically sick. For one awful moment she thought she was going to retch. Once she was sure the queasiness was under control she blindly began walking in the direction from which she had come.

Her imagination ran rampant. They were up there in the loft, together on the bed, of course; perhaps they were undressed, perhaps they had just made love. Jennie's heart leapt into her throat.

Intuition had told her all along that there was something between Ancel and his sister-in-law. First there was the Bumgarner sister's confusion over which of the Gunter "boys" was married to Ellen, then Ancel's uncommonly solicitous attitude toward her the night of the dinner party, and last but not least were Paul's snide implications. All had pointed to some sort of special relationship. Where there was smoke there had to be fire, and all that.

But since the night Ancel had asked her to marry him, and particularly since last night when she had awakened at some point during the night to find his arm thrown possessively across her and felt his gentle, even breathing on her neck, she had convinced herself that she was conjuring up monsters where none existed. Even while grappling with her fears and suspicions she never had doubted her ability to make Ancel love her and truly "forsake all others."

But now she knew she had been living in a fool's paradise. Her ears hadn't deceived her. There couldn't be any more naive denials of the truth. Ancel loved Ellen, had been deeply involved with her for possibly a very long time. Jennie's fertile imagination visualized an entire scenario: Ancel had fallen in love with the beauteous Ellen while Paul was courting her, and she, at the time, "hadn't known he was alive." Now, however, with the marriage gone sour, Ellen needed someone and there was adoring Ancel, all too ready to step in. Now he was just waiting for Jennie to go back to Fort Worth so that he could have time for his lover. Furthermore, he had no intention of giving up Ellen, not even after he and Jennie were married.

Paul had been right all along, and the realization of that made Jennie's blood boil with furious indignation. Ancel was no better than his brother, just more charming and, therefore, much more dangerous. At least Paul didn't hide his ulterior motives behind a vigorous, hail-fellow exterior. At least with Paul you had some idea of what you were up against.

Why? Why was Ancel going through with the sham of a wedding? Was he lonesome? Jennie had heard that clandestine lovers often suffered severely from loneliness. Did he just need someone around to take care of his creature comforts? Did he want a wife to throw a smokescreen around the pursuit of his affair with his brother's wife? She had told Meg she didn't care, but she did care. Thinking Ancel *might* have been in love with another woman was one thing; *knowing* he was contemplating adultery even before the wedding was something else entirely.

But no—Ancel would never get married for any of those foolish reasons. There was little impediment to his love affair as it was—certainly Paul didn't seem overly distressed by it. A wife would only serve to complicate that facet of his life. So there had to be more.

The Croft! *Of course!* It had to be! Ancel was a man with that mystical attachment to the land, just like Rob Cameron. Rob had been a young man when his wife died, and yet he never even came close to remarrying. He had had his land, and that had been enough. Ancel was like that. He couldn't afford to buy The Croft... but he could marry it. Jennie suspected that Ancel Gunter would marry a woman with two heads for three hundred acres of hill-country ranchland. And his ownership of The Croft would assure that Paul never got his hands on it. Quite a feather in his cap—acquiring something Paul desperately wanted.

And all he had to do to get it was marry stupid, gullible Jennifer Cameron.

Oh God! She had done it again! She had given her heart to a man who cared nothing for her, who was interested in something else entirely. For Paul it had been Ellen's millions; for Ancel it was Jennie's land. She was such an imbecile! In five years she had only grown older, not a bit smarter.

Shame and humiliation gripped her as she recalled begging Ancel to make love to her, and of his being the perfect gentleman. Small wonder that he could leave her bed so willingly. What had he planned to do about *that* after they were married?

Almost as shameful was thinking of what lay ahead of her, telling Meg that the wedding was off and enduring her sister's pity, going back to Fort Worth and hoping she still had her job at *Women Now,* a job that no longer meant anything to her. Losing The Croft, for there was no way she could stay now. It would be beyond bearing.

With tears stinging her eyes and the ache in her chest threatening to squeeze the life out of her, Jennie began to run, heedless of where she was running. Run! Run! It was as though she expected the mere physical act of running to purge her soul of its misery, that when she stopped running the pain would be gone. She ran until her legs would no longer carry her, but when at last she stopped and collapsed on the mossy ground, out of breath, she realized she had been wrong; the pain was still there, as insistent as ever.

Moments passed before she realized something else too. She had absolutely no idea where she was. She long since had missed the spot where she was supposed to cross the water. Struggling to her feet, her breath coming in short, painful pants, she tried to retrace her steps, but it soon became apparent to her fogged mind that she was totally disoriented.

Moreover, Ancel's cabin was nowhere in sight. Mindlessly following the river, steeped in her personal anguish, she had inadvertently made a turn of some sort. Too late she remembered the river's erratic course through the hills. On a map it looked like a squiggly worm. Frantically she scanned the sky for the dying western sun. The cedar and oak were so thick that the sky was barely visible, but a dull golden glow sent her scurrying in what she fervently prayed was the right direction.

Where were all the landmarks she had noticed so carefully on the way over? Nothing out of the ordinary about these trees and rocks. Everything was just more of the same. *Damn it!* Where was that spot in the creek where the stones formed a natural bridge? She couldn't have gone that far!

At last she came to a shallow crossing in the river, and though it did not look precisely as she remembered, every instinct told her that by crossing the water at that point she would be on her property. Then, if she kept moving south, she would come to the homestead's clearing.

Tentatively she scampered across, only to find alien territory on the other side. Pure, primitive wilderness, unchanged since the time of the Comanches. Dear God! She couldn't be that far from home, yet nothing, absolutely nothing looked familiar. The steadily darkening sky reminded her that if darkness fell soon, she might very well have to spend the night alone in the woods. For the first time in her life, Jennie knew the meaning of real fear.

Slow down, her inner voice warned. *Slow down. Don't panic. You've just temporarily lost your bearings. Your mind isn't functioning properly at the moment. Now, look around carefully and you'll see a landmark, something you'll recognize—a windmill, a shed, a holding pen, something!*

But there was nothing. She remembered stories from her childhood, stories about people getting lost in these hills, and when they were found they often would be only minutes from home. She could not decide whether or not that was a comforting thought. Home might be just beyond that clump of cedar, or over those jagged rocks, or behind that big stand of oak...or it might be in the opposite direction.

The wind! Of course. The prevailing wind always was

from the southwest. Only during a storm did it change course, and there would be no storm tonight. As she had seen her father do hundreds of times, she sucked on her forefinger and held it aloft. But there was not enough wind to take a reading, just the barest stirring. A feeling of impotency and defenselessness swamped her.

It rapidly was growing dark. Cautiously Jennie continued walking, her forehead glistening with perspiration though the early evening air was soft and cool. If she didn't see something in five or ten minutes, she would stop and wait. Rob's words from long ago came to her: "If you get lost, don't move! Stop the moment you realize you're lost, and someone will find you."

Who? Ancel wouldn't have the slightest idea where to start looking for her, and he would be the only one who would know she was missing—and it might take hours before he suspected something was amiss. No, her car was at the house; he would know she couldn't go far without a car. But for all she knew, Ancel was still at his cabin with Ellen.

Damn him! *Damn him!* He was responsible for this mess. What had she ever done to him that he would dare treat her in such a despicable manner? She almost was afraid to see him again; she honestly thought she might hit him. And he had had the nerve to call Paul a bastard! Ancel had written the book on falsehearted, double-dealing, deceitful bastards! How could she have fallen so insanely in love with the worst sort of hypocrite?

Jennie shook herself free of this worthless mentation. It did no good. Certainly it wasn't helping to ease her predicament, which she now admitted was a grave one. Trees arched above and ahead of her, their branches stretched as though to provide protection, but Jennie did not feel protected. She was hungry and tired and frightened; her fright was something she could taste. Survival absorbed every fiber of her being.

At that moment something—a rabbit, a squirrel, a wild turkey—scampered through the woods in front of her, triggering an explosion in Jennie. She sank to the ground as though she had been shot, helpless, and began to scream. The sound tore from her throat again and again, like the eerie cry of a trapped animal, and the tears came in a torrent. She sat on the soft, mossy floor of the woods, hugging her knees, rocking back and forth, and crying as she hadn't cried since she was a child.

Finally, exhausted, she raised her head and made several rapid swallowings in her throat to keep down the fear-induced nausea. She was wondering what all the wildlife—who doubtlessly resented her encroachment anyway—had thought of her noisy wailing when she spotted him. A little velvet-horn buck, peering intently at her through a thick clump of cedar. *Velvet!* It had to be! Otherwise, wouldn't he have been scampering frantically away from her? A great rush of hope swept through her.

Jennie wiped at her eyes with a dirty hand, then struggled to her feet. At this movement the little buck turned and began moving purposefully away from her, snaking his way through the woods. An odd instinct was urging her to follow; an almost physical force was pushing her in the direction of the retreating deer. Common sense should have told her to remain where she was, just as common sense should have told her there was small chance that this one deer was the same one she had been feeding for a week, but she was in no mood for common sense. She was desperate, and in her desperation she believed that all she had to do was keep the little buck in sight, and she would end up on her own back porch.

She traveled for what seemed to be miles but could only have been yards when she heard her name being called over and over, whether by one voice or many she couldn't tell. Finding renewed strength, she began to run, lashed on both sides by stiff tree branches, and the calls became louder and more urgent.

She opened her mouth to cry out; her throat was so parched she barely could manage the word. "*Here!*" She stood rigidly, straining her ears. There was a long moment of silence, and she wondered if she had been imagining things.

But then a booming masculine voice—Ancel's— came to her. "Keep talking, Jennie! Keep talking! We're coming!" Jennie didn't think any words had ever sounded so wonderful.

"Here I am... here I am!" she called over and over, her throat aching with each word. Leaning against a tree trunk, she continued to call until she thought she could not possibly utter another sound.

An eternity later a figure appeared out of the woods, a man whom Jennie did not know, followed by another, and finally an ashen-faced Ancel ran through a clump of trees and gathered her to him in a crushing hug. He looked like he was on the verge of tears, and for a moment Jennie could almost have forgiven him anything.

"My God!" he cried in a choked voice. "I've been half out of my mind! How in the world did you get here? Oh, Jennie... Jennie!"

The other two men began talking all at once. "... told you we'd find her."

"... can't think how she came to be all the way over here at Karl Wendt's place."

"... 'nother half hour and we wouldn't have found her 'til morning."

"... you all right, little lady? Sure gave Ancel a scare."

Ancel was whispering in her ear. "Come on, darling, let's go back to the house. You're as cold as ice. You need some coffee... and I need a drink."

Jennie was brought sharply back to reality then. The shame and humiliation of the afternoon returned in clear focus, and she gazed up at Ancel with a dull, clouded expression. "Please take your hands off me!" she hissed so that only he could hear. She pushed him away with a violent shove, then turned to follow the other two men down the hunter's trail through the woods, leaving Ancel to stare after her in hurt and bewilderment.

The men were two of Ancel's hired hands, Jennie discovered as she sat in the warmth and comfort of the kitchen, sipping coffee. The man named Jim was responsible for her rescue, and she thanked him gratefully.

"Yes, ma'am. Harve and me were on our way home when we saw Ancel runnin' down the road like a frightened pup. Naturally we stopped, and he asked if we had seen a little dark-haired gal wanderin' around. Well, I told him I saw someone fittin' that description runnin' down the creek bank about an hour earlier. I thought at the time that it was kinda peculiar, but, hell, you looked like you knew where you was goin'. When I saw how worried Ancel was, well, me and Harve got out and started helpin' look for you. I don't mind tellin' you I was watchin' that settin' sun pretty close by then.''

''I'm very grateful, Mr.—ah, Mr.—''

''Jim Bledsoe, ma'am. I'm one of the few folks around here who don't have a German name.''

''And I'm another,'' Jennie told him with a wan smile. ''I do thank you . . . you and Velvet.''

Jim Bledsoe shot Ancel a questioning glance. ''Velvet?''

''That's a deer Jennie's taken up with,'' Ancel explained, his piercing gaze fastened on Jennie. ''It's not supposed to make sense.''

Jim and Harve stayed only a few more minutes; they were quick to point out that they would be very late getting home to their suppers and would have a great deal of explaining to do.

''Don't we all,'' Ancel said pointedly.

Once Jennie and Ancel were alone in the house, the silence was strained and uncomfortable. She steadfastly refused to meet his questioning look, and she answered his questions in monosyllables, explaining nothing, volunteering nothing. Time and time again Ancel tried to delve beneath her icy exterior, but Jennie brushed him aside. As much as she wanted to lash out at him, she wouldn't give him the satisfaction of knowing how deeply he had hurt her. But neither could she manage to be cooly civil to him. How could she, when he had killed everything inside of her?

Finally Jennie gave in to her emotional and physical exhaustion. ''I'm going to bed,'' she announced coldly.

''Without eating anything?''

''Yes,'' she said and mounted the steps, devoid of all feeling save for a weary sadness. She would have given anything to simply throw herself across the bed, but she was filthy. The thought of climbing into her clean bed in her present state of uncleanliness was abhorrent to her, so she pulled the white terrycloth robe off the hook in the closet and carried it to the bathroom. Lethargically, every movement requiring supreme effort, she ran a full tub of hot water and eased her weary body down into its burning comfort, then scrubbed and scrubbed and scrubbed.

But the physical act of scrubbing was no more effective at easing her pain than running had been. She got out of the tub, briskly toweled dry, slipped on the robe and went into the bedroom, where she stretched out full length and buried her face in the pillow. She wished with all her heart that sleep would claim her quickly, but she feared that was impossible. Tomorrow morning, when she was rested, she would pack and drive back to Fort Worth, and she never, ever, would come back to White Rock. It had been a mistake to come this time.

Jennie groaned under her breath when she heard the unmistakable sound of Ancel's footsteps on the stairway. She supposed it had been too much to hope that he wouldn't pursue the questioning. She lay as still as death, afraid to move, afraid to breathe, resigned to a confrontation and dreading it. When it was over, so would her dreams be.

Her back was to the doorway, but she knew he was standing there. She could feel his presence in the room. In a moment she felt the bed sag as the weight of his body settled upon it. She did not turn to face him.

"You should eat something," he said.

"Your solicitude is touching," she said caustically, "but I don't want anything."

"Perhaps a drink then. I'll fix you a vodka and tonic."

Jennie closed her eyes. She shouldn't, for her stomach was very empty, but perhaps a drink would relax her. "All right."

He was not gone long, and when he returned he was carrying two tall glasses. "You'll have to sit up to drink this," he said.

Sighing, she struggled to a sitting position and accepted the drink he handed her. She sipped and let the cold liquid refresh her parched throat. As yet she couldn't bring herself to look at Ancel, but she could feel his eyes beating down upon her, and she knew the quizzing was about to begin in earnest.

Again he sat on the edge of the bed and took a long swallow from his glass, then set it on the bedside table. "I have a million questions, Jennie," he began slowly, "and not the least is what on earth made you go into the woods at night to begin with?"

"It wasn't night when I—when I got lost," she said dully.

"But where were you going when Jim saw you? He said you were running like a bat out of hell."

"I wasn't going anywhere in particular. I guess I—I was on my way home."

"You must have been completely turned around. Where had you been?"

When she said nothing he reached out and tipped her chin with a curved forefinger so that she was forced to look into his eyes, and she clearly saw the pain there. *Good!* she thought bitterly. *I hope he was worried as hell about me. I hope he was sick to his stomach. I hope I made him suffer the way he's made me suffer.* But she knew that was impossible; they were different kinds of pain.

"Where had you been?" he repeated.

"I was...looking for you."

"In the woods?"

"Of course not!" she exploded. "I went to your place. I missed you...as idiotic as that now seems."

His brows came together briefly, but his unwavering gaze never left her face. "Jennie, I've tried all evening to come up with an explanation for why you're treating me this way, and I'm sorry, I just can't. This morning I left a warm, sweet lover lying in this bed, and tonight I came home to an empty house, no sign of you anywhere. I went through the tortures of the damned while we were looking for you. Then we found you, and you treated me as if I was poison. I can't figure it out."

"No, I don't suppose you can," she said sourly. "You have no way of knowing that I came to your cabin this afternoon, that I heard you *with Ellen!*"

She shot him a look of bitter triumph. She expected that statement to be something of a bombshell. She expected him to look chagrined, a bit embarrassed, and flustered. She certainly had not expected one slightly raised eyebrow to be his only reaction. "So," he said calmly.

His unruffled manner infuriated her. Oh, he was such a cool one! Jennie's control snapped. "So?" she cried in disbelief. "You have your fair share of gall, I'll give you credit for that! So? So I *heard* you!"

Ancel rubbed his forehead tiredly. "Maybe I'm just dense, but I don't see what that has to do with anything. What could Ellen and I possibly have said that would get you in such a snit?"

Stiff with righteous indignation, Jennie thought surely she would choke. Her eyes blazed with fury as she spit out the words. "What do you take me for, Ancel— a blathering idiot? Try this on for size—'Ellen, Jennie is leaving for Fort Worth this weekend. She'll be gone two weeks. I promise, you'll have my undivided attention while she's gone.'" She paused to give dramatic emphasis to the revelation, hoping he was cringing inside.

Ancel stared at her with incredulity. "But, Jennie, for God's sakes, I—"

But once Jennie had started she couldn't stop. "You couldn't have been more explicit, and I can understand plain English. But that wasn't the worst of it. At least while I'm in Fort Worth you still will be a single man. What about later? That's what really topped it! 'I don't know, Ellen. We'll just have to work that out as best we can.' Oh, Ancel, that's despicable. Planning adultery before you're even married! My God!"

Jennie felt as though a great weight had quit her. It was out in the open now; at least he knew that she knew. It would lead to a final break, of course, and though she feared she would want this man until she died, it was better to get it over and done with.

Ancel's shock was genuine; she could see that he wasn't faking it. Well, who wouldn't be shocked? He had been caught red-handed, dead to rights, without a leg to stand on. "Good Lord!" he groaned. "There's nothing more incriminating than a conversation taken out of context. Tell me, Jennie, just exactly what did you hear this afternoon?"

"Enough," she said harshly, immediately off on another tangent. "Enough to know that our marriage would have been a sham, a farce. Enough to know you are breaking Ellen's heart and that you never had any intention of being a faithful husband to me. Paul warned me. He warned Meg, too, and that's why she came to see me. But I was so blind in love with you I was willing to marry you even while thinking I was second choice because I honestly thought I could teach you to love me. I was wrong, and stupid and naive into the bargain. I knew you didn't love me—you all but spelled it out for me—but I thought it didn't matter, just as long as you belonged to me. I...."

A dry sob caught in her throat. She had blurted out words she hadn't meant to say; one more blow to her devastated pride. "Oh, what difference does it make? It's over. I'm leaving for Fort Worth in the morning, so you won't have to go through the pretense of a wedding. And lest you panic over losing The Croft, rest assured I'll sell it to you if you still want it and can come up with the money. Otherwise, I'll put it back on the market. I won't sell it to Paul. I love the place too much, and I'm not any fonder of his motives than I am of yours."

She raised the glass to her trembling lips, but the drink tasted flat. She set it on the table beside Ancel's and clasped her hands tightly in front of her. Her head was throbbing so painfully she thought it would burst, but the rest of her was an aching void.

Ancel had not moved. He sat immobile and stared at her for a long wordless moment. Then suddenly he was on his feet, pacing the room and running his fingers through his hair. His agitated stalking continued for what seemed forever. Finally he twirled to face the back of her head with astonished eyes.

"Good Lord, Jennie! We haven't been communicating at all. All this time I've been thinking that we had this special thing of—of not needing words... but now I see that I should have said a lot of things. Oh, Jennie sweetheart, I had no idea, no idea at all...."

"No idea that I ever would find out? Is that what

you're saying? Gullible little Jennie! 'She'll never think to question me or my comings and goings.' No wonder you found it so easy to— Did you breathe a sigh of relief every time you escaped my bed? What excuse would you have used once we were married? I—I might reasonably have expected my new husband to...make love to me occasionally.''

"Jennie, don't! You're going to have to give me a chance to explain...about Ellen...about everything.''

"I don't want to hear anything you have to say!''

"Well, that's too bad! You're going to hear it!'' He returned to the bed and grabbed her roughly by the shoulders, giving her a shake. There was nothing warm nor cheerful about his eyes now; they were like green fire.

"Stop it, Ancel! You're hurting me, and this time it's physical.''

"You're going to listen to me if I have to sit on you! You've accused me of plenty tonight. You've given me the worst damned night of my whole life, so the least you can do is let me try to defend myself. Then if you still want to leave, at least you will have heard the truth. Whether or not you choose to believe it is up to you.''

She looked at him expressionlessly. She was numb. All the fight had gone out of her. She grabbed the pillow, propped it against the headboard and leaned against it, feigning indifference.

"All right, that's better,'' he said, visibly relaxing. He took one of her hands in his, and she made no attempt to withdraw it. "You're right, Jennie,'' he said, his voice growing soft and mellow. "I'm involved with Ellen, deeply involved, and I want you to know about it.''

Chapter Eleven

Jennie stared at him with her mouth agape. Never would she understand this man. He was so unpredictable. He wasn't even going to go through the motions of making lame excuses.

"That's monstrous!" she cried. "You're heartless! You're using both of us! You—"

"Shut up and listen to me!" he said in such a cold and commanding voice that Jennie was immediately subdued. "I'm deeply involved with Ellen, yes, but it's not in the way you assume. I feel sorry for her. Thanks to my dear brother, she's on a collision course with disaster. She's flirting with alcoholism. I'm surprised you hadn't noticed that."

"I—I've only seen her once since I've been here," Jennie said feebly; *and was much too jealous to notice anything but your kind attentions toward her,* she added silently.

"She reminds me of my mother," Ancel said sadly. "Dad drove her to the bottle and to an early grave, and Paul is doing the same thing to Ellen. God, the awful things people do to each other! I sometimes think that the worst cruelties in the world go on in the name of family. I wasn't around to help my mother until it was too late, so I'm trying to atone by helping Ellen. She's nothing more than a sweet, helpless girl who led a thoroughly sheltered life until she got married. She hasn't the slightest idea how to cope with a man like Paul, a man who treats her like a possession, just another item of inventory.''

Ancel's eyes grew distant and vacant. ''Paul married Ellen for the same reason my father married my mother—money. He, like my father, has engaged in numerous extramarital affairs, and, unfortunately, like my mother, Ellen regards this as some sort of failure on her part. When it gets to be too much for her, she seeks escape in liquor, just the way my mother did. It's like a rerun of a very bad television show.''

He paused, and Jennie winced at the pain and anguish mirrored on his face. He took a deep breath and went on. ''I don't pretend to understand men like my father and brother, but I think I understand Ellen. That's why I've asked her to call me whenever she feels herself going under, and I suppose she's come to consider me her only friend. Now she's frightened that once I'm married I won't be able to help her quite so freely. She's right, of course. I won't be.''

Ancel's hand was gripping Jennie's so hard it hurt, but she gave no thought to trying to pull away. She only remained still and silent and let him continue.

''The night of the party Ellen was in about as bad shape as I've ever seen her. That afternoon she had had some sort of mishap—dropped a glass or something trivial—and Paul had lashed out at her, accused her of being drunk. She wasn't; I know for a fact that she had been sober for a very long time. But Paul had threatened to put her in a sanitarium, and I thought I never would settle her down. Then, the night I came home from the club and found Paul here with you, we had quite a row, as I'm sure you heard. Ellen had gone to pieces over his constant taunts, and Paul's solution to his wife's condition was to leave, so I had no choice but to stay, try to calm her down and see that she got home safely. When I walked in that front door and saw him with his hands on you, I wanted to kill him. I told him to get home and start behaving like Ellen's husband, and he told me to mind my own damned business.''

Jennie felt her defenses crumbling. "If things are that bad, why doesn't Ellen divorce Paul?''

Ancel shrugged and sighed a labored sigh. "Who knows? I guess she loves him, God knows why. And, too, she was taught that marriage is forever, that it's up to the woman to make it work, and on and on and on. Paul knows there's nothing romantic between Ellen and me, but it pleases him to intimate that there is.'' Now the eyes that had been so cold and distant became warm and pleading as he looked at Jennie. "I'm not in love with Ellen, sweetheart. I never have been. I love her the way I would love a sister who was in trouble.''

"I—I don't know whether to believe you or not.''

"I can imagine what bits and fragments of our conversation must have sounded like to someone who didn't know the situation. Ellen knows how I feel about you, and she would be happy for us if she weren't so scared. She knows she has a problem, and she thinks I'm the only one who can help her. I've tried everything I know to get her to go to Alcoholics Anonymous, but Paul undermines my efforts at every turn. It would cause a *scandal,* he says. It would *ruin* the Gunter name.'' Ancel smiled bitterly and his voice dripped with scorn. "A lot there is to ruin. That's why I said what you heard this afternoon. While you are in

Fort Worth I plan to get Ellen to one of those AA meetings if it's the last thing I do. Or to a doctor, at least. I want her to know that I still will be available to help her, but someone else will have first claim on my time. You'll always come first, Jennie. Call Ellen and ask her. I've confided in her a lot, and she knows how I feel. If you had heard more of our conversation this afternoon, you would know too. I've never loved any woman but you."

Jennie's eyes widened. "Me? Oh, Ancel, don't lie. Please don't. You made it perfectly clear on more than one occasion that your interest in me was purely the physical desire of the moment."

Now it was Ancel's turn to look surprised. "I find it impossible to believe I ever said that, particularly since nothing could be further from the truth. Jennie, I love you. I suppose I should have told you that before now, but frankly, sweetheart, I was afraid I would frighten you off. I wasn't at all sure you weren't carrying a torch for Paul. Don't you remember when I told you I had been in love once, but that the lady in question didn't know I was alive?" He asked the question with the gentlest smile she had ever seen.

"Are—are you trying to tell me . . . she was me?"

"Jennie, I fell in love with you years ago, when you and Paul were engaged. That's the main reason I let Dad ship me off to work in the bank in Amarillo. I simply couldn't stand by and watch you marry the bastard! When I finally came home, I fully expected to find you here as Mrs. Paul Gunter. I—I tried to find out where you were, but you didn't keep in touch with anyone in White Rock, and no one seemed to know where you had gone after you left the university."

"No," she admitted. "I was rather stubborn about

that. Once Papa was gone I assiduously avoided the place. I was awfully young, and I felt very alone, hurt and confused by Paul's rejection. I was going to 'make it on my own.'" She smiled ruefully. "I was so certain White Rock had nothing I wanted. But, you know, there must have been some record of my address at the bank since my trust fund is administered out of there."

"Now, why didn't I think of that? But I have as little to do with that bank as possible. I just assumed you had gone for good, probably were married and busy raising a family. Then, when Jeremy told me you were coming back to sell the ranch, I made it a point to be here, and once I realized you still were single, I did everything I could to get you to stay. The suggestion about fixing up this ranch was just a ruse, darling, to keep you here as long as possible. I—I don't know what I hoped would happen. I doubt I was thinking much beyond the moment. I was just enjoying the hell out of being with you. I'm sure I never dared hope it would turn out so wonderfully, that I would get you and The Croft and—"

Jennie stiffened, and old fears came back. "How much does this ranch mean to you, Ancel? Be honest with me. Paul suggested things to Meg that—well, she's convinced you're marrying me to get your hands on my land."

Ancel smiled. "A rather drastic measure, wouldn't you say?"

"Men have married for less."

"No doubt. But, Jennie, if I had only wanted The Croft, I could easily have bought it from you and let you be on your merry way the day after you arrived."

"Ancel, it costs a lot of money, and with Paul wanting the place himself, you might have had a hard time borrowing it...."

Ancel rubbed his chin thoughtfully. He reached for his drink, took a long swallow from it, then placed it beside Jennie's on the table and wiped his damp palm on his jeans. "I—I haven't told you the complete truth about myself, Jennie. Not because I wanted to deceive you, rather because I liked letting you think I was nothing but a poor hill-country rancher. It's a pose I've struck because it suits my purposes. I don't lie, but neither do I volunteer information. Actually, Mama left me a good deal more than that plot of land I work. She was quite a wealthy woman in her own right. Why do you think Ernst Gunter married her? The mercantile fortune she inherited from her father matched the Gunter millions perfectly. She left it all to me, every cent she had when she came into the marriage."

Jennie gasped, not at the thought of all that money but at the thought of Ancel's having it. Ancel of the scuffed boots and faded denims? Ancel of the dilapidated pickup truck? Ancel of the dawn-to-dusk menial labor? A millionaire? The entire thing was so ludicrous she had to suppress a laugh.

There was no humor in Ancel's expression, however. His mouth was set grimly, and his eyes were unspeakably cold as he continued. "If Mama had been suffering from heart disease or cancer or any one of a dozen other things, pride would have forced Dad to seek the finest medical care for her, but she was an alcoholic—a disgrace rather than someone in dire need of medical attention. Dad and Paul shunted her aside, kept her a virtual prisoner in her own home, tried to pretend their 'embarrassment' didn't exist. But when she was sober—and she was sober more often than either Dad or Paul realized—she was perfectly lucid, the most perceptive person I've ever known. She knew

I loved her and would have loved her under any circumstances. I've lost count of how many nights I sat by her bed, how many times I took her to the doctor or to the hospital while my father and my brother turned their backs. I was the one who sat and watched her die.''

"Oh, Ancel,'' Jennie said helplessly.

"Do you wonder why I hate them so? I wish you could have seen the look on Dad's face when her will was read. He made a big show of contesting it, but Mama's lawyer was a pretty shrewd man. He knew the whole story, and he let it be known that a court fight would be rather messy—at least as disgraceful as Mama's alcoholism. Jennie, I suppose I could buy and sell Gunter State Bank any day of the week if I had a notion to, but that sort of thing just doesn't matter to me. I live the way I do by choice, not by necessity. I don't spend money because there's never been anything I wanted to spend it on, at least not until now.''

With this Ancel reached out his arms to her. "Will you let me hold you?''

Jennie closed her eyes, letting the tension go out of her, and she allowed him to gather her to him. Melting against his hard, comfortable warmth, she reveled in the feel of him. He was so absolutely warm. Only when she was in Ancel's arms did every part of her come alive. She lifted her mouth to accept his demanding kiss, moving her lips insistently, hungrily against his.

"I'm sorry, darling, so sorry,'' she murmured against his mouth. "I guess I didn't trust my ability to hold you. I was all too willing to believe that a woman who looks like Ellen does would appeal to you more than I ever could.''

His hands, which were moving along her spine,

stopped at the small of her back to press her ever closer to him. Slowly they inched downward. "I ought to spank this appealing little fanny of yours! Sweetheart, haven't you ever looked at yourself in the mirror? You are the loveliest creature on earth! Why didn't you come to me when Paul first implied that Ellen and I were lovers? It would have saved you a lot of doubt."

"I can see that now," she said slowly, burrowing her head in his shoulder. "I was afraid of what you would tell me, I guess. I was falling in love with you by then and was very sure you didn't feel the same way about me."

"I don't understand how that could be. I've been so crazy about you for so long."

"But you never said anything but that you wanted me. You never mentioned the word *love*. You even admitted it was nothing more than two sets of glands calling to one another."

"No, love. *You* said that, remember? Cooled me off damned quick too, as I recall."

"But surely you knew I meant it was that way for you," she said insistently.

"Surely I didn't. How could I have known that?"

"And the night we first talked about getting married— you told me to be patient and love would come. I assumed you meant that, though you didn't love me now, you would learn to."

Ancel laced his fingers through the thick curls atop her head and brought her face so close to his that she could feel his warm breath on her skin. "Oh, Jennie, see what I mean about lack of communication? We just weren't getting through to each other at all."

"One thing came through loud and clear," she said pettishly. "I all but begged you to make love to me, and you refused. Can you deny that? You walked away from my bed not once but twice, just as calm and easy as you please...."

"No, sweetheart, believe me...it was not as calm and easy as you please. In agony and torment, maybe, but not—"

"Then why did you do it?"

He pulled back so that he could look into her eyes, then bent his head and kissed her lingeringly. His hands resumed their restless, seeking caressing, and Jennie felt the stirring in her loins, the rushing of desire he always aroused in her. She stroked his broad back and pressed herself closer, molding her body to fit against his. This time she was determined he wasn't going to escape. "Why?" she repeated in a throaty whisper. "Feel me and tell me why you rebuffed me."

"To protect you, my darling innocent, what else?" he muttered thickly. "I was afraid you wouldn't be able to handle the attack of conscience afterwards and would blame me. And...I wanted to give you that wedding night to write a poem about. But if you don't stop...what you're doing now...Jennie! I won't be so noble tonight."

Jennie snuggled against him. "Good!" she said boldly. "You once called me a wanton vixen. I'll try to live up to the advance billing. And...I'll just write a poem about...tonight."

Slowly, because she had to shed years of inhibitions in the doing, she began to explore him. Her eager hands splayed across his chest, then moved down his rib cage and across his firm stomach. As their lips fused and their tongues intertwined, she teased at the waist of his jeans before continuing down his hips to investigate the sinewy strength of his powerful thighs. He was clutching her so tightly she was sure her arms would be bruised tomorrow, and his breath rasped in her ear. And still she continued her rubbing and petting.

"Dear God, Jennie," he said in a distorted voice, "do you know what you're doing to me?"

"Mmm. I think so." With deliberating care she undid the buttons of his shirt and pulled it free of his jeans, then pushed the garment open to give her hands and mouth free access to that broad expanse of warm, bronze skin. Exerting only the slightest pressure she forced him down to lie on his back, and with agonizing slowness she covered every inch of his chest with tiny, light, fluttery kisses. He was pliant and malleable in her hands.

Then she heard him groan, and in one lightning quick motion he had her lying beneath him, and his mouth was covering hers with a hot, intense kiss that she returned in full measure. When he lifted his head his eyes were blazing with desire. "You're really asking for it, you know...."

"I know."

"Are you sure, Jennie darling? Really sure?"

"I've always been sure, Ancel. Even when I was afraid, I was sure I wanted you."

With one hand he untied her belt and flung open the white robe. Then his trembling, inquisitive hands explored her body. Her breasts swelled to fit his big hands; his thumbs teased the nipples to erectness before his head bent to capture first one, then the other, between his lips. Jennie alternately sighed and moaned as the ache of desire overtook her, and her stomach cramped into a tight coil of desperate need.

She was never really sure how Ancel accomplished their complete disrobing, but they were lying together naked on the bed, wound around each other, and his hands were performing their love rite, while his mouth chanted her name incessantly. He molded his long length to her; Jennie felt the force of his passion and heat and strength, and his mouth claimed hers in a fierce, thrusting kiss. Dear God, she loved him so, wanted him so! The seductive movements of her creamy smooth thighs conveyed this message.

Then he paused and looked down at her, pleading, inquiring, searching her face for some sign of misgivings or regret. In answer she sighed, "I love you," and arched her body to his. And in joy and triumph they melded together in the act that made them one.

Sometime later Jennie stirred in his arms, her body glutted with satisfaction. Ancel's head was resting on her shoulder and one leg was thrown possessively across her. Unable to resist the lure of that beloved male mouth, she kissed him softly, bringing him to a state of semiconsciousness.

He uttered some sort of unintelligible sound, and his hold on her tightened. She smiled against his mouth, then moved it to his earlobe to gently nibble. "Are you awake?" she asked softly.

"Hmmmm."

"How can you sleep? I'm too excited to sleep."

He opened his eyes. "Dear God, you really are wanton!"

"Was I?" she asked happily. "Was it delightful, darling? Please tell me."

"No, it was terrible," he teased. "I don't know how I endured it."

"You're a very good actor then," she teased back.

Ancel laughed a lusty laugh, then swung his leg off

her and sat up on the edge of the bed. "Come with me, vixen."

He stood and pulled her to her feet, and together they crossed the room to stand at the window. Their naked bodies were bathed in moonlight. Ancel pushed aside the billowing curtains, and he drew Jennie close. "Look at that, darling. Our land. Could you ever have left it? I don't think you could. It has its magical hold on you too."

The green and gold of the day was long gone, replaced by the purple and black of the night. A timeless place. Home. Jennie sighed in deep contentment and nestled her head against Ancel's chest.

"No, I could never leave it, not now. Had I gone away in the morning, I would have come back. I'm sure of it." She tilted her head and looked up at him. "I have a friend in those woods, you know. Ancel, tonight I was thoroughly lost until Velvet showed me the way home."

He smiled down at her. "Now, Jennie, that's a figment of your imagination. Velvet hasn't been here for two nights, and we saw no deer when we ran through the woods after you."

She shook her head vehemently. "No, you're wrong. It was Velvet. He was there. I couldn't have been imagining it. He waited for me to follow him . . . he showed me the way."

"Sweetheart, deer do not behave that way."

"It was Velvet, I know it was. We've got to put food out for him again."

"All right, Jennie. Believe it. Believe it was Velvet. Believe anything you want. Just please believe that I love you."

Jennie closed her eyes as his enveloping embrace

tightened around her, lost in the peace and joy that only his nearness could bring. "Yes," she said dreamily. Yes, she knew he loved her. Even before experiencing the intenseness of his lovemaking she had known it. Truthfully, she had seen it in his face when he found her in the woods, only she had been too steeped in misery to admit it at the time. When he had emerged from the clump of trees he had looked like a man who had found the only thing in life that mattered to him.

Ancel's lips brushed against the hair at her temples. "I had almost despaired of ever hearing you tell me you loved me."

"Now I wish I had said it the moment I first felt it. But I was afraid you'd flee in horror."

"Jennie, promise me something. In the future, if you have doubts or fears or worries, spit them out! Don't let these things fester. Let me know what you're thinking every minute. Let's not ever let the lines of communication between us go down again."

"I promise," she said, hugging him ferociously and basking in the solace of his warmth.

"I wonder if we can be married before you leave for Fort Worth," Ancel mused.

"I don't know . . . marriage license, blood tests, to say nothing of arranging for the church. Or"—her eyes lit up—"we could be married there. Oh, Ancel, please come with me! I'll show you a fantastic time. We'll visit the museums and go to the Botanical Gardens, and I know some wonderful restaurants. I'll even take you to Billy Bob's!"

He frowned. "What's that?"

"Just the biggest night club in the whole world, that's all. Three acres under one roof. Please come with me."

"All right, I'll come, but I don't care anything about museums or gardens or Billy Bob's. I just want to be with you. If the ranch collapses, I'll just rebuild it. I've done it before. I don't want you away from me for two weeks, not now that we've finally begun to understand each other."

Jennie hesitated. "Ancel, what about your obligation to Ellen?"

"That's a problem, I'll admit. Ellen's just a step away from going off the deep end. I'll have a talk with her tomorrow, if that's all right with you, darling. If she won't go to AA, I'm going to try to get her to see a doctor. I'll take her there myself if I have to. I just can't turn my back on her, Jennie."

"I know you can't. One of the first impressions I had of you was that you're a man to lean on."

"Always lean on me, Jennie."

"Ancel," she said thoughtfully, "you say that Paul knows there's never been anything romantic between you and Ellen. Why do you suppose he went to such great lengths to make me and Meg believe there was?"

"I have several theories about that. First of all, spreading those rumors would make him seem less the heavy if he decided to seek a divorce. Secondly, I don't think he wanted us to get married. Once married, I naturally would not have as much time for Ellen. As things have stood, whenever Ellen became difficult, she ran to me, and that relieved Paul of a lot of responsibility. And, too, I think he lusts after you a bit himself. You're the only woman Paul ever had anything to do with who couldn't further him in some way— money, prestige, something. I think that as much as Paul could care for someone other than himself, he cared for you. My God! What if you had married him? He might have destroyed you too."

Jennie pursed her lips. "It's sad really. I feel sorry for Ellen and very ashamed of the terrible things I was willing to believe about the two of you. It just hurt so much. Can you forgive me?"

"Absolutely. I'm just glad you cared so much."

Jennie turned her face up to his, and the look she gave him was one of pure overflowing love. "Oh, Ancel, I was cold and unfeeling for so long. I wasn't sure I was capable of this much love."

"You're a warm, beautiful, passionate woman, and I'm a lucky man."

She slipped her arms up his chest and locked her hands behind his neck. Almost shyly she said, "I wasn't a disappointment to you?"

A flicker of surprise crossed his face; then the corners of his eyes crinkled as a sly smile curved his mouth. "Did I seem disappointed to you?"

"No...no. You seemed...ecstatic," she admitted.

"And so I was. And, my darling, so you should be too."

With a glad cry he scooped her up into his arms and carried her back to the bed, where he set about immersing her in ecstasy.

The long, lovely, love-filled days they spent in Fort Worth while Jennie tied up the loose ends of her old life constituted their honeymoon—not a really proper one some might have said, but for Jennie that brief interlude was the nearest thing to pure bliss she expected to find on earth.

Theirs was the most perfect mating imaginable, the

union of two souls who had waited such a long time for love. Ancel responded to Jennie's unfettered adoration with a searing passion, as though he never could get enough of her and still was a bit awestruck by the realization that she belonged to him and only him.

Often there was a poignancy to their lovemaking, an unbearable sweetness to their breathless consummation. The first time he brought her to the pinnacle of ecstasy, she lay in his arms, her body sated with gratification, and murmured, "Oh, Ancel, not all the things I've heard and read prepared me for it. I'll never be the same again...never."

"No, that's right, darling. You never will be the same."

She felt newly born, and once they were settled back at The Croft, Jennie fell in love with him all over again. With him and the life he had given her. There was something so satisfying about waking each morning and knowing that every second of that day was to be spent occupied with meaningful work, then to fall into the four-poster bed at night, weary but pleased that a few more things could be crossed off the list. Little by little the changes came, and soon there were big things to be checked off, jobs done that wouldn't have to be worried about again for a few years.

Rob's stone house went through a major renovation. Manolo Guerra and his wife Rosa came to work for them and were given Ancel's log cabin to live in. Manolo proved to be an excellent foreman, and Rosa's presence in the house was invaluable help to Jennie, to say nothing of giving her feminine companionship at the male-oriented ranch.

When Jennie and Ancel combined their property they wound up with five hundred or so acres of land, nothing very carefully surveyed or behind fence. Parts of it still were too rocky and hilly to do much with, and other parts were pure wilderness and would, hopefully, be that way when their grandchildren were roaming the hills. As far as Jennie was concerned, it was Paradise and the Garden of Eden rolled into one.

One night, when they had been married a little over five months, Jennie crawled between the covers of the four-poster and waited for Ancel. When she felt him sink into bed beside her, she turned to be gathered into his embrace. Fresh from his bath he smelled marvelous, all damp and masculine. She snuggled against him as his hands caressed her sensitively and came to rest on the soft mounds of her breasts.

"What do you think?" she asked dreamily.

"Feels good," he said, smiling down at her.

"I don't mean that. What do you think of the house? The workmen say they'll finish tomorrow. You've been so busy that I've had to make a lot of decisions on my own."

"It's beautiful," he assured her. "Fit for a queen, and almost good enough for you."

"Ancel, we got a letter from Ellen today."

"How is she?"

"She sounds in good enough spirits. She's happy to be back in Galveston and seems to be making a new life for herself."

Ancel frowned. "I hated advocating divorce, but in Ellen's case I think it was the only way to save her sanity. I knew she'd stop drinking once she got away from Paul."

"She wants us to come to see her as soon as we can get away. She suggested Christmas, but...I want us to spend our first Christmas together alone."

"That reminds me—I think we're in for a helluva winter."

Jennie looked puzzled. "What's that got to do with anything? And how do you know that, anyway?"

He shrugged. "The signs are everywhere if you know how to read them. The squirrels are busier than ever earlier than ever. And the animals' coats are growing thicker than normal."

She shook her head admiringly. "You amaze me. You know everything."

"Anyway, I'm betting it snows before Christmas... and when was the last time that happened?"

"So?"

"So, it occurred to me that you might like to spend Christmas some place where it will be nice and warm."

"Mmm. Sounds nice. But I don't have the slightest idea what you're talking about."

He rolled away from her, switched on the bedside lamp and began fumbling around in the drawer of the table. He withdrew an envelope and handed it to Jennie. "I picked these up yesterday when I was in town. I thought you might like them."

Jennie propped up on one elbow and inspected the envelope's contents. "What are these—airline tickets? For December? Let's see... San Antonio to Tucson. Ancel, how nice! Aunt Mary is dying to meet you, and Tucson should be lovely in December."

"Read on," he instructed, looking for all the world like the cat that swallowed the canary.

She shot him a wary glance. He was up to something, that was for sure. He looked too pleased with himself. "Tucson to... Los Angeles? How wonderful! Whatever made you think of this? I've never been to California."

He nudged her. "And...go on."

She read further. "Los Angeles to"—she let out a gasp and her hand flew to her mouth—"to *Sydney!* Oh, my God!"

Ancel was trying to feign nonchalance and doing a pitifully poor job of it. "It was just a thought. Of course, if you don't want to go..."

She shrieked and threw her arms around him. "Ancel! Australia at last! Oh, you wonderful man!"

He grinned and rumpled her curls with his hand. "It will be the honeymoon I never gave you. We'll spend a month there if you like—see the whole damned place. I can leave Manolo in charge without worry."

Tears glistened in Jennie's eyes. "Ancel, it's too much. Too much."

"Nonsense. I'd give you the world if I could."

She bent to find his mouth with hers. "You have, my love. Oh, but you have!"

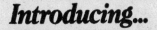

ROBERTA LEIGH

Collector's Edition

A specially designed collection of six exciting love stories by one of the world's favorite romance writers—Roberta Leigh, author of more than 60 bestselling novels!

1 Love in Store
2 Night of Love
3 Flower of the Desert
4 The Savage Aristocrat
5 The Facts of Love
6 Too Young to Love

Available in August wherever paperback books are sold, or available through Harlequin Reader Service. Simply complete and mail the coupon below.